Time passed and the a———————, as it does. She worked hard at creating the shell to cover her scars, pretty and smooth and fragile as a robin's egg. She grew up, she found friends, and she had a step-mother – another doctor – who was kindly, if detached. She married young.

She left Missy behind, long-forgotten in the mists of a childhood she never chose to recall. But Missy did not go away. Missy waited, silent in the shadowy corners of her mind, for the crack made by some blow of fate through which she could emerge, full-fledged, in a form older, stronger, and more evil still.

About the author

Aline Templeton grew up in a fishing village in the East Neuk of Fife. She read English at Girton College, Cambridge, and has worked in education and broadcasting. She lives in Perthshire where her husband is Warden of Glenalmond College. She is a Justice of the Peace, and has a grown-up son and daughter. Aline Templeton has written numerous articles and stories for national newspapers and magazines; this is her third novel. Her second, *Last Act of All*, is also available from New English Library.

Praise for *Last Act of All*:

'Aline Templeton has conjured up a chilling atmosphere of suspicion and malice, in which a cast of memorable, mostly troubled characters play out a cruel drama. The rising tension is conveyed with masterly skill, and the author's literate style is a delight to read'
James Melvill, *Hampstead & Highgate Express*

'Templeton has wit, a strong narrative sense and a dab hand with the atmospherics'
Philip Oakes, *Literary Review*

'Templeton crafts a nifty plot amid the dour and inward-looking denizens of a Fenland village'
Gerald Kaufman, *Scotsman*

'Well written and utterly compulsive. A writer to watch out for'

Northern Echo

Past Praying For

Aline Templeton

NEW ENGLISH LIBRARY
Hodder and Stoughton

First published in Great Britain in 1996
by Constable and Company Ltd
First published in paperback in 1997
by Hodder and Stoughton
A division of Hodder Headline PLC
A New English Library Paperback

10 9 8 7 6 5 4 3 2 1

A CIP catalogue record for this title
is available from the British Library

ISBN 0 340 68270 1

Typeset by Hewer Text Composition Services, Edinburgh
Printed and bound in Great Britain by
Clays Ltd, St Ives plc

Hodder and Stoughton
A division of Hodder Headline PLC
338 Euston Road
London NW1 3BH

For Philip and Clare
with much love

PROLOGUE

Christmas 1967

The huge depression that settled down over Europe brought with it snow – soft, wet, dangerous stuff that clung like a damp sheet as it spread itself down into Northern Italy, over the Alps and Switzerland, Austria, France, then at last across the Channel into Britain on Christmas Eve.

But the man who stood bleakly at the upstairs window of the drawing room of the big house was not considering the prospect of a white Christmas. Giles stared unseeing into the snow-flecked darkness, the lines about his mouth taut with suffering. It was eight months now. Surely in eight months the raw agony should have subsided into some manageable ache.

Restless in his mental torment, he turned. Mrs Beally, the housekeeper, had set up a Christmas tree, a poor puny travesty of a thing, its artificial limbs decked with gaudy lights and cheap ornaments. He looked at it, but saw instead, as if he could touch it, the tree that had stood there last year, and the years before that; huge, towering kings of the forest, hung with chains of popcorn and little patchwork dolls and proclaiming home and family and the joy of Christmas in a triumphal procession stretching back over twenty-four years.

He shook his head impatiently to clear his vision, and

when he looked again the little tree with its tawdry finery seemed to symbolize all that he had lost.

He had conscientiously, or perhaps desperately, finished his hospital paperwork. He had nothing left to do, and tomorrow yawned empty before him, a chasm of misery as black as an open grave.

Gervase had had the right idea. He usually did, particularly when it came to his own comfort.

It was hard, though, for Giles to view the boy dispassionately. He was tall, blond and athletic, and managed his Oxford finals without neglecting either his sport or his social life. He had come up to London that autumn to St Theresa's, the teaching hospital where his father was a highly-successful consultant, to complete his medical training.

Melody had been more objective, viewing her big handsome son with some amusement. But then, Melody was alive with humour, from her taffy-coloured curls to her size three feet, commonly encased in pastel suede shoes with three-inch heels.

At nineteen, she had laughed into enslavement the tall, serious young doctor, come to her home town of New Orleans to do a year's specialization in its famous hospital. Within the year, he had married her and swept her off to England, to the dismay of her warm, affectionate and extended Southern family.

The double-cream drawl had become a little less pronounced over the years, but nothing changed her sunny nature. Coming home from hospital, tired and frequently depressed, Giles's heart still lifted twenty years later to the lilt of that voice calling, 'That you, sugar?' and the clip of small feet in perilously high heels scurrying across the parquet floors.

A son to follow in his footsteps was the only other thing

he had ever wanted, and, for twelve years, all they seemed likely to have. As an only child (the son of elderly parents, now dead) it seemed to him a natural family.

The late addition of a daughter was, if he were honest with himself, unwelcome as well as unexpected. With Gervase away at school, he had Melody's undivided attention once more, and he resented sharing it now with a girl child who appeared to regard him as little more than an alarming stranger.

But Melody doted on her daughter. She called her Missy, in Southern style; Giles used her given name, finding the pet name awkward on his tongue.

Missy was not, like Gervase, a fearless and outgoing child. In temperament, though he failed to recognize it, she was not unlike Giles himself, and worshipped her lovely, laughing mother with round adoring eyes; in company she held her skirt as if presciently afraid that she might lose something so infinitely precious.

So the world ended for Missy, in the spring just before her ninth birthday when, aged forty-four, her mother died after a mercifully brief but painful illness, from the type of cancer which was Giles's own speciality.

It was a bitter irony; one of the foremost experts in that field of research, he could do nothing to save this one vital life, and it tormented him.

His work became a blind obsession. Gervase was part of it; for Melody's sake, he must join Giles in research for a cure which might, all too easily, be the work of more than one generation.

His daughter, however, was irrelevant to him, almost like a pet for whom his wife had conceived an unwarrantable affection, and he made provision for her in that spirit. He dealt with her physical welfare by appointing the first housekeeper he could find, and saw to it that she was taken daily to her little private school, but did not think to warn them of her loss. It never occurred to him that she, in his eyes a baby still, could experience grief as great as his own, and infinitely more destructive.

His mourning was self-centred, all-absorbing, and there was no space in his heart for her suffering. Indeed, he found it hard to curb his irritation when, in the rare times that he was at home in her waking hours, she followed him about like a shadow, even pressing herself to him with the ill-judged insistence of a fawning cur.

Gervase, too, missed his mother, but he was embarking on the excitements of a flat in London and a new career. Arriving home a week before Christmas, he took one look round the house, desultorily run by Mrs Beally and haunted by wisps of laughter no longer heard, and announced that he was going skiing in Kitzbuhel with a party of friends.

So Giles was left facing Christmas alone with his daughter. He had refused the pressing invitation of the American relatives, believing that there he would feel worse, not realizing then that there could be no worse. Perhaps he should have sent the child on her own; perhaps he might think about it later, if she was too demanding.

But the question did not really occupy his thoughts. His mind had drifted again, mouthing the dead-sea apples of memory, when the door opened and his daughter insinuated herself into the room. She was pale and too thin, with an aura of insubstantiality about her, and she paused on the threshold, sniffing the air, as it were, like an animal poised for flight.

Lost in his own thoughts, Giles did not hear her approach, and jumped as she slid her hand into his.

'Don't do that!' he said sharply, dropping her hand and taking a step back. Then, controlling himself with an obvious effort, he said more gently, 'I'm sorry, but

4

you startled me. Shouldn't you be in bed? What time is it?'

'It's only nine o'clock. I'm going up soon.' She shifted uncomfortably from foot to foot.

Trying not to sound impatient, he said, 'Did you want something?'

Her eyes swept up to study his face. 'Er – no, not really. I just – I just wondered what was happening tomorrow?'

For a fleeting second he had the impression that this was not what she had originally intended to say, but it was swept away in a flood-tide of dismay as he looked down at her beseeching expression.

'I – I'm not sure. I must make a phone-call,' he said, turning abruptly and almost running downstairs to his study.

Left alone in the big room, the child stood silent for a moment, then, half-turning as if in conversation, she said, 'What do you think? Do you think he's got it yet, Missy?'

She knew, really, that she was sort of talking to herself, but after – well, afterwards, it had been a comfort to have an imaginary friend. Missy, she called her, because when she had been Missy everything had been all right, and she had been happy and strong and clever and loving and loved.

Missy said, 'Why don't we wait until he comes out of the study and go down and see? If he hasn't opened it we could take it away and silly old fat Miss Jenkins would never know.'

'That's bad. We shouldn't do bad things like that.'

'It's not bad, it's sensible. Otherwise he'll be cross, and you know you hate it when he's cross.'

The child shuddered. 'I know. But it's because of what you told me to do that I got in a mess anyway.'

Miss Jenkins had been angry, very angry. Miss Jenkins was short and plump with round gold spectacles, and she was usually a cosy, rather jolly headmistress. But as Miss Jenkins talked fiercely of bullying and cruelty it seemed as if she changed into some kind of monster before the eyes of the frightened child.

'I simply cannot imagine what has possessed you, and I shall be writing home to say that this sort of evil behaviour – I can only call it that – must stop. You've made several children very unhappy, and poor little Sophie was distraught after that note you put in her desk. She's been deeply upset by her parents' divorce, and we must all be very kind to her.'

The girl felt a shaft of self-pity. Sophie would see her father every week; it wasn't as if he'd gone away for ever, like her own mother, but no one was told to be specially nice to her. It did not occur to her that no one knew.

'Yes, Miss Jenkins,' she said dutifully.

'There can really be no excuse for this. We've all been upset by it – very upset – because we are a happy community, with no place for wicked, spiteful little girls who enjoy making people miserable. Do you understand?'

'Yes, Miss Jenkins.'

'So will you promise that this will never happen again? Because if it did, we would ask you to leave the school.'

'Yes, Miss Jenkins,' she said a third time, dully. Miss Jenkins didn't want her either; was there anyone, anyone at all, who did?

Behind her spectacles her headmistress's eyes were softer now, though puzzled. 'I hope you mean that. I'm very disappointed in you, you know. You used to be such a nice child. Well, we'll leave it at that, and hope that this has just been a temporary fit of naughtiness, shall we?

'Off you go, now. Have a happy Christmas and come back your old self, will you?'

It had all been Missy's idea, of course. She herself would never have thought of writing the notes. When she saw that Lucy's new coat came from a thrift shop and she hadn't money for tuck, she knew she should be sorry for her, and for Sophie Chambers who looked miserable all the time, now that her daddy had gone away with someone else. But misery loves company, and something inside her was glad other people were sad as well, even if she was afraid she was sadder than any of them.

'Make them cry,' Missy advised. 'If they're crying, they're sadder than you are. You're not crying.'

She had tried crying, until she had no tears left, and it didn't change anything. So she didn't cry now, but once Missy had told her what to put in the letters – nasty, poisonous things that nice people didn't say – the other girls cried and in some horrible way it made her feel better.

But then Miss Jenkins had found her out. She didn't know how – perhaps she was a witch – and things were even worse. She'd never had a best friend – when Mommy was alive she didn't need one – but now everyone hated her.

Missy refused to take the blame. 'It was only because you were so dumb you got caught. Do it better next time, Dumbo.'

After that, she was so cross she didn't speak to Missy for days. And now she had, Missy was just trying to get her into trouble again.

'Go away,' she said. 'I'm not going to talk to you any more.'

Her father had not returned. Slowly she climbed the stairs to the pretty attic bedroom which Mommy had filled with every treasure a little girl's heart could desire.

She crossed the room to her white and gold chest of

drawers and opened the bottom one. Tucked away at the back was a Christmas stocking, with her name knitted into the welt at the top. She took it out, unfolded it and stroked it as lovingly as if it had been a living thing.

There was no point in hanging it up. She could not bear to find only a horrid skinny emptiness in the morning, instead of the mysterious wool-clad bulges that had always greeted her.

She sighed, a sigh from the bottom of her heart which ended in a dry sob, then she folded it neatly and put it away.

Mrs Beally, savagely stuffing the turkey in the kitchen, was muttering resentfully. She had been hurrying to get everything prepared, so there would be nothing for her employer to do but lift the turkey out of the oven and carve it, and she could get away first thing to her Karen's to have a proper Christmas Day with the family. She even had stashed in her bag a bottle of bubbly which no one would miss from the cellar, so they could get a good start to the festivities.

And now, here was His Nibbs telling her she couldn't go. She had protested, of course. What, miss the pleasure of seeing Karen's face when she opened the box and found the beautiful leather jacket she wanted and couldn't afford! Not that Mrs Beally could really afford it either, but that snotty little bitch upstairs wouldn't know how much had been spent on Christmas cheer, and he certainly wouldn't ask to see the receipts.

But 'People do not choose their times to be ill, and this is a surgeon's house, Mrs Beally,' he had said coldly. 'When you accepted employment in it, you were told that the hours would be awkward and there would be sudden demands upon your time, and you have been paid accordingly. If you refuse to carry out your duties tomorrow, then you can find alternative employment. I shall not expect you back. Is that clear?'

For all she would have liked to fling his lousy job in his face, caution held her back. She had a good place here; wages well above what anyone else was offering, no one to criticize her cleaning, and good pickings, with no questions asked about a fiver here or a tenner there. He had her over a barrel, the bastard, and she had had to submit.

But she wasn't beaten yet, not she, and though she phoned to order the morning taxi for His Nibbs, she did not cancel her own, booked for a little later.

She was quite confident the child could be made to keep quiet. She barely talked to her father, anyway, and she was too scared of the rough side of Mrs Beally's tongue to try playing up.

So there was nothing to stop her going, once he was safely out of the way. And after all, it was downright unchristian to keep you apart from your family on Christmas Day, wasn't it? It was in a spirit of righteous self-justification that she thrust the turkey into the oven.

When her employer's taxi had gone in the morning, she woke her charge, telling her to get downstairs quickly now, and adding, without conscious irony, 'Merry Christmas!'

She had put on her outdoor coat and gathered together her pile of Christmas parcels by the time the girl had dressed and come downstairs. Mrs Beally did not meet her eyes.

'Now, your dad's had to go to the hospital, and the taxi's coming for me any minute. There's your breakfast – look, I've made you bacon and eggs for a treat – so you eat that, and then when it's dinner time just get your dinner out of the oven. It's all plated up for you, and all you have to do is turn off the oven after, like a good girl.'

9

'But you can't leave me here, all by myself!' Sheer terror lent her courage. 'My father wouldn't let you!'

At these signs of rebellion, the woman's lips tightened.

'Oh, can't I, my fine lady! We'll soon see about that. Your father doesn't care tuppence, or he wouldn't have gone away today, would he? And if you complain, he'll be ever so angry. And I'll be angry too, so just you remember that.'

She shrank back, as if she had been physically struck, and Mrs Beally was quick to follow up her advantage.

'That's right. You're a big girl now, not a baby. The day'll pass, quick as a wink – you just watch the telly, or read a nice book – you've plenty of nice books. You'll have had a big meal, you won't be needing supper, so just get yourself to bed if I'm not back. You've done that often enough, and I'll see you in the morning. And not a word to go worrying your poor pa now, mind.'

The taxi hooted outside, and in a flurry of parcels she bundled herself in and was off into the falling snow.

The house was very, very quiet now Mrs Beally had gone. Her head felt funny, strange and light, as if it might float away off her shoulders, and her hands felt clammy. There was no sound of wind or birdsong outside in the snowy hush, and inside only the ticking of the kitchen clock which grew insidiously louder and louder, until with a little shriek she clapped her hands over her ears and fled the room.

Across the hall, the door to her father's study stood ajar. She paused, hesitated, then went in.

In a tray on his desk there lay a pile of envelopes, unopened, and feeling very wicked she tiptoed across and leafed through them. Most of them looked like Christmas cards, but one had a crest on it that she recognized from her blazer.

She took a long, shaky breath. She didn't want to listen

to Missy, but she couldn't bear Daddy being angry. She stared at the horrible missive, then, without opening it, crumpled it up and stuffed it deep in among the papers in the waste-bin. Then she shot out, as if all the demons in hell were after her.

As she ran upstairs, she made a little bargain with – something, she didn't know what. If people were nice to her again, and no more horrible things happened, she would put Missy away, and never ever ever speak to her again. She felt a little better after that.

But outside the long staircase window, snow was falling, and the wind was getting up now, blowing round the house with strange sighs and moanings. She shivered. How dark it was! The far side of the landing was in shadow, the doorways black.

Perhaps she should go to bed, pull the covers over her head and try to sleep the time away like some suffering animal. But it was Christmas Day, and she was still child enough to remember that the Christmas tree was in the drawing room. She scuttled in, closing the door carefully behind her.

The tinsel on the tree sparkled in the livid light and the cheap baubles gleamed. She switched on the lights, then stepped back to look.

But the little gaudy bulbs somehow took any magic out of it. The family Christmas tree had always dipped and danced in the flickering, perilous light of candles; this tree was plastic, unreal, nothing to do with Christmas.

She sighed, and her eyes fell on the presents beneath the tree. There were only two; the pen she had chosen and wrapped so lovingly for her father, which was still there, and just one for her. There had been parcels from her American aunts and uncles, but Mrs Beally had indifferently allowed her to open them as they arrived

11

– indeed, had abstracted some gifts that she 'wouldn't be needing' to give to Karen's family. There was nothing yet from Gervase. He had said she would prefer something from Austria, though she wasn't sure.

She picked up the single parcel, weighing it in her hand. It was not very heavy, and it rattled softly when she shook it.

The label didn't say happy Christmas, but it did say 'with love' in her father's writing. She thought Mrs Beally had probably bought it, but he had written the label. He had remembered her. Her heart lifting a little, she opened it.

It was a nurse's outfit. Red cape, apron and cap, a mock watch to pin on. A tray, with syringe and tweezers. A grey ligature with tube and rubber bulb, to take blood-pressure. Bandages, thermometer. All neatly packed together.

Her eyes dilated, but she did not see the details of the small plastic replicas. Like Mrs Beally, she did not notice that it said, 'Recommended age 4–6' on the box. She recoiled from the loathsome thing, then in utter revulsion threw it from her, fled to the bathroom and was violently sick.

To be fair, Mrs Beally had meant no harm. The nurse's outfit was cheap, with lots of items – a good bargain, in her book – and the girl was a doctor's daughter. It didn't occur to her that it might be inappropriate for a child who had last seen her mother surrounded by objects of this kind.

When she came out of the bathroom, she was weak and trembling, but her movements were decisive. She marched in, picked up the hated gift, placed it neatly in the fireplace, and fetched matches and firelighters from the log box.

The flames took a moment to catch hold, then flickered up, brighter and stronger. The colourings in the box tinged them with chemical blue and yellow; the plastic shrivelled and smelled, forming melted blobs in strange, contorted shapes. Fascinated, she put on more firelighters, watching them flare up too, consuming what was left.

She looked at the horrid little tree, and started pulling things off. The tinsel burned merrily and the paint on the baubles sent up sparks of green and gold. She smashed them with the poker, and soon the tree was exposed and ridiculous with its fake lights, rigid branches and unconvincing pine needles. She would have liked to burn the whole horrible thing, but it was too big to fit in the fireplace.

Her lovely blaze was dying now, and with it her brief pleasure. There had been a strange comfort in the leaping flames, and she would have loved to go on feeding its ravenous appetite, but somehow she did not quite dare. What if her father noticed the bare tree, or asked to see her present? She didn't think he would, but she cast a lingering glance at the ashes of her fire then drifted aimlessly out of the room.

Her purged stomach was empty and uncomfortable, so she went to look for food. Breakfast lay, in a pool of cold fat, on the kitchen table, so, though it was not yet ten o'clock, she went to the oven and took out the Christmas lunch which had been left for her. It was burning round the edges already, gluey gravy baked on to the plate, turkey dry and brussels sprouts brown, but she ate it indifferently, and the plum pudding with thick custard.

When it was finished, she rose to wander restlessly about the house. Upstairs, her own room felt cold and unfriendly; even the familiar Raggedy Ann doll that always slept in her bed seemed to look back at her with a dead, fixed stare.

On her little desk by the window, there was a book, covered in pale blue suede. 'My diary', its cover said in gold, and it had been in her Christmas stocking last year.

She opened it and looked at the entries, frequent to start with, then more sporadic, then, eloquently, missing. She took out the gold pen from its slot at the side, sat down and turned to the date which was burned in her mind.

'Mommy died on this day,' she wrote in her unformed hand, 'and I wish I could be dead too.'

She wrote for some time, with concentration, over several pages. But then there was nothing more to say, and she put back the pen and closed the book.

It was ten forty-five when she settled down in front of the television. She did not move. She did not smile at the massed talents of British television comedy. Perhaps she did not hear. The telephone rang, once; she listened to it echoing through the empty house but did not try to answer it, and soon it stopped.

Somehow the hours passed. Once she fetched biscuits and milk, then sat down again to watch the flickering black-and-white shadows that helped keep panic at bay.

For outside, it was getting dark. All day it had snowed, and now the wind was howling in earnest. The house was stirring and muttering to itself in the gale.

As the light faded, the shadows in the corners of the big room seemed, eerily, to thicken and encroach, and although she was not cold, she felt a shiver run up her spine. Was there someone – something – over there, behind the big armchair?

Suddenly, into her head came the vicar's words to her on that dreadful day when they had put Mommy in a box in the ground. 'Your mother isn't really gone,' he had said, patting her shoulder. 'Your mother will always be watching over you.'

For the first time, she thought of her mother, not as an aching absence in her life, but as a *dead person*, a creature with strange powers she had not possessed in life. What if she came now, dead and with long bony fingers, to carry away the daughter she had loved to be with her for ever in some place of blackness and shadows where everyone else was dead too?

She shoved her knuckles into her mouth to stop herself from screaming. It was better to be silent, motionless, in the weird glow of the television screen than to get up to turn on the light. Light might chase away the shadows – *but what might remain when the shadows fled*? Cramped and rigid, barely daring to breathe, she sat huddled in her chair, glassily unseeing in an interminable torture of terror.

It seemed a long, long time later that at last she heard a taxi coming up the drive. With frantic energy she leaped from her chair, ran out of the room and downstairs to see, miraculously, her father, not Mrs Beally, climbing out.

'Daddy, Daddy!' she shrieked, throwing herself at him as he opened the front door, desperate for his protection and assurance that now everything would be all right.

But Daddy hardly seemed to see her. Looking over her head he detached the clinging arms and put her inexorably aside.

'For God's sake, not now,' he groaned, and reaching his study like a wounded animal crawling to its lair, he shut the door on the stricken child.

It was from Mrs Beally the next morning that she learned of her brother's death in an avalanche.

'Your pa went off to Austria first thing. You'll need to be good now, because there'll be a lot to do, people coming for the funeral, I don't doubt.'

She did not mention the day before. The child could not.

The night before Gervase's funeral, Giles sat at his desk with his papers before him, but gazing over them unseeing to the framed snapshots of his son, his hair tousled from running, and his wife, her mouth in its sweet curve, her blonde curly hair springing back strongly from the smooth brow. The picture of his daughter as a baby he did not even see.

As he looked bleakly at Melody's smiling face, his hand dropped from the side of his chair and rested, for an incredulous moment, on her soft curls. He came to himself with a cry, and looked down on a smaller head, then into the pleading upturned face of his daughter.

It was too much; he could not bear it.

'Get out!' he said with barely suppressed violence. 'Get out, and for God's sake never do that again.'

And the child fled.

She was only nine years old, but she had learned already the futility of tears. She had learned that nothing was too bad to happen, and that she could trust no one. She had learned, too early, the frightful truth that we are all of us, in the end, alone.

She had not learned yet that life went on, and they could patch you up so effectively that no one would realize that inside, somewhere, you had been warped and twisted to destruction.

She seemed entirely calm by the time she reached her room. She went over to the desk and picked up, once more, the blue suede diary. Sitting in her chair she read, quite slowly, what she had written, and took up the pen again to add another half page. Then she picked up a crayon, and solemnly, meticulously, coloured every remaining page black until she reached the end of the book.

Time passed and agony faded, as it does. She worked hard at creating the shell to cover her scars, pretty and smooth and fragile as a robin's egg. She grew up, she found friends, and she had a step-mother – another doctor – who was kindly, if detached. She married young.

She left Missy behind, long-forgotten in the mists of a childhood she never chose to recall. But Missy did not go away. Missy waited, silent in the shadowy corners of her mind, for the crack made by some blow of fate through which she could emerge, full-fledged, in a form older, stronger, and more evil still.

1

Margaret Moon had always liked dressing up. When she was a plain, square, freckle-faced little girl with long brown plaits, she had loved to put on her mother's old white nightie and play weddings; long, detailed, luxuriously-imagined ceremonies, with herself the unlikely cynosure of all eyes, the groom an accessory much less interesting than the traditional blue garter.

And now, when the freckles and the plaits had vanished, but the squareness and a certain child-like gusto remained, here she was, standing on the altar steps, wearing a white gown. Only she was facing the other way.

She looked down the length of her little church, past the Crusader's tomb into the thicker shadows of the cross-aisle beyond. Under the Norman arches, the stained glass of the windows was opaque, and only the polished memorial brasses on walls and floor took light from the flickering candles in the jam jars on pews and ledges, a hundred luminous points. The cool, damp breath of old stone was overlaid by their warm, waxy smell. Perhaps that was what was meant by the odour of sanctity, which had always seemed to her a curious phrase.

Penny Jackson, at the organ which was one of Margaret's more immediate problems, struggled womanfully into the first asthmatic chords of the tune 'Forest Green'. Along with everyone else – about fifty of them, Margaret reckoned, with her ex-banker's automatic eye for figures – she drew an obedient congregational breath for the opening words of the beloved Victorian carol.

> O little town of Bethlehem
> How still we see thee lie . . .

Lit from below, her new parishioners' faces had a strange, disembodied innocence; the mouths round dark 'O's of sound, sharp features blurred, wrinkles smudged smooth by shadow. Only the eyes told a story: the young eyes, glowing in the candlelight, wide with wonder and over-excitement; older eyes, veiled or hooded depending on whether caution or age had made the greater mark.

Here and there, she caught the glimpse of tears, but she did not yet know her flock well enough to guess where these were prompted by grief, where regret, and where the easy, generalized nostalgia for an idealized Christmas as it wasn't now, probably wasn't a hundred years ago and most certainly wasn't almost two thousand years before that, in the draughty squalor of childbirth in a cattleshed somewhere in Bethlehem. If you believed that.

She did, in fact. It couldn't be described as a fashionable position, and she wasn't certain it had the Bishop's full support, but it was one of the persistent convictions which had driven her to where she stood at this moment, which came as a fresh surprise to her every time she thought of it.

Sometimes it seemed like one of her dressing-up games, even now, with her feet in their sensible black shoes planted on the flagstone floor of St Mary's, and the weight of the cassock across her broad shoulders, ready when the hymn stopped to turn and say the words which would introduce the sacrament, here for her own people in her own cure of souls.

How silently, how silently
The wondrous gift is given . . .

But it hadn't felt like a gift, more like some sort of monstrous burden laid upon her, so that however unpromising the prospect, she never had the alternative of turning back. There was an illustration in the family copy of *The Pilgrim's Progress* which had terrified her as a child, and even now occasionally haunted her dreams, of Christian with his burden of sins growing fleshy tentacles into his back; at times it seemed that her calling was quite as hideously inescapable.

'Do you hear – voices?' a friend had asked with hushed, fascinated horror, and even as Margaret laughed a dismissal, she found herself half wishing the answer was 'yes'. Then it would have been simple; a visit to a psychiatrist – the modern white witch – and a diagnosis of stress, a prescription. Religious delusions dissipated, inconvenient vocations removed.

It was more a sort of relentless discomfort, a niggling itch she couldn't scratch. At every stage, her approach had been grudging and tentative, every query prefaced, as it were, by 'Num . . .', the word her Latin mistress at school had dinned into her as introducing any question expecting the answer 'no'. Yet, uncannily, the path had been made smooth and doors that appeared tight shut had opened, sometimes so unexpectedly that she fell on her metaphorical nose.

She had joined, dutifully, in the prayers that the Synod might be guided to approve women's ordination, but with a sense of praying after the event. The decision, however little the wise and great and good might realize it, had already

21

been made – probably before the dawn of time, though it didn't do to get caught up in that sort of speculation, or you could spend your life contemplating the tiny trivial circles which were all your mind could achieve on that subject, like stirring the ocean with a very small twig.

> And praises sing to God the King
> And peace to men on earth.

What she had certainly never expected was to find herself in a peaceful village in the prosperous Thames Valley, which dozed amid well-kept gardens and quiet leafy lanes, deserted during office hours when, it seemed, almost the entire population abandoned it for somewhere in the City.

It had been in an inner city charge that she had worked as deacon, then curate; a frenetic, dynamic place throbbing with the urgency of the human need which lay, visible as an open sore, on every side. There were soup kitchens and encounter groups and missions to people as ignorant of the Good News as the savages her missionary great-aunt had so forcefully enlightened seventy years before.

The babies with Aids, the homeless, the drug addicts and the battered wives she had counselled had been a joyful confirmation that the hand she had felt laid upon her shoulder was indeed summoning her to an important battle.

So when the Bishop told her about Stretton Noble, the charge he had chosen for her, her first, incredulous reaction was that this could only be some sort of episcopal joke. She did not know him well; perhaps he had an odd sense of humour?

Fortunately, she had restrained herself from bursting into laughter and slapping her thigh. He meant it, all right. As he talked about her duties and the Parish Council and the Mother's Union, she fought to stifle the unchristian thought that perhaps the lip-service he had paid to the idea of women priests was no more than that. If she was an inconvenient body, where better to bury her than beneath the mouldering turf of a rural English parish?

Only as she left the Palace, unspoken protests fermenting in her soul, did it cross her mind that whether or not the Bishop had a sense of humour, there was little doubt that the Almighty did.

> O Holy Child of Bethlehem
> Descend to us we pray . . .

They had been pleasant enough in their civilized, rather patronizing way, these sleek, well-fed city folk aping what they imagined were country ways with their waxed jackets and Barbour wellies and Range Rovers to tackle, morning and evening, the threatening terrain between the village and the nearest Thames Valley railway station, all of four miles away. They had treated her with such impervious civility that she had no means of knowing what they thought either about women priests, or about Margaret Moon herself, as a person, if this last concept ever came into their heads. She had found herself warming to old Sam Briggs, who was one of the rare indigenous breed; he occupied sheltered housing in the Old Almshouses and with patent sincerity spat on the ground whenever she passed. He was not, she noted, here tonight.

It was a good congregation, though. There were people here whom she had certainly never seen in the church before, and probably wouldn't again until Easter, if then.

The hymn was nearing its end. Behind the gold rims of her spectacles, she closed her short-sighted eyes briefly in inchoate prayer, waiting humbly for the transforming moment of peace and power.

23

> . . . abide with us,
> Our Lord Immanuel.

As the reedy echoes of the organ faded on the air, the Reverend Margaret Moon turned towards the altar.

The Ferrars had not gone to church. Laura had made the excuses about having too much to do at home, and the girls being tired, though Sara had immediately insisted that she was going to church with the McEvoys, which had made her mother look foolish. But she was past caring by now. Just as long as she didn't have to sit in church, trying to be pious and grateful for all her blessings, of which she had many – she knew that, because James kept telling her so – when all she could feel was rage and humiliation.

It was like a sickness, a physical sickness, which made even Lizzie McEvoy's delicious cooking (stuffed quail with almond wild rice and an orange Sauternes sauce) taste of sawdust and sit in lumps in her throat. She hadn't wanted to go at all tonight, but James had forced her to do it.

'The girls have been looking forward to it, and I'm not taking them and leaving you behind, on your own. Anyway, you can't go into hiding for the rest of your life.'

The trouble with James was that he was a lawyer. If you were a lawyer, everything you had to deal with was so cut and dried that in the end you became, as he would put it in his prissy lawyerish way, more than a trifle cut and dried yourself.

It was hard, sometimes, to hold the thought that he'd played a mean and moody saxophone in his Oxford college jazz band, and had been sleek and dark and excitingly moody himself, or that she had been a Maenad who could dance for hours at a stretch and make her hair spin out in a dandelion clock as she grooved to their beat. He was going

24

to be the most brilliant defence lawyer in criminal history, and she was going to write scintillating, incisive television drama. Funny what life did to you, really. Funny, if you thought that someone grinding a steel-edged heel in your face was funny. That was what life was like.

And she would never know how she came to be a failure, and he came to be a stuffed shirt, and she didn't know now, when he was being so amazingly reasonable, whether what he said was prompted by loving consideration of his wife's well-being, or cool calculation of what would suit him best.

He was certainly determined that she should rejoin the human race, and it didn't seem to matter that forcing her to do it at a dinner party at the McEvoys was the equivalent of hoisting someone on to an unbroken stallion to get back their confidence after a fall from a horse.

Her pride had come to her aid, and she had carried it off. But it made her feel schizophrenic; the slim, elegant, social Laura there at the dinner table laughing and chatting and making all the right noises, while the black voices of her fury raged on in her head. The effort of keeping the two parts separate had given her a genuine headache, and all she craved now was a couple of extra-strength paracetamols and peace to think her poisonous festering thoughts and swear and cry if she wanted to, without James's calm voice saying maddeningly, 'It won't do any good, going on like that. It's not the end of the world, after all.'

What she really didn't need was James to point out in that unbelievably annoying way that they were all healthy and solvent in a world where lots of people weren't. Having it pointed out that she was unbalanced about it and behaving badly didn't help one bit.

'You can't reason yourself out of feeling something!' she

had hurled at James. 'We're not all cold-blooded lawyers, you know.'

And when James had sighed and smoothed down his already immaculate hair and agreed and refused to be drawn into an argument, it all made everything worse, because an argument would have given her somewhere to direct her anger. His sympathy might be genuine enough, but the trouble was that there was no right thing anyone could say or do, except to decree that the facts weren't the facts and it had all been a stupid mistake.

The worst of it was that she had, for once in her life, allowed herself to feel truly confident. She had lived with a heady cocktail of excitement, elation and pride ever since last summer when, over a glass of sparkling wine to celebrate the conclusion of another successful year at Cranbourne Girls, Joan Lambton, the headmistress, had told Laura, her deputy and friend, that she was going to retire next year.

'I'm fifty-eight and I'm single. I've got my years in for my pension now, and it gets harder every year for me to leave my little house in Périgord for the "A" level results and those ridiculous league tables. So next year, I shan't. I shall stay on when the tourists leave, and I shall sketch and read and enjoy the September weather, and get particular satisfaction out of thinking of you all, slaving away on the chalk face.'

'Oh Joan!' Laura's first reaction was dismay. 'That's all very well for you, but —'

'My dear girl, this is your big chance! You've been an outstanding deputy, and I've told my governors they need look no further. They'll advertise, of course, but I have no doubt that I'm looking at my successor. To the next Principal of Cranbourne Girls!'

She raised her glass, and Laura, laughing and pink and protesting, had returned a toast to the present one.

Laura hadn't exactly told anyone herself, but she had hinted to Lizzie and Suzanne, because they were her closest friends, and Hayley Cutler had somehow found out, because she always did.

She was proud of the way she had acquitted herself at the interview. It was only the third she had ever had, and previous ones had been a damp-palmed, twitching nightmare. But this time, she believed in herself; she was confident that she could do the job, and in any case, she knew most of the governors – Piers McEvoy was one of them, for goodness' sake – and they were well aware that on occasions when she had had to deputize for Joan, she had done it well. She had made modest noises after the interview, of course – after all, there were three external candidates, and one might prove to be outstanding – but she had already begun making her plans, looking forward to the long chats with Joan about the future, and the congratulations, and the status she had never dared to hope would be hers.

She would never have dreamed of applying for promotion elsewhere. They could have turned her down out of hand, and rejection mattered to her. Rejection really mattered. James might say it was simply a question of pride, but then James had never in his life had a visible problem about his sense of self-worth.

She had known the day the decision was to be made, and when Joan Lambton's voice greeted her on the phone first thing that morning, her heart had leapt.

It had taken a moment or two to understand what she was hearing, not least because Joan herself was so upset. She had not been authorized to phone; Laura would learn by letter that the new Principal was to be, not Laura, not even one of the unknown and possibly exotic outsiders, but Elaine Siddons, the Head of History, a young woman of advanced ideas who had been a thorn in Joan's flesh since her appointment two years ago. It was a slap in the face to Joan herself, and she was also riven with guilt at the damage her explicit raising of expectations in Laura might have done.

Automatically, Laura said the right things, replaced the kitchen phone gently on its stand, and sat down at the round pine table in the corner of the room, looking at the Hokusai exhibition poster on the wall as if she had never seen it before.

She would have to return to a staff-room where even those who liked her would be unable to resist *schadenfreude* and where everyone, without exception, would fawn nervously on the member of their own ranks who had been so suddenly elevated to power over them. Where she herself would have to mouth warm congratulations to her junior colleague.

She had written six versions of her resignation letter, varying in tone from coldly dignified to vituperative, by the time James came home from the office.

He had turned pale at the notion of anything so extreme. 'Extreme' was James's ultimate word of condemnation, and he had persuaded her not to send any of them, for the moment at least. She would want to apply for another job, and it wouldn't look good to be unemployed when she did it.

It was practical advice. It went without saying that James's advice would be practical, but she wasn't sure she could bring herself to apply for another job. She wasn't sure that she was ever going to be able to put herself back together again in a convincing enough pattern to get one.

And besides, she didn't want to be sensible any more. She wanted to be irrational, and violent, and to punish the world for what the governors of Cranbourne Girls, may they rot in hell, had done to her.

And Piers McEvoy was the worst. She wasn't sure why Piers was the hub of their social group, because nobody really liked him. He was physically unappealing – short and squat – as well as being boorish and overbearing and far too often drunk.

He was a man with something to prove, of course. It was his father, a plain-spoken Northerner, who had built the haulage business up from two second-hand lorries bought when he was demobbed; all that Piers had ever done was sell out after his father's death to an international company for who knew how many millions and a seat on the board. A credible rumour suggested that otherwise it would have been two lorries to two lorries in two generations. Not very bright, Piers.

But somehow, it was hard to refuse the constant invitations to the Lodge. It was such an exquisite house; it seduced you, really, against your better judgement, with decor by one of the London interior decorators and furniture you might read about in collectors' magazines which you pick up but feel are too expensive to buy. It was flattering to be part of the inner circle, and Lizzie's superb cuisine and the quality of the champagne didn't do any harm either.

Money talked, there was no doubt about that. You could buy friendship, influence, anything you liked with that sort of money. Including a place on the board of Cranbourne Girls – a place meantime, until he could get himself made chairman.

His Paula went there, along with the Ferrars girls and Martha Cutler, and he had homed in on the governing body as an interesting toy. His opinion might count for nothing in the London boardroom of Trucking Worldwide, but it was clear he was carving up the Cranbourne Girls' governing body like the conjuror with a lady and an electric saw.

You could, she thought bitterly, carve them up with a butter-knife.

She should have been able to count on his support for her application – they were nominally close friends, after all – or at the very least he could have warned her about the way things were going and cushioned the blow.

But she knew now, as if she had been privy to the governors' discussions, that he had gone against her. She knew by the way he had looked at her tonight, knew he was getting some sick, sadistic pleasure out of watching her, noticing the dark circles from lack of sleep and the bitten nails with the knowledge that he had got in to inflict this injury on her mind. It was a sort of mental rape.

If he had said anything about it, anything at all, she was not sure that the social Laura could have remained in control.

But nothing had been said. In this village, nothing ever was said to rock the social boat, except with doors closed and shutters bolted, or under the seal of confessional coffee at the kitchen table to another woman.

They walked home through the village, hearing the sound of the organ from the church as they passed. James took her elbow solicitously as they reached the front door, and having unlocked it, put his arm round her to usher her in ahead.

He's treating me as if I were ill or deranged, she thought. Perhaps I am.

She knew she must pull herself together somehow. She was becoming unbalanced, obsessional; she wasn't eating properly, and she felt light-headed and strange. And now she was afraid – she was very much afraid – that she was beginning to do things, weird things, without realizing she had done them. Like placing a bunch of dead flowers bound suggestively in black thread on the middle of her desk.

She had stared at it when she came down yesterday

morning, and the rest of the family had looked at her oddly and denied all knowledge, and she found that she could not quite dismiss the notion that she might have done it herself. Which was a nasty thought, but not as alarming as the thought that if she hadn't, someone else had got into the house and left this cruel suggestion of a wreath for the funeral of her hopes.

Outside, the midnight, far from being clear, was damp and unpromising. The electric light in the church had been switched on, streaming through the open doorway in a golden rectangle.

Margaret, her wide embroidered vestment making her look squarer than ever, took up her usual stance by the ancient yew to the left of the south door. There was a little worn hollow in the stone just there, and she liked to feel that here she stood in the footsteps of her predecessors in office – however shocked some of them might have been by such blatant disregard for the views so trenchantly expressed by St Paul.

'Happy Christmas, Margaret – lovely service!'

'Thank you *so* much, Miss Moon. Good-night. Oh Caroline! Happy Christmas!' Mwah, mwah. 'Drinks tomorrow, remember, twelve o'clock.'

'Not much chance of a white Christmas this year.'

Someone made the inevitable comment, and a woman somewhere behind shuddered.

'Don't even mention it! I hate snow.'

'Nice for the children, though.'

Like a stream in spate, irrepressibly, the flow of polite banalities poured out, lapping the congregation in a flood of well-intentioned insincerity as its constituent parts filed through the door-way and fanned out on to the flagstone path.

Margaret scanned them all shrewdly as she processed them: smile, murmur a greeting, shake hands with just the slightest sideways impetus to move them along, smile, murmur, shake hands again.

She had, she reflected, heard only one genuine, heartfelt remark ('Has anyone got an onion they can spare me? Please? I used my last one in the stuffing and forgot all about the bread sauce.') and that was not excluding the embrace and, 'Dear Margaret! May Our Lord's birthday shower you with the *fullest* blessings!' from the oppressively evangelical Mrs Cartwright. Perhaps, Margaret allowed guiltily, the woman really meant it, but she would be surprised to see her at early communion tomorrow morning.

She could put a name to a good number of them by now; others she recognized, a few she did not know at all. Visitors, perhaps, or what they called Occasional Christians, though whether because they appeared on occasions like this, or because these appearances were so infrequent, she was never quite sure.

And here was Piers McEvoy now, in camel coat and rollneck cashmere sweater. He was a short, flabby man with fair colouring and glassy, protuberant eyes, like a fat pale frog in a blond wig, Margaret thought. He had freckled hands, too, one of them now clutching at the shoulder of the scarlet military-style coat worn by a willowy brunette rather taller than he was. She wasn't Mrs McEvoy – was she the young doctor's wife, perhaps? – and if Froggy had wooing on his mind it was clear from the expression of his victim that he was out of luck.

She had taken some time to sort out the women in the group that revolved around the McEvoys – they seemed to be of similar age, and tended to cluster at church or social functions – but she had it more or less straight now.

That was Elizabeth McEvoy coming out, her face pale

and tired-looking under a Black Watch tartan silk Alice band. She liked what she had seen of her, and perhaps presumptuously felt rather sorry for her, since however lavishly interlined her Colefax and Fowler curtains might be it could hardly make up for having to live with Piers. She was always beautifully dressed; tonight she was wearing a coat which looked as if it cost more than most women's clothes' allowance for a year, but she wore it as if, like a doll, she had been dressed in it by someone else.

Suzanne Bolton, just behind, was the nurse, and looked it, with her crisp light brown hair always immaculately styled. She was the one who would give a hand with anything practical in the church, if you didn't mind your other volunteers dropping out one by one because she couldn't help trying to organize everyone else as if they were in an operating theatre. She was married to a businessman – what was his name again? Patrick, that was it. Had a business in the town nearby supplying some sort of engineering parts, which was going well now after a bad patch. He was coming out with his arm round the shoulders of Ben, their son. They were very alike, those two, with their dark red hair and brown eyes. The likeness was accentuated by the air they both had of expecting that someone would bark, 'Get that sterilized' at any moment.

Then there was Hayley Cutler. She was the easy one to remember, leggy with wavy blonded hair worn long and that thick-as-clotted-cream American accent, which always seemed just a little exaggerated. She was chatting now to a man Margaret didn't recognize, but as usual was making great play with her long thick eyelashes, and laughing her warm, throaty laugh. Mr Cutler had apparently fled the scene some time before, but Hayley certainly wasn't the type to let that dent her social life. *Au contraire*, if Minnie Groak – an amateur at cleaning

Margaret's house but a rigorously professional gossip – was to be believed.

The fourth of the group – which was undoubtedly *the* group to be in with in Stretton Noble – was Laura Ferrars, wife of James, a lawyer who was one of the churchwardens. She was a deputy headmistress, with a manner which seemed cool but which might stem from being shy. Margaret hadn't noticed them tonight; perhaps they were away.

'Ah, vicar,' said McEvoy, with the sort of heavy facetiousness that made Margaret's hackles rise. 'Well done! That will have set me up nicely for another year's sinning.'

I feel sure you don't need any encouragement. The tart rejoinder sprang to her tongue, but she was practised now in the control of that unruly member, and smiled noncommittally as he laughed in appreciation of his own joke. The gust of his breath was stale and whisky-laden.

A group of teenagers, giggling and jostling, passed on the far side without meeting her eye, though she was regarding them benevolently. There had been stifled whispers and muffled snorts of laughter from that quarter of the church, but their intoxication was mainly with the wine of youth, and if they had been to a party, at least they had broken off to come to church.

She recognized one of them – Andy Cutler, a shamelessly good-looking sixteen-year-old with a black pony tail, black leather jacket and silver earring. Her eyes lingered on him fondly; just the type of young rebel she liked. The church was badly in need of a youth club, and it would take someone like this lad to give it any sort of street cred. She bet herself a half-bottle of her favourite Chablis, to be collected after its inaugural meeting, that she could pull him in as a founder member. He was definitely the brightest thing she had laid eyes on in her six weeks' tenure.

The last of them were straggling out now; a mother

clasping a child, sprawled in sleepy abandon across her shoulder, elderly Mrs Travers, immaculate in her Jaeger coat and Gucci scarf, but clinging to her husband's arm and walking painfully with a stick. They were the old guard, living in the original village manor house in its own park. He tended to see himself still in the position of squire even if nobody else did, but they performed what they saw as their duties with an old-fashioned courtesy which was hard to resent. Nobody had the heart to tell them that the commuters who had now gentrified the cottages the Travers family had once owned didn't really consider themselves peasants any more. Now they paid the compliments of the season with appropriate cordiality, as Penny Jackson, the organist, shot past, her hair as usual in mad disorder, calling over her shoulder, 'Left the pudding on! Merry Christmas!'

Margaret went back into the church where Ted Brancombe, one of the churchwardens, was waiting to count the collection with her. He bent to kiss her cheek, a big solid farmer with grizzled fair hair and hands as hard as horn from years of toil and weather. He had checked the heating already, he told her, so it was all in order for tomorrow morning's services.

His wife Jean, a thin, anxious, small-boned woman who was blowing out night-lights and collecting the jam jars on to a tray with the practised efficiency of one who had performed the task many times before, pattered over with her Christmas greetings, and Margaret embraced her too with genuine warmth. She was aware of the dangers of having favourites among your parishioners, but there were, thank God (and that was not a phrase she used lightly), people you simply couldn't help liking.

With the collection safely counted and stowed away, and the service-books neatened for Christmas Day, they left Margaret to lock up.

She went into the vestry to disrobe and came out again, buttoning her practical tweed coat up to her throat. She bobbed to the altar, snapped off the lights, and stood for a moment in the hushed holy darkness of the church. Her church.

The light source was outside now, and she could see faintly the deep reds and blues of the ancient glass in the windows. It was all very beautiful and very peaceful.

Right now, in St John's Marketgate, they would be serving hot coffee and mincepies to people who, for one or another sad reason, had nowhere else to be. There would be people drunken and maudlin, or stoned and impervious, or weeping over past or present failures. Her successor, a decent young man, would be summoning up the last remains of his energy to cope with six simultaneous demands despite sinking fatigue, both mental and physical.

And here she was, bursting with energy and nothing to do with it except go home and give her cat, the irresponsibly-named Pyewacket, a saucer of Christmas cream and perhaps a sliver of the smoked salmon she was allowing herself for Christmas lunch.

She had sent presents for her old friends, the familiar dossers and winos who frequented the churchyard, and money for their Christmas feast, but would any of them at St John's, she wondered, have time to spare her so much as a thought? She doubted it.

But that was a self-indulgent, mawkish sort of reflection, and finishing the communion wine was hardly enough to give her an alcoholic excuse for such a pathetic and self-pitying attitude. But could this really be her destiny – the plan she was so sure God had in mind for her – or was she merely suffering the result of a Bishop's whim? Though that, of course, was religion's catch-all; God could use as an instrument the Bishop's prejudices just as easily, and certainly more commonly, than Cecil B. de Mille-style thunderbolts.

It was an odd sort of challenge, this parish of hers. She had followed an elderly priest, wise and much-loved, who had looked after his flock without ever feeling that their heels needed nipping. Margaret couldn't quite see it that way.

If only Stretton Noble weren't so neat, so self-sufficient, so perfectly organized in its discreet worship of Mammon, with God kept tidily in this pretty stone box and propitiated with offerings (meagre enough, she thought wryly) to His Fabric Fund and His Organ Appeal.

She had begun to stir things up already, with a sermon at the regular Sunday morning service today about the dual nature of Christ as God and man, which led naturally enough to contemplation of our own dual selves; the temptation to show a surface which was smooth and pretty, and totally at odds with the darker needs and failures and shame of our fallen state, which we denied at our peril.

It was a departure from the usual 'wouldn't it be nice if everyone was nice' sermon they tended to expect, and she had sensed the frisson every preacher recognizes when the message somewhere has struck home. At least she hadn't had a single hearty, 'Splendid sermon, vicar!' on the way out, which had to be progress.

The trouble was, she didn't really know where to go from there. It reminded her forcibly of one of those very tasteful, highly-expensive educational puzzles in hand-crafted wood which children loathe and parents will insist on buying for them instead of Sonic the Hedgehog and Barbie and Power Rangers. Everything in Stretton Noble fitted together with just such smooth, forbidding intricacy, with no awkward protuberances and no disfiguring gaps.

She sighed, looking down the length of the nave towards the altar. Oh Lord, she prayed silently, help me to be a catalyst for change. Help me to break apart this deathly smugness, and open up their hearts to real emotions once more.

She did not recall a favourite saying of her mother's, whose constant complaint it had been that her children never listened to a word she said. 'Be very, very careful what you ask for,' she had cautioned, 'because you just might get it.'

But Margaret's round, cheerful face was sombre as she locked the huge oak door and set off with uncharacteristically leaden steps towards the two-bedroomed box in a recent housing-development which was the new vicarage, still thinking about the neat, smooth, impenetrable artefact.

She did not, unfortunately, follow her own image through to its logical conclusion. Hand-crafted puzzles, once they are taken apart, are not readily reassembled. Without great patience, determination and skill, they are doomed to lie for ever in pieces at the bottom of the toy box. And already, though she had failed to notice it, the sections were beginning to slide apart.

2

'Come on, come on! The night is young, and there's still a few inches of whisky left in the decanter,' Piers McEvoy was urging the group gathered outside the lych gate, which included those who had dined with him at the Lodge, now saying their thank yous and goodnights.

Patrick Bolton, at the edge of the group, took deep breaths of the cooler air. He had drunk a little too much – somehow you always did at the McEvoys' – and he was in the mood of philosophical disengagement which that state so often induces. He lit up a cigarette and drew on it, exhaling smoke which hung about his head in the dampness.

Throwing him a look of contempt, Suzanne went past to join the others and was soon laughing and talking animatedly. He found himself looking at her with the eyes of a stranger; in his current detached state, he felt only an intellectual regret that this was so, and that the marriage which had seemed so solid before he became a failure in his wife's eyes had become such a cold, uneasy relationship.

Yet nostalgia was part of the Christmas package, wasn't it, with all those corny carols and 'There went out a decree from Caesar Augustus' and all that stuff. It set him thinking back to their better times, their army days. They had both been so well-suited to army life, that was the thing. As the eldest in a family of six, he had been used to responsibility, and the protection duties of the modern military had suited him admirably. It had given him a deep satisfaction to think that, thanks to him, an aid convoy had got through or an IRA attack on civilians been thwarted.

Suzanne had been the perfect soldier's wife, following the drum cheerfully, and constantly resourceful and uncomplaining. It had never occurred to either of them that he would not be offered a further commission and promotion.

It had been painful to adjust to life without the ceremonial and the comradeship, and even Queen's Regulations, God bless 'em, and he had taken a long time to find his feet in the engineering parts business, because his heart was not in it. It had been a great relief to find that Suzanne could immediately pick up a good nursing job in one of the London teaching hospitals, and even become the major breadwinner through the rough days of the recession when he was still on his learning curve. He had been neglectful then, perhaps, but when you're fighting to keep your head above water you don't have time to look at the scenery.

It was only when business picked up and he had at last got on top of the job that he realized that somewhere along the line he had become – diminished, that was the word, now that she had taken over the responsibility that had previously been his. She had to exercise considerable authority, of course, in her position as theatre sister, but it had begun to spill over into everyday life to a positively worrying extent. She was becoming a control freak; it was losing her friends, but she flipped if he so much as suggested that spontaneity was also a virtue, and a little bit of muddle never hurt anyone. They didn't make love very often these days; he had begun to feel she had a stopwatch on him, and a 'duly-performed' checklist in her head.

Much of the time, he simply accepted that they lived at arms' length, but he regretted that she had no use now for the protective warmth that had characterized his relationship with her in the past. He knew she was having problems at work, and was indeed worried about what it seemed to be doing to her, but offering TLC to Suzanne was about as profitable as snuggling up to a Scorpion tank.

His eye fell on Elizabeth McEvoy, on the farther side of the group behind her husband, also a little detached from it. He could never understand how such a gentle creature could have brought herself to marry a brute like Piers, whose coarse bullying manner even he found offensive. It was her neat, delicate profile he could see, her mouth drooping and her eyes wide and wistful, as if she were looking sadly out to distant horizons. The Little Mermaid, he thought suddenly; that was what she reminded him of, the enchanting statue on the Langeline in Copenhagen, and she looked all too often as if, like Andersen's tragic sea-maid, she too were walking on knives. His gaze softened as he looked at her.

Elizabeth did not notice his regard. As her husband issued invitations, she dug her nails into the palms of her hands until she thought they must bleed. And she should never have worn these stupid sandals; her feet were killing her, her back ached and her head was throbbing so that she felt almost sick. She had to go on and on, with all this desperate entertaining, trying to keep Piers busy and amused, but increasingly these days everyone seemed tense and jaded. Tonight she had been terrified that the whole thing would blow up in their faces; you could have cut the atmosphere with a knife. Surely no one who didn't have to go home with Piers would choose to do so!

She was desperate that the children should have a proper Christmas. Peter, at nine, was still sentimental when he was allowed to be, and this was probably the last year Milla would believe in Santa Claus wholeheartedly – that was, as long as Paula wasn't inspired to make this the night she extended her sister's education, and surely even Paula in her current phase of twelve-year-old cynicism couldn't be as merciless as that.

But she must get them to bed, and have time to sort things out. This Christmas was going to be worse even than usual, the first since Mother Mac died. Piers's mother had been, like his father, blunt and plain-spoken and formidable, but she could be relied on to keep Piers in line, and she had been improbably kind to the daughter-in-law who was as unlike her as anyone could be. She had always given Elizabeth a sense of security, and indeed it was only after her death that Piers had started drinking in earnest – but she mustn't think about that now. She must put on a good show tomorrow, if this Christmas wasn't to be like far too many other recent occasions, with her left frantically trying to put on a brave face and salvage something from the wreckage to slip into the thin file in her mind marked 'Happy Family Memories'.

But nobody wanted to come, thank God, thank God, thank God. They were all, even Hayley Cutler, collecting up assorted children and making their excuses.

'You're a glutton for punishment, Piers, I'll say that for you,' Patrick said with an attempt at jollity as Piers, unsuccessful elsewhere, turned to him. 'I've got another heavy day's partying ahead, and I want to be fit to enjoy it.'

Suzanne said acidly, 'That's what's known as the triumph of hope over experience. Good-night, Lizzie. That was a perfectly lovely party – I don't know how you do it. Try to get ten minutes shuteye before tomorrow morning, won't you? You can always get Piers to peel the potatoes.'

Elizabeth smiled tiredly and hugged her, but Piers had moved out of earshot.

'Anthea, you'll come won't you darling? You're off the leash without the old man for once – make the most of it!'

Anthea Jones, in her red coat, was moving off already, as if trying to keep space between herself and her would-be host.

'That's very kind, but I must get back to my babies. Richard's second on call, so I really shouldn't be out at all. And we've still got to do the Santa bit.'

'Sssh!' Suzanne frowned, pointing down to the six-year-old leaning sleepily against Elizabeth McEvoy's coat, but the child was clearly not listening.

'Come on, Milla darling,' her mother said. 'Time we got you home.'

Her husband, seeing the party break up despite his efforts, turned away with a petulant shrug, returning none of the shouted 'Good-nights'.

Hayley Cutler's rich American tones carried in the night air as she summoned her family.

'Gather up, Cutlers! Back to the ranch. Andy!' she called towards the teenagers still clustered round the gate.

He detached himself and lounged across. There was a low-voiced discussion before she turned away, calling over her shoulder, 'OK honey, an hour but that's all. Past 1.30 and you're grounded.'

With the two younger children, she crossed towards the Briar Patch, as she had christened the cottage where they had lived since her divorce five years ago.

'Patrick, for heaven's sake don't be so bloody stupid. I'll drive – the place is swarming with policemen on a night like this. Into the back, Ben.'

Bolton, protesting that it wasn't far and he was perfectly

fit to drive, handed over the keys meekly enough, and Suzanne swung the car round neatly and set off back the way they had come, past the Lodge and out the quarter of a mile to Bentham's, on the edge of the village.

It was only a few hundred yards back to the Lodge, but with Milla clinging to her waist and stumbling along half-asleep, Elizabeth walked slowly. She was wrestling with a deep reluctance to go back to the house, which was natural enough considering all that she still had to do when she got there.

Yet it wasn't only that. There was something about the house these days, a sort of feeling that something – somewhere – was badly wrong. It wasn't her house at all, of course, it was Piers's house, his possession and his pride. And things were badly wrong with Piers; perhaps, she thought fancifully, his darkening spirit poisoned the air.

But even that wasn't everything. There were strange things happening, things she couldn't explain, like the spilled sugar with the primitive face drawn in it: a circle, with two dots for eyes, a down-turned mouth, and other little strokes representing tears. It was the sort of thing a child might draw, but she had gone to bed after the children and got up before, and she always woke if they were moving about . . .

They had reached the gate now, and in she must go. Peter, at her side, had been talking companionably – he was a child who was seldom silent – about a moth which had tried to barbecue itself over his own personal candle.

'So I shooed it away, Mummy, but then it came back, again and again. So I put a hymn book over the top, but it began to smell funny so I took it off, but I had to keep on shooing it away all the rest of the hymn. Why do they do that, Mummy? It's silly, isn't it? Why don't they know it's silly, Mummy?'

'I don't know, darling,' she said mechanically. Piers had gone on ahead, of course, presumably to shut himself into the games room, which was his particular preserve, with what was left in the whisky decanter, just in case she was unreasonable enough to ask him to help her clear up, or do something for tomorrow, or even fill the children's stockings.

She bit her lip. She couldn't afford to let herself start crying now. She mustn't fall apart. She had far too much to do.

Paula McEvoy had outdistanced the family party, while not walking fast enough to risk catching up with her father. She was tired, though she wasn't prepared to admit it to herself, and as a result felt crosser than usual. Even crosser than usual.

It was all just so naff, the whole Christmas bit. Why couldn't Mum just chill out, instead of pretending like this? They'd be a lot better off like the Cutlers, with everyone accepting that Christmas Day was dismal and you just had to get through it, so you would have no need to feel sorry for your mother and guilty because you weren't making yourself into some sort of domestic slave, or something.

She'd said that to Martha Cutler this evening, when the two of them had sneaked out into the garage for a smoke. It had been cold, and she wasn't that keen on fags, actually – she'd had to be very careful not to breathe in too deeply and choke, which would give away the fact that she hadn't quite worked out how to inhale – but Martha, who was a year older, really smoked, four or five a day sometimes, and she definitely wanted Martha to be impressed.

'I wish my parents would just split up and get it over with, like yours,' she had said, making it sound quite casual, as if this was the sort of thing she said all the time, instead of the first time she had spoken it out loud.

Martha, who was whippet-thin and wore black a lot and had a husky voice, blew a smoke ring towards the rafters of the garage, where cobwebs festooned an ancient car roof-rack and a couple of rusty garden tools suspended there.

'What makes you say that?' she drawled. Her accent wasn't quite American, because she'd lived in England all her life and her Dad was English, but she had a hint of something more exotic in her voice which Paula admired enormously and tried from time to time to imitate.

'You wouldn't believe how horrendous tomorrow is going to be. Mum will bang on about the Christmas spirit and insist on puke-making family traditions that she's only just thought of, and the kids will squabble and Dad will get pissed.'

She used the word with a sense of daring, and shot a sideways glance at Martha, to see how it would be received. But Martha, whose mother's language had always been uninhibited, seemed not to notice.

'At least she tries. I like your Mum; she talks to me as if I was a human being instead of a teeny-bopper, which is what Hayley keeps calling me.'

That was another thing Paula admired, calling your mother by her first name. She had rehearsed it secretly – Elizabeth, Lizzie, Liz – but somehow it hadn't worked. She still thought of her as Mummy, which had to be some kind of brainwashing.

Martha dragged the last puff out of her cigarette and ground it below her heel.

'Come on, we'd better get back. If Hayley finds me smoking she'll go ballistic. She's got this awfully American thing about it.'

Obediently, Paula had ground out her own half-smoked cigarette, with secret relief, and followed her friend back into the house.

She had managed to sound cool, talking to Martha, but she still felt sick when she let herself think about the feeling she had constantly these days, that something was dreadfully, dreadfully wrong. And putting it into words hadn't helped at all. Perhaps nothing would.

Now she had achieved her objective of outdistancing her mother and the kids without catching up her father. She reached the house only a few minutes behind him, but she saw the lights go on in the games room so she let herself in quietly. Her father had shut the door, which was a good thing. She could get herself upstairs and out of sight without anyone forcing her to help clear up their stupid party, or go through the toe-curling exercises of stockings and Santa Claus rituals.

Just as she crossed the hall, she heard the 'ping' of one of the telephone extensions being lifted, and stood for a moment very still.

Earwigging was no sort of taboo as far as she was concerned, but she could hear the rest of them coming up the garden path, Milla whining that she wanted to be carried up to bed. Swift as a lizard, she slid up the stairs and was in her bedroom with her own door shut tight and the comfort blanket of Capital Radio filling in any awkward silences.

Hayley Cutler switched on the lights as she came in the door, looked round the open-plan ground floor of the cottage, and groaned. Sometimes she thought it would be easier just to quit and do it herself, but hell's teeth, she wasn't the only able-bodied mortal around.

'Would you look at this place? Mikey, go get some logs

from the shed for the fire. And Marty, all that stuff in the corner is yours. Clear it, can't you?'

'Don't call me Marty.' Martha went across to pick up the litter of wrapping paper and ribbon as her younger brother went silently out. 'You only do because you like to sound really American instead of half-and-half.'

'So? That's a crime, suddenly?' Hayley went to switch on the coffee machine, her invariable first action on getting home. 'I think Marty's a really neat name, and if I'd known you aimed to grow up so prissy, I'd have never called you Martha in the first place. I had a great-aunt Martha once, and she died guessing.'

Martha was moving purposefully round the room, picking things up and straightening the big Kelim cushions on the floor by the log fire, now cold and dead. The expensively-faked Christmas tree in the corner, purchased complete with red bows, silver chains, imitation parcels and gold lights, looked even more tawdry with the lights off.

'Why can't we have a real Christmas tree?' she grumbled. 'The one at the McEvoys' looked really brilliant, all covered with proper ornaments that they've had for years, and real little parcels and chocolates.'

In her stormy life, Hayley Cutler had fought every inch of the way. She didn't play by the rules – as someone once memorably said, there are no rules in a knife fight – and you didn't take home too many popularity prizes, but you fought, or you went under. She swung round from the kitchen area to face her daughter's truculence.

'Why now, honey, I'm sure there are some sugar canes around someplace, if you rake among those packages, and you could hang them on the tree. Switch it on anyway, for goodness' sake, and it'll look better. And tomorrow, if you're heading for a traditional phase, you and Mikey can fix popcorn and thread it

48

on strings just like I did when I was knee high to a grasshopper.'

Her intonation parodied the notion as well as the expression, and her voice sharpened.

'And before you ask me about tomorrow, we've got a delicious lunch all worked out between kind St Michael and the microwave. And if you're about to match me up against sweet St Elizabeth McEvoy, I'd just ask you to remember that some of us have to work for a living and haven't the time to make a career out of being a domestic martyr. I've filled stockings and basted turkeys with the best of them, but you all are old enough now to see the whole Christmas farce for what it really is. If it's just an excuse for a party, and we're the only guests, well, hell, let's enjoy it, OK? Let's all of us enjoy it, instead of everyone checking out my performance and giving it points out of ten.'

She waited, a verbal pugilist weaving and ducking on her toes, to see if Martha would reply, before she poured herself a mug of the strong black coffee that was never far from her elbow, as Michael came in with the basket of logs which he set down on the wide hearthstone.

'Do you want me to light it?' he said politely. He was always polite to his mother; it set her at a distance far more effectively than Andy's tempestuous rages or Martha's confrontations.

'I guess not, unless you kids –' She was cut short by the ringing of the telephone.

'Quarter of one? Now who could that be?' She wondered aloud. 'Oh, it's most likely Grandad, phoning to say Merry Christmas. I'll take it in my bedroom.'

She disappeared and brother and sister looked at each other.

'Most likely Grandad!' Martha mimicked her mother's tone. 'Most likely Nigel, I reckon.'

'Or Eddie. Or one of the others we don't know about yet. He's probably married, phoning after his wife's gone to bed.'

Michael's voice hadn't broken yet; the world-weary sentiments sounded odd, so delivered. 'I'm going to bed. Don't let any fat red-faced men into your bedroom.'

'I'll yell for help if I need it. I might wait up for Andy anyway.'

The door shut behind her brother. Through the floorboards Martha could hear the rise and fall of her mother's voice.

She looked at the cold white ashes of the fire and the unlit Christmas tree. It was all very well for Paula McEvoy to moan about her mother making a fuss about Christmas. Paula was only a baby who hadn't the least idea what it was like out here in the big world where you had to look out for yourself because no one else would.

Her eyes filled with tears, though she would have let them pull out her fingernails with red-hot pincers before she would admit to them. She wanted to be looking forward to Christmas Day, to the magic she remembered, if vaguely, when she was a very small child. But there wasn't a chance in this family. Sometimes she thought her mother simply hated Christmas.

Upstairs, Hayley Cutler replaced the receiver with a grimace. She couldn't quite believe she was stooping this low; doing the dirty on a friend, behaving like . . . Well, she wasn't going to figure out that side of it too closely.

Lizzie might be a sweet girl, but she wasn't exciting, and Hayley had always been coolly aware of her own attractions. Piers McEvoy just couldn't believe his luck, and he couldn't keep his hands off her, either. Surely she could convince him that he owed it to himself to have a wife who could really make things swing.

Not that her idea of a dream lover was someone who looked and tended to behave like Toad of Toad Hall, but time was moving on. Too many men had treated her badly of late, and she could almost hear that clock ticking. It was time for a long-term solution.

And as far as Lizzie was concerned, if she got a good settlement and custody of the kids, she'd probably end up happier. Being weak, she brought out the worst in Piers, whereas Hayley had no doubt at all about her ability to put him in his place once the ring was on her finger. It would be good to ease off, face the future without this corrosive worry.

Downstairs she could hear the children moving about. Just for a moment the old Norman Rockwell pictures rose in her mind; the family gathered round the fire below the laden tree, the mother reading 'The Night Before Christmas' . . .

A lump rose in her throat. She had lost them, somewhere a long way back; after the divorce, perhaps, when Chaz Cutler had removed his worthless self from their lives and even the CSA had given up trying to get money out of him. She had had to be tough then, and the children had stopped expecting cuddles and home-baked cookies from a mother who was permanently stressed-out. She tried to think of the last time she'd hugged one of them, and couldn't. Tears spilled over, slid down her cheeks.

She dashed them away. She couldn't afford the sort of weakness that candles and carols and too much champagne produced, which was one of several reasons why she hated Christmas. But this Christmas was bleaker than ever.

Beside her bed lay the letter from her bank manager

about the future of the employment agency, which she had read so often in the hope that this time she could make it mean something different that it was dog-eared and curled. All those readings told her only one thing; at whatever cost of self-loathing, there was no way but to follow her reluctantly-chosen course, or lose everything.

She had borrowed in the belief that the recession was at an end, but somehow there still weren't the jobs available, and if there were no clients, there was no commission. If she lost that, all of the sacrifices – of close, warm family relationships and the right to act feeble and pathetic when you felt that way – would have been for nothing. She hadn't been able to loll around the place being a homemaker and learning gourmet cuisine, she had gone out and hustled for herself and her family instead of sitting on her butt with her hand out, and this was her reward.

And she had made an enemy. She tried not to think about it because it made her feel sick to her stomach. She had always, somehow, been an outsider, and this forced her to admit that she didn't even know which of the people who disliked her hated her this much. The anonymous letters were bad enough of themselves – three of them, bitchy and poisonous. But this last one; that had really scared her.

This one had been threatening, talking about striking at her heart in the best melodramatic style. She had torn it up and burned it, of course, told herself that nutters who were perfectly harmless acted this way, and tried, unsuccessfully, to put it from her mind.

Then she had come downstairs the other morning to find a pretty, polished red apple sitting in the middle of the kitchen table, with one of her kitchen knives stuck through its core.

When she had checked that none of the kids had suffered from a suddenly-abandoned snack-attack, she had sat down and stared at it in mesmerized horror. The back door was locked, the windows were latched.

The hideous, inescapable conclusion was that the person who hated her had a key. And there were only three people who kept a key of hers; they all kept them for one another. Suzanne Bolton, Elizabeth McEvoy, and Laura Ferrars.

Suzanne Bolton parked the car neatly in the garage, so that the cork she had suspended from the roof to show where to stop just touched the windscreen. It was an old-fashioned wooden garage, and Ben had had to get out to open the big double doors. She padlocked them closed herself, as usual, while the men, engaged in some earnest low-voiced conversation, went on ahead into the house.

It was not, naturally enough, in the same league as the McEvoys' exquisite Lodge, but Suzanne was entirely satisfied with it. When you had lived in a succession of army houses, even a cottage like Bentham's which was short of space and cursed with the sort of sloping ceilings that meant that half the room was unusable was a dream come true. They had spent what money they had on good carpets, immaculate decoration, and a good kitchen and bathroom, and if the furniture came from one of the cheaper discount warehouses at least it was new and smart-looking. She had seen Piers McEvoy's lip curl when they came to dinner, but then she wouldn't have given houseroom to some of those shabby rugs he put on his floors.

All over the house the evidence of Suzanne's skills as a needlewoman, seamstress and homemaker were displayed. As she entered the hall now, the lights of the Christmas tree which stood at the foot of the stairs greeted her, and she viewed it with satisfaction.

She had chosen it carefully; it was a good shape, and it was certainly worth the extra to get the kind that were treated to stop them shedding needles everywhere. She had bought new lights for it, silver and gold instead of the old coloured ones, and this year she had gone for huge tartan bows. There was an evergreen garland over the fireplace in the hall, also caught up with a tartan bow, and there was a pile of presents under the tree. A few, the ones wrapped in dark green tissue and tied with tartan, were her own for Patrick and Ben, and the people they would see tomorrow. She always felt faintly aggrieved that by Christmas Day the packages were such a motley lot; it really looked nicer two weeks before with all her own coordinated parcels ready for posting.

She went through to the kitchen to check that the timer had gone on for the turkey. Patrick's parents and one of his aunts were coming for lunch at two o'clock, and she wanted it cooked ready to slice cold by then. They were expected for drinks again at the Lodge – she spared a sympathetic thought for poor Lizzie – and she didn't want to be fussed by having too much to do when they came back.

The black and white kitchen was immaculately tidy, with the culinary *mise-en-place* set up for tomorrow with the same precision she employed when she set up the instrument table for an operation. If you were theatre sister in a London teaching hospital, disorder of any kind made you feel threatened and uncomfortable.

From the scullery Tigger set up a yapping and she let him out – a quick, neat little Jack Russell bought as a companion for Ben once she had managed to establish, quite firmly, that he would have no siblings.

'Tea, Patrick?' she called, switching on the kettle as he followed her into the kitchen.

He contemplated the suggestion. 'I don't know if I want tea. Perhaps I'll just go straight up to bed.'

'You'd better have at least a couple of glasses of water

before you do,' she warned him, 'or you'll regret it in the morning. In any case —'

She jerked her head meaningfully towards Ben, who had drifted into the kitchen and was kneeling on the floor accepting the dog's extravagant greetings.

'Do you want some hot chocolate, Ben? Or a biscuit? No? Then off you go upstairs, and bring your stocking down to the hall and we'll get it hung up by the fireplace.'

She surveyed him fondly – tall and thin for eleven, with the horn-rimmed spectacles he had insisted on having giving him a quaintly severe expression. He was such a good boy, and she was coming to rely on him more and more, as Patrick became more and more unsupportive.

Ben unfolded himself obediently from the floor, went slowly to the door, then hesitated.

'I can't remember where it is.'

'Good gracious, where it's always kept, silly! In the middle drawer in the chest on the landing. Hurry up now – it's very late.'

Patrick had filled a glass with water and was sipping it doubtfully.

'It just seems such a lot to drink, when you're not thirsty,' he complained.

'You'll pay for it if you don't,' she said crisply. 'Now, once Ben hangs up his stocking, if you take him up and see him into bed, I'll get the presents from the cupboard under the stairs.'

'Er –' Patrick said awkwardly. 'I wonder, isn't he perhaps getting a bit big for Santa Claus? I'm not sure that other boys his age hang up their stockings. Apparently Mike Cutler stopped years ago.'

If Suzanne had thought about it, she might have guessed that he had been reluctantly put up to address this subject. But she was finding it hard at the moment to see their

55

relationship in perspective, and she flushed. That little pinprick was so like Patrick. Everything he said seemed designed to deflate her, to make her feel that all her efforts to hold down an important and demanding job without compromising anywhere else, were unappreciated. No, worse than that; they were actively resented, and the only reason she didn't know was because she was too insensitive and people were too polite to tell her. She knew it was spiteful and untrue, of course, but she had to work hard to keep up her self-respect under attacks like these.

'Hayley Cutler,' she said stiffly, 'is too lazy and too wrapped up in her own gratification to put herself out for anyone. It's got a lot more to do with that than whether or not poor little Mike wants a stocking. You're a long time grown up, and the Christmas traditions are the things you remember all your life – if you're lucky enough to have them.'

Patrick, still looking uncomfortable, said, 'Well, whatever you think.'

He set down his empty glass on one of the surfaces, beside a big, shallow pottery bowl made by Suzanne in one of her evening classes a few years ago.

Seizing the chance to change the subject, he said, 'By the way, what were you burning in this last night?'

She stared at him. 'Burning? What are you talking about?'

'I emptied some ashes out of that bowl this morning when I came down to let Tigger out. They looked as if you'd been burning one of those endless lists of yours – you know, the timetables for what ought to be done by everyone of your acquaintance every moment of every day.'

She coloured again. 'I certainly wasn't burning any lists,' she said stiffly. 'Maybe Ben was playing with matches; you'd better have a word with him.'

But she didn't believe him. He had said more than once that people thought she was bossy, and she assumed this was some silly spiteful joke, and as such better ignored.

Perhaps, if she had accepted what he said, if he had persisted in trying to establish what had happened during the dark and silent hours of the previous night, things might have turned out differently. Perhaps not. Perhaps even then, it was all too late.

Suzanne heard Ben coming down and went through to the hall. They had always made a ceremony out of this, hanging up the big green felt stocking, so lovingly made for Ben's first Christmas when he was only six months old, on the special hook by the side of the fireplace, used only for this purpose. It was a magnificent stocking, large enough to hold real treasures, with his name appliquéd at the top, above the stars and the assorted Christmas fauna, all hemmed around with neat red blanket stitch.

Tigger, who had accompanied him upstairs, came racing down ahead of him; Ben was lagging as he came down the stairs.

Suzanne smiled at him lovingly.

'Come on, darling, you're exhausted! You come and get your stocking hung up, and I'll go and get the mince pie and the carrot.'

Ben stopped, wincing, three steps from the bottom, just above one of the pine and fir-cone bunches.

'Oh, for heavens' sake, Mum!' he groaned.

Suzanne stiffened, looking up at him. His glasses glinted in the light, giving him an opaque, impersonal expression.

'What's the matter?'

Ben was a dutiful child, who had become accustomed to shouldering the burden of his mother's expectations. He had kindly instincts, and he was, if he were honest with himself, a bit scared of what the result of rebellion might

57

be. Only the terror of Mike Cutler's scorn, if, horror of horrors, he found out about this particular wrinkle, drove him on.

He came down the last few steps slowly.

'Look, Mum –' He paused, trying to deal with this as tactfully as he knew how. 'It's just – it's a bit yuk, if you know what I mean. I mean, who's it all for? The stocking, OK, if you like, but I've known for years that Dad ate the mince pie and you put the carrot back in the basket. I marked one years ago, and it was there the next morning. So . . .'

His explanation trailed away, and just for a moment there was a terrible silence. His stomach lurched in fright, but when Mum spoke again, she sounded brisk as usual, though her voice was a bit funny.

'I see. Well, you're certainly right. If it's not for you, there's no point, is there? There's absolutely no point at all.'

She flashed a smile at him, and he smiled back warily.

'Right, off you go to bed. You're a big boy now – see? No more stockings.'

She unhooked it as she spoke, and Ben, shocked by the lack of resistance to his argument, opened his mouth to say that he hadn't meant that, not exactly, then thought the better of it.

She had her back to him now, adjusting some of the parcels under the tree, and he hesitated for a moment, then said, 'OK, then. Good-night, Mum.'

His father came out of the kitchen, holding the dog lead, and Tigger raced off with him for his late-night walk. Ben called good-night to him too, then continued uncertainly on his way upstairs.

He'd got his own way, hadn't he? But he hadn't meant that *this* Christmas – tomorrow morning – he was ready to come downstairs to a fireplace which didn't have a stocking hanging beside it, full of surprises and little treats. There had always been a stocking there on Christmas morning, and he couldn't quite believe that there wouldn't be.

Perhaps Mum would do it anyway. She must have all the stuff, after all. At the top of the stairs he sneaked a look over the banisters.

She was standing in the middle of the hall, with two bright red spots on her cheeks and brilliant, glittering eyes. She was making a strange, soft, high-pitched keening sound and she was ripping the stocking apart, right down its blanket-stitched edges. She looked – he shuddered – almost as if she was, well, mad.

He got into bed, and cried himself to sleep.

3

───•═•───

She had been sleeping a heavy, dreamless and exhausted sleep, but now she was suddenly and completely awake, as if someone had laid a hand on her shoulder.

She turned her head instinctively, but she knew that there was no one there.

She felt strange, somehow, in a way she could not quite define, though she thought, vaguely, that this had happened before. She could sense her eyes becoming glassy, her gaze fixed, and then . . . She didn't know what would happen, but she knew that it scared her.

She could still move. She slid out of bed with infinite caution, then out of her bedroom and down the stairs. About her, the house was hushed, but in her fancy the silence was strained and unnatural, as if a scream were being choked back because of a steely hand about the throat.

Perhaps if she kept moving . . . She went into the kitchen, busied herself with the kettle, a mug, a teabag, the teapot. But it needed more and more desperate concentration; her movements were getting slower, slower . . .

Suddenly, as if a switch had been thrown, she perked up. Her eyes were bright now, her shoulders straighter, her movements quick and decisive.

Her lips curved, and she began to giggle.

'Clever old Missy!' she said softly. 'Clever old Missy!'

61

She looked at the mug, and the teapot warming in front of her, and pulled a naughty face.

'Tea!' she said disdainfully. 'How crummy, how entirely crummy!'

She liked the sound of that, and declaimed it once or twice, as she opened a kitchen cupboard to take out a bottle of cooking brandy and slosh a large measure into a drinking glass. She sipped at it, smacking her lips and apparently oblivious to the rawness of the spirit.

'That's better. And now –!'

She went through to the hall, moving cautiously and murmuring 'Sssh!' to herself under her breath. There was a long, deep cupboard which ran below the stairs and she bent low to step into it, then crawled her way purposefully to the deepest, furthest corner. Under a pile of dust sheets there was a black plastic bag which she pulled towards her. It was quite heavy, and an awkward shape in such a confined space; she was strong, very strong, but she struggled a little to get it out. She banged it against the door and swore out loud, then froze, listening. But there was no responsive sound; the spell of silence still lay over the place, and she carried her booty into the kitchen.

Before she opened it, she went to the sink where a pair of rubber gloves were draped to dry, and put them on. She admired her funny pink hands, wiggled the fingers a little bit. Then she went to the table and sat down for a moment to think.

She had planned to write another letter tonight – another little part of her grand design – but now there was something else that was bothering her.

She didn't recall the past very clearly. Memories and times were blurry, somehow, but she remembered feelings. She remembered fear and shame and a plump body and gold glasses that glinted, and someone who seemed somehow to know what you had done in secret. It was confused in her mind, but she was clear about one thing; she must make her keep her distance, scare her off, or disaster for Missy would follow as it had before.

The typewriter she took from the bag was a battered black Imperial, almost a museum piece. She set it up on the kitchen table, then made another trip to the sitting room to fetch notepaper, envelopes and stamps. Smiling in appreciation of her own cunning, she pulled the sheet from the centre of the pad, chose envelopes from the heart of the packet.

She tapped with silent concentration, giggling occasionally her soft, high-pitched giggle, then stood up. She was still in her nightgown, with her funny pink hands and bare feet; from the pegs at the back door she took a hooded raincoat, and slipped her feet into a pair of gumboots.

She took the letters and opened the back door stealthily, just enough to let herself out, then closed it quickly to shut off the light from inside. She stood in the shadows, listening and looking down the deserted street. She had one or two things to do tonight and she slid into the blackness like a fish released into its natural element, darting and flickering in and out of the shadows, herself a deeper darkness made visible, had there been eyes to see.

But beyond, the calm domestic night-world with its streetlamps and pavements and parked cars was empty, its houses blank in their own innocent darkness, except where a window sparkled with the lights of a Christmas tree.

This was her playground, the world in which she moved for her mischief, her own special homage to her unholy deities of Misrule. And that mischief was breeding crueller mischief, as she watched from her strange hiding-place the people she knew best become twisted by distress, even fear. She had learned how to exploit vulnerability long ago, and

63

if she had forgotten why she needed to do so, she recognized the deep, evil excitement that was growing now, demanding blacker devilment and wider powers.

So tonight she had thinking work to do, and she slid back through the shadows like the ripple of a running wave. Seated at the table with more of the rough brandy, she plotted, her eyes bright and blank, as if their intelligence were unconnected to a spirit within. She must practise, experiment; she must be clever and elusive, until with her grand finale she could change her world dramatically and take control. She could feel the need strong within her, consuming her like the healing fire itself – but that was enough. Like other night creatures, she dare not risk even the first whisper of cock-crow.

She put the typewriter back in its bag. There was a little book covered with blue suede in there too; she stroked it thoughtfully with her pink-gloved hands, but did not open it.

As she came out of the cupboard, having restored the bag to its original place, she was getting sleepy, and back in the kitchen she hung up the coat, returned the boots and gloves to their proper place. She was tired now, very tired. The bed upstairs was warm and inviting, even if it led her back into the prison from which she could do no more than peer out at the world through the eyes of Dumbo, as she always called her.

At least she could spy on Dumbo, even if she couldn't always fight her way out. Dumbo, poor fool, could see nothing when Missy was in control, though even that lamebrain was beginning to sense the musky taint of wickedness in the air about her, and be afraid. Very much afraid.

Smiling drowsily, Missy made her way quietly back upstairs.

*　　*　　*

Laura Ferrars, yawning a yawn which almost dislocated her jaw, shuffled into the kitchen with her dressing gown unfastened and her feet shoved into an ancient pair of furry slippers. It was six o'clock; she would put the turkey in the oven and then go straight back to bed. She didn't wake refreshed these days, after restless and dream-haunted nights.

Melissa and Sara, thank heavens, were past the stage of 4 a.m. reveille on Christmas Day, and if Sara woke she would open her stocking quietly in her own room. The Wicked Witch of the North was a pussycat compared to Melissa untimely roused.

With arms braced she lifted the prepared turkey from the kitchen table and slid it into the Aga. For a nasty moment she thought it hadn't clearance, but no, it was all right.

She was going to make a big effort today, she decided as she closed the door. After all, it was Christmas, and James and the girls couldn't be expected to tiptoe round the corpse of her self-esteem speaking in hushed whispers indefinitely.

She had not as a child been in the habit of expressing her feelings, and living with James certainly wouldn't encourage anyone to parade them. 'Thank goodness you're level-headed, Laura,' was his highest praise, usually after he had left her to cope with a teenage tear-tantrum from one of the girls.

She was past mistress by now at suppressing her problems under a veneer of confidence when she felt shy, or calmness when panic threatened to engulf her. And it worked, in its way, though when articles in thoughtful magazines suggested that this was hardly wise, she could believe them. The injuries life inflicted on her never seemed to heal very well; they suppurated and left scars, but you can't change your nature to order.

So all she could do now was to cover this particular wound – deeper and wider and more crippling than any she had suffered before – with the flimsy fabric of cheerfulness and hope that gangrene didn't set in.

At least she should have another three or four hours before she had to get the show on the road. She had reached the kitchen door when her eye was caught by something on the floor.

One of the girls must have left her school blazer lying there, though what on earth she had been doing with it in the holidays she could not imagine. Tutting mumsily, she went to pick it up and restore it to the pegs in the lobby by the back door.

The Cranbourne Girls blazer was a pleasant shade of dark green, with its crest and motto ('*Video, audio, disco*': officially rendered as 'I see, I hear, I learn' but the source of much mirthful satisfaction to those of a less classical bent) embroidered on the pocket in gold thread.

This pocket, when Laura picked it up, flapped loose. Uncomprehending for a moment, she stared at it, ripped savagely along its stitching from the body of the garment.

Her first thought was of concealment. She had been shaken already by the flowers, but this was worse. If it were, indeed, something she had done herself, the others must never know. No one must discover if she was having blackouts, going mad.

She had the needle threaded and was sitting in her rocking chair, the blazer in her hand, before her shock dissolved in tears. Surely she could not have done this, surely . . .

But if not she, then who? She looked about her comfortable, homely kitchen as if, even now, some spirit of malevolence might lurk within its walls, and began to shake.

* * *

The Christmas Day Open House at the Lodge was proving less than entirely successful. Too many of the guests had seen each other too recently, and the children who had last night relished the novelty of all being together, were jaded and fretful after a late night and an early start to the day.

Half a dozen other couples appeared, some fresh from the eleven o'clock carol service at St Mary's, which inspired Piers to new heights of wit as he greeted them with glasses of champagne heavily adulterated with peach schnapps.

'Well, how was our lady padre this morning? Miss Margaret Moon – it's just too good to be true, really, wouldn't you say? Do you suppose it's a *nom de plume* – or a *nom de guerre*, perhaps, fight the good fight, and all that.'

He gave a roar of laughter which shook his fleshy jowls, and one or two of his audience laughed too.

'It does seem a bit strange, certainly, having a woman priest,' said pretty Anthea Jones, who had given her husband Richard instructions that he was not to leave her side for ten seconds if Piers McEvoy were anywhere in the vicinity.

'I really don't get this, you know. Tell me why it's such a big deal? If she was setting up as a football jock, I could understand it.' Hayley Cutler, resplendent in a holly-berry red silk shirt and dark green velvet trousers, was in a mellow mood already, thanks to the American breakfast-time Christmas tradition of egg nogg made with liberal proportions of brandy.

'I have to say it's crossed my mind that she'd make quite a useful prop,' Piers put in.

Hayley persisted. 'We've had women priests in the States for years, and it seems like a nice enough job for a lady to me. Sure, some of them are dreary enough, but the guys in that line of business aren't usually any ball of fire either.'

67

'I don't think I would actually describe Margaret Moon as dreary.' Richard Jones, a cheerful, open-faced young Welsh doctor who in his spare time was a handy second-row forward for the county rugby football team, had already had some dealings with her over elderly and hospitalized parishioners, and was ready to admit that she had impressed him.

'To keep up the sporting metaphor, she's ready to run with the ball, I would say. She might actually stir things up around here. She's a good person to talk to, and she's started taking a real interest in people's lives already. Perhaps the fact that she's a woman is an advantage.'

Suzanne sniffed. 'The whole thing gives me the creeps. There's something unnatural about it, and she looks simply ridiculous, standing there in a white nightgown. It takes all the meaning out of it, as far as I'm concerned.'

'Never knew you were one of the God Squad, Suzie.' Piers was splashing champagne into every glass he could find that was not brimming already.

'She isn't. She's just in a bad mood and looking for someone to kick who can't kick back, aren't you, sweetheart?'

Patrick's malice was embarrassingly apparent, and Suzanne, whose colour was already high, glared at him with more naked antagonism than was socially comfortable for the bystanders.

Anthea shifted uneasily, and true to his rugby player's instincts, Richard flung himself into the conversation with gallantry if not tact.

'It's all a question of getting used to the idea, don't you agree? Think how much prejudice there was initially against the idea of women being doctors instead of nurses, and yet no one thinks twice about that now.'

It might have been described by one of his team-mates

as gathering a hospital pass. Suzanne's face darkened further.

'Oh no?' she snapped. 'Well, all I can say is that you do if you have to work with them in theatre. That's one area where political correctness can't be used to cover up deficiencies, and nothing would induce me to allow a woman doctor to lay hands on me. Take my advice; if there are mascaraed eyelashes above the theatre mask when they wheel you in, get up and get out.'

In the awkward silence which followed, Anthea, who was taking five years out from medicine to enjoy her two small children, bit her lip, and Richard bridled, ready in her defence to make matters worse. But before he could say anything, Piers intervened with spiteful glee.

'Oooh! Do I detect just the teensiest weensiest whiff of sour grapes? Come on, Suzie darling, we all have to accept our limitations!'

Suzanne, her cheeks crimson, stared at him with open loathing for a long moment.

'Oh, I do wish you would,' she said at last, and turned away, leaving the group, with some relief, to drift apart in search of less contentious conversation.

Fumbling for a handkerchief, Suzanne fled to lock herself in the cloakroom where she could have a good howl.

What on earth had possessed her to vent her feelings like that? She had forgotten Anthea was a doctor, though she and Richard would never believe that now. And she liked Anthea: she was young and sweet and funny, and she had hoped that Anthea liked her too.

But probably she didn't. Suzanne found herself doing things that made people dislike her, but somehow she couldn't stop herself. She didn't much like herself, come to that.

And she was upset today. She was so upset that

talking to people at all was difficult, without bursting into tears.

She'd been desperately hurt about Ben last night, of course, and angry because she felt so foolish about his deception of her over these last years. But oddly enough, it had been Patrick who had made her feel better.

'Oh, come on!' he had said. 'That's a very loving deception. Think about it; he probably felt much the same when he found out he'd been kidded about Santa Claus.'

That did set it in a happier light, and she was grateful to him, though she still felt bereft in a way that obviously he did not understand. Perhaps no man ever did, and that was forgivable. Perhaps if they both made an effort to accept the differences between them, things would be better.

After he had gone up, she finished off her preparations then followed him to bed in a mood of comparative optimism, which made the next morning's discovery all the more shocking.

The meticulously prepared kitchen she had left last night was today a shambles. The little bowls of chopped vegetables, measured herbs and spices had been stripped of their cling-film and tipped into a heap in the middle of the table. The crumbs for the bread sauce had been sprinkled along the edge of the surfaces in loopy patterns, and the ingredients for the stuffing had been taken out of the fridge and mixed together in the bowl where she had some scraps for the dog. After a long search, she found her cooking knives in the dustbin.

Ben, that was her first thought, in some sort of stupid reaction to last night, but when she went up to his room to ask him about it, the child's bewilderment was transparent. He was awake already, his little face white and miserable, and even if she herself felt distracted, she could not have him looking like that on Christmas morning.

'Maybe you're too big for a stocking,' she said, 'but it's a long time till we open our presents in the afternoon. If you'd like to go and look in the cupboard under the stairs, you might find a few things to keep you busy.'

She was rewarded by the transformation in his face, and a strangling hug, and a little of the pain about her heart eased.

But as she came downstairs to tidy up and salvage what she could, her face darkened again. So it was Patrick, was it! What a spiteful, heartless thing to do, even if you did constantly sneer at your wife for her lack of spontaneity.

They had had one of their most bitter and destructive rows about it. Patrick, presumably taken aback by the scale of her anger, foolishly denied it, and then became absurd, suggesting that someone might have broken in, or even, when confronted with the absence of any sign of breaking and entering, accused her of having done it herself.

Remembered rage and indignation dried the tears on her cheeks, and she splashed her face with cold water and renewed her make-up. She would go and seek out Lizzie – always a soothing friend – and offer to help. That was what she was good at – the practical side of things. There weren't many women who could run a house and family as she did, and hold a job like hers, to everyone's satisfaction – or almost everyone's, anyway. Or at least what ought to be to their satisfaction, even if, quite unjustly, it wasn't. But this wasn't the moment to be thinking about all her worries.

When she opened the kitchen door, it was to find her hostess kicking the sleek green Aga at the far side of her expensively countrified kitchen.

71

'Lizzie?' Half-laughing, Suzanne stopped in the doorway and stared at her. 'Whatever are you doing?'

Elizabeth jumped and looked abashed, then turned, holding out a tray of slightly overdone piroshkis.

'Oh – no one was meant to see that. But just look at these! I can never get the temperature right, never. I hate this bloody thing!'

'I don't think you're allowed to say you hate Agas. They're an icon of our class. And those look perfectly all right to me, for anyone who isn't a perfectionist like you.'

Elizabeth gave the pastries a disparaging glance and set them down. 'I'm sure it's all my fault. Piers insisted we had to have it, and he says it's every woman's dream, but I still can't get the hang of it.'

'Ask Laura. She talks to hers.'

'Oh Suzanne, I can't ask Laura anything just now! I don't know what to do about it.'

Their eyes met significantly across the kitchen table.

'It's a pretty awkward situation, isn't it? Did Piers tell you what happened?'

'Not a word. But then I suppose he couldn't, really. If you're a governor you've got a duty of confidentiality.'

'Of course,' said Suzanne diplomatically. 'But Laura isn't taking it well, you know. She always looks so tremendously together and confident, but she's really quite shaky about herself underneath. She was doing her best to put a good face on it last night, all bright and brittle, but you could see she was thinking about it all the time.'

'I know.' Elizabeth's grey eyes were troubled. 'I wanted to say something, but I was afraid I'd make matters worse. And they wouldn't come today. Something about a relative or an old friend coming, but I shouldn't think she feels very festive. And I know she's blaming Piers, even though he's only one of fourteen governors and if all the rest wanted this other woman, there wouldn't be anything he could do.'

'No, of course not.' Suzanne admired Lizzie's wifely loyalty, and she couldn't exactly say that it would be just like Piers to ruin Laura's chances purely for the fun of it.

'I honestly think you should just leave it, Lizzie. She'll get over it. She'll have to, won't she? There isn't an alternative, really. After all, we've all got our crosses to bear, haven't we, and we don't have time to sit about whimpering. There's always the next meal to cook.'

Suzanne's eyes scanned the cluttered kitchen. Heaven only knew how Lizzie conjured her elegant cuisine out of this mess – the sink full of pans, vegetable peelings, bowls and spoons and kitchen knives on the work surface. However neat it was when she started, she always got into a fantastic mess when she was cooking, and it reminded Suzanne sharply of her own problems.

'Lizzie,' she said slowly, 'can I ask you something? Am I —'

As she spoke the door opened and Camilla came in. She was pouting, and clutched protectively to the front of her navy Viyella sailor dress was a doll of horrible vulgarity.

'Mummy, Mike Cutler says he's going to cut Samantha's hair off.'

'Mike's just teasing you.' Elizabeth began decanting the despised canapés on to a plate.

'He isn't, he isn't!' The protruding lip was beginning to tremble. 'He says —'

Elizabeth intervened hastily. 'Milla, we won't let him, I promise. Now, why don't you show Suzanne what you got in your stocking? She's dying to see, aren't you, Suzanne? You put most of it over there on the dresser, I think.'

Diverted from her grievance, the child skipped over.

'Look, Suzanne! This is a pound, and I got that down at the toe of my stocking, and this is an orange . . .'

Elizabeth paused in her task to direct, across the small fair head, a look of fond maternal complicity at her friend.

Suzanne managed to smile back. She showed no outward sign of the shaft of purest envy that pierced her heart.

Margaret Moon carefully put the last of the plates she had used back in place behind the glass of the corner cupboard. They were part of her grandmother's wedding china, gloriously gilt and beflowered, and she made a practice of using them whenever there was an excuse.

Like the Cutlers, she had enjoyed an excellently trouble-free Christmas dinner for one, also courtesy of St Michael. Would he, she wondered idly, as she covered the remains of a small plum pudding and popped it in the fridge, become by use and wont the patron saint of shoppers? 'By St Michael, that is a fine piece of steak!' Or working mothers, perhaps . . .

She put the Christmas Oratorio on her elderly hi-fi, made herself a cup of Blue Mountain coffee luxuriously topped with whipped cream – it was Christmas, after all – and carried it through, with a small box of Belgian truffles, to put on the table beside her armchair.

'You do know how to show a girl a good time,' she murmured appreciatively as she went to sit down.

Pyewacket was in possession already, naturally, since this was the most comfortable chair, and asleep with that air of boneless relaxation specific to cats. It did seem harsh to wake him, when he was so sound asleep . . . Then she noticed one eye open, watching her, and recognized the power play.

'Scat, cat!' she said, suiting the action to the words and sinking into her chair with a sigh. She kicked off her shoes and put her feet up on the little Victorian footstool her mother had covered with petit point, and chose a chocolate.

She was very tired. Three services in the last twelve hours – she had not realized how much conducting them, on top of all the planning and preparation, would take out of her, though perhaps she should have.

It had all gone smoothly; no hitches, nothing forgotten, and everyone cheerful, healthy, happy and prosperous, all these bright, middle-class families with their 2.4 children with shining hair and perfect teeth, clutching expensive playthings whose price would feed a family for a week, and which by the day after tomorrow would probably be broken or neglected. They looked as if the only problem they had in the world was how to pay off January's Barclaycard.

Margaret had always believed that the good things of life were there to be enjoyed, and she was far from being a Puritan – indeed, an ascetic friend had accused her, with asperity and some justice, of being a hedonist – but that sort of pointless, conspicuous waste was hard to stomach.

She hadn't felt exaltation, or even satisfaction, at her successful organization of the Christmas worship. She had felt – she groped for the word – irrelevant. That was it. They viewed the church as little more than a social club in refined surroundings where you could be sure of not having to encounter the undesirable element.

It was personally depressing, too. She liked her own company; she had chosen to be alone on this her first parish Christmas instead of inviting guests. She even liked this plain little box of a sitting room, furnished with some cherished belongings from her family home, including a few good watercolours, and her books, of course, ranged in long bookcases on either side of the exuberantly tasteless electric fire. She was far happier here – she took another chocolate – than she would be making polite conversation at someone else's lunch table.

But she did wonder whether a bachelor vicar, new to the charge, would have received not one single invitation for Christmas Day? She thought not; John Anselm, the previous encumbent, had warned her of the pitfalls of accepting one invitation rather than another. She would have valued a chance to talk to him about it, but he had underlined his wisdom by retiring to the West Country to which he felt he still belonged.

Oh, she wasn't paranoid enough to feel that it was especially personal, at least mostly she wasn't. Although – well, probably she wasn't the sort of person the smart sort of person liked, and if she were honest the feeling was mutual. She hoped it didn't show, but it could be that she hadn't learned to fake sincerity as well as she thought she had.

On the other hand, it could be simple unease with this oddity, a woman whose office made her a spiritual parent. It could even be hostility; Margaret, whose antennae were usually quite sensitive, had detected aggression in several humorous comments. By their jokes ye shall know them, she thought wearily, but to tackle hostility it must be openly expressed, which in this society was about as likely as turning up to a drinks party and finding they were all wearing shell suits. That was one of the reasons she had preached her sermon.

She sighed again, and ate another chocolate. Three o'clock; her sister Ruth would be phoning later from Canada, where she was married with five children; driven to this excess, she claimed, by the unphiloprogenitive nature of her siblings.

But it was probably a good time to phone Robert, the remaining member of her family. He would have lunched, as usual on Christmas Day, at his club with another bachelor, but should by now be back in his extremely comfortable flat in Bath.

She dialled the number, and when he picked up the receiver heard the strains of the same piece of music sounding from the other end. It had always been traditional Christmas listening in the Moon family.

'Snap!' she said by way of greeting, and held the receiver nearer her own recording.

He was never disconcerted. 'Ah, Margaret!' he said. 'I thought it would be you. Happy Christmas! And has Stretton Noble survived the shock of Christmas with the female touch?'

'Oh, yes,' she said brightly. 'It's all gone very smoothly indeed. Not a response missed, lovely singing, lots of happy families. I'm just putting my feet up in the consciousness of a job well done.'

'I see.' There was a pause, then, 'Depressed, are we?'

She sat upright and glared at the phone as if she could see him, wearing his red smoking jacket, no doubt, and the inevitable bow tie.

'Remind me,' she said tartly, 'in my next incarnation, not to choose a brother who's a psychologist.'

'Well, I can readily imagine that you might be tired of the Church of England, but I can't think that Buddhism would suit your temperament. What's the problem?'

She fought a rearguard action. 'I don't know what you mean. What have I said to indicate that everything isn't absolutely fine? As it is, of course,' she added hastily.

'My dear girl, I've known you since you were a singularly unrestful addition to the nursery I had happily considered my personal preserve. Unless you're saying that you're totally exhausted, haven't got a moment to yourself and are just dashing off to something else which will probably finish you off completely, you're miserable.'

Her laugh was a little forced. 'It's just a question of adjusting, that's all. I need to be needed, Robert, and I don't think anyone needs me here at all. Everyone's well-fed and well-housed and comfortable, and I even suspect that there are people I could help who don't come to church because it's a middle-class preserve.'

'Oh, I feel sure you can be relied on to take it down-market fast, if that's what's needed. A couple of tambourines, a bearded guitarist and some hip-hop for Jesus . . .'

Margaret groaned.

'Hah! Got you there, haven't I? You don't like that any more than they do, do you? Look, when am I going to be allowed to come over and inspect this place for myself? You've got to let me come sometime, you know.'

Suddenly it seemed a very attractive offer. 'I did want to get things going myself. And you can't stay for a service yet, I'm not ready for that. I'm not sure I totally trust you not to try to make me laugh. But if your friends in the police force are going to give you a breathing space over Christmas, why not come down tomorrow for a couple of days? I even have an invitation – the redoubtable Mrs Travers is having a drinks party to which I "and any house guests you may have, my dear" have been, amazingly enough, invited.'

'I'll look up the section on paranoia before I come. I'll be with you around tea time tomorrow, barring forensic emergencies.'

She felt much more cheerful when she put down the phone. It rang again almost immediately, and she picked it up expecting Ruth's exuberant mid-Atlantic tones.

But it was a parishioner, elderly and distraught, whose husband had been taken into hospital with a heart attack after Christmas lunch.

It was a timely reminder that a turkey on the table and a roof over your head were no guarantee of human happiness. With a sense of relief at the opportunity for service, she grabbed her coat and hurried out.

Their guests had gone. Suzanne, leaving Patrick and Ben watching the Christmas movie, had gone to tidy up the kitchen. She ached for her bed; Christmas was bad enough, without the additional stress of having to conceal from Patrick's mother, who believed the sun rose only to shine on her eldest son, that she was barely speaking to him.

When Patrick unexpectedly opened the kitchen door, her lips tightened and she turned away, busying herself at the sink.

He stood awkwardly in the doorway. 'Look, Suzanne, can we call a truce for a moment?'

She did not turn. 'Fine, if you've come to apologize . . .'

'Let's not start that again. Come here and sit down.'

She ignored him, but he came over, removed the dishcloth from her hand and drew her to a chair. Still wearing her washing-up gloves, she sat down reluctantly.

'Please don't say anything till I've finished what I have to say. OK?'

Suzanne eyed him sullenly, shrugged, and he took it for assent and went on.

'The mess this morning – you believe I did it. No –' as she opened her mouth to speak indignantly, 'hear me out. I swear to you, by all I hold sacred – the Bible, my son's life, if you like – that I did not do it. Neither of us think for a moment it was Ben.

'You say you didn't do it either, which, so help me God, is what I believed. You've been under a hell of a lot of strain

79

lately, and you might – oh, I don't know, be sleepwalking or something. Or setting me up.

'But I've been going round and round this in my head. Let's assume for a moment that neither of us did it. The logical deduction then is that someone else did, but as you pointed out a tad trenchantly this morning, there were no broken windows or forced locks.'

He paused, but she did not say anything. She was listening properly now.

'Is there anyone, anyone at all, who could conceivably have acquired a key to this place? I know it sounds silly, but still —'

She stared at him. 'Well, of course there is! I can't believe you don't know. How do you think the plants get watered when we go off on holiday?'

Taken aback, he said, 'I don't think I ever gave it a moment's thought – though I do always ask the neighbours on either side to keep an eye on the house.'

'We all have keys,' Suzanne explained. 'Lizzie, Laura, Hayley and me: we all keep keys to one another's back doors. Someone's always needing a repairman let in, or forgetting their own key, or something. Or we pop in, when someone's away, to check on things . . .'

She trailed off, into a silence that became prolonged, as they both drew their own conclusions. Then Patrick said heavily, 'In that case, Suzanne, I think you had better get on the phone and call them in. It's you, or me, or someone else who's been burning things and vandalizing things, and I choose someone else.'

'You don't understand, Patrick!' she cried. 'How can I phone up my best friends and tell them I don't trust them any more? Women don't work like that.'

'Men do,' he said grimly, and got up, going towards the phone.

'Oh no, Patrick! For goodness' sake, don't! All that will happen is that we'll lose all our friends overnight. I'll think of something – just leave it to me.'

For a moment there, they had been communicating. Now Patrick withdrew.

'As you wish,' he said curtly. 'I can quite understand that you would prefer to doubt your husband rather than your friends. Have it your own way. You always do.'

He walked out and left her sitting at the kitchen table, eyeing the wall-phone as she might have contemplated a harmless grass snake which had suddenly reared up and opened a flattened hood.

4

'Sorry, sorry,' said Elizabeth, compulsively murmuring the placatory words, with no real hope that they would achieve their propitiatory object, 'I'm sorry, I —'

'For God's sake!' Piers's face was blotchy with temper and his bulging eyes bloodshot from the hangover he was suffering. He pushed his chair back from the kitchen table with a violence which would have overturned any less solid piece of furniture.

'What's the use of grovelling? It doesn't help, you know. If you directed your energy towards getting things right beforehand, instead of all this snivelling about afterwards, these things wouldn't happen. How the hell can anyone *forget* to stock up on Alka-Seltzer over Christmas?'

Because other people don't drink so much that they need it. Because some people have used up more in the last three days than most people would need in a year. Because the last lot didn't magically remove all your symptoms and you said you couldn't think why I wasted money on them.

She said, 'I'm sure the shop in Chorton will be open later, even though it's Boxing Day. I'll run over and get some then.'

'And what's the use of that? It's now I need it, not in three hours' time. Oh, forget it. It'll just have to be the hair of the dog – and don't go all pious about drinking this early in the day. This is all your fault.'

Even after he had lurched out, headed for the drinks cupboard in the games room, there was silence at the breakfast table. Peter and Camilla, the mechanical movements of their spoons from cereal bowl to mouth arrested, were pale and wide-eyed; Paula's gaze was downcast, her expression veiled.

Elizabeth found that she was holding her breath, and released it slowly. They had survived the crisis, and the brandy bottle should buy an hour or two's peace.

'Come on, darlings, eat up your breakfast. Daddy's not feeling well this morning, so he's a bit cross.'

The words tripped off her tongue readily enough, with the well-honed instinct to protect, cover up. Perhaps it helped, perhaps it didn't, but she couldn't bring herself to think that saying to a six-year-old, 'Your father is a drunkard and potentially violent,' would help anyone.

With nervous obedience the two younger children went back to spooning up their cereal, but Paula looked up, her dark grey eyes flashing fury at her mother.

'How *can* you?' she cried. 'You're so dishonest – this whole family's nothing but a sham! Why do you let him get away with it – this and everything else? Tell him to get his sodding Alka-Seltzer himself, why don't you?'

Elizabeth winced. 'Paula —'

She jumped to her feet. 'Oh, what's the point? I can't believe that anyone in the whole world can be so pathetic. If you would stand up to him, he wouldn't behave like that. But you haven't got the guts, and everything's getting worse and worse and worse while you try to pretend that it isn't happening. I'm going out.'

Helplessly, Elizabeth watched her slam the door. Somehow, she comforted Camilla, who had begun to sob, and bought the two of them off with morning television and chocolate bars. Probably it would only mean that they had rotten teeth as well as psychological scars, she thought drearily, but the instinct to sweeten life's bitterness with sugary food lies deep in a mother's soul.

Even Paula believed it was all her fault. It was ironic, really; Piers and Paula both despised her for apologizing when things went wrong, yet both, for different reasons, held her to blame for not putting them right. She blamed herself for a lot of things too, though no one could try harder than she did not to make mistakes.

If only she did have the guts to stand up to him, be a strong person, like Hayley or Suzanne who weren't afraid of anyone. But then, if she'd had any sort of courage, she wouldn't have married him just because he was so sure of himself that she couldn't see how she could possibly refuse. She wouldn't even have let herself be bullied by her father into going to the Young Conservatives' Ball which had sealed her fate. Her wildest act of rebellion had been secretly voting for Labour ever since, which as a testimony to her strength of character said it all.

The serious problems, though, had only started after Mother Mac died, when his drinking began to take over his life. So far, he had never hit her publicly or where it would leave an obvious mark. She tried not to think about it too much, because there was so little she could do.

She had no illusions. If she left Piers, she would be on her own. However much she might have right on her side, he would be too strong for her. He wouldn't really want the children, but he had the money to see to it that she didn't have them, to punish her.

Her head began to swim, as it always did when she allowed herself to think about it. She must stop this, stop this . . .

She was wiping the Laura Ashley oilcloth on the table

free of crumbs and putting things away – how odd, there was a smiling face in the sugar bowl this morning – when Suzanne phoned.

This was not a surprise. The phone-call to let off steam after a stressful family occasion was a ritual, and Elizabeth's face brightened. Suzanne's rueful descriptions of her in-laws' Christmas foibles were always amusing, and today it was just what was needed by way of distraction. Her tone was conspiratorial as she greeted her friend.

'Suzanne! You've survived then, have you?'

'Survived? Oh – oh, yes. And thank you for the parties. We all had a wonderful time.'

'Oh good,' Elizabeth said, but her brow furrowed. That wasn't Suzanne's usual style.

'Are you all right?' she asked with some concern. 'You don't sound like yourself at all. Was it even more horrendous than usual?'

'Er – no, not specially. It wasn't too bad, I suppose.'

Suzanne gave a laugh but she still sounded distant, almost formal, and Elizabeth felt rebuked as if by the tone of her question she had presumed on a non-existent intimacy. But perhaps she was being over-sensitive.

'Were Patrick's parents on good form?' she asked, more cautiously.

'Yes, fine.'

This time there was no mistaking the constraint. She wasn't imagining things; Suzanne was definitely keeping her firmly at arm's length. Wondering wildly what she could have said or done to offend her, Elizabeth could only repeat hollowly, 'Oh, good.'

'Er – Lizzie –' At the other end of the phone, Suzanne cleared her throat nervously. 'I wonder, could you dig out the back-door key you keep for me? The thing is, the insurance company has started getting stroppy about the way we spray our keys around, so we're having to get them back. Silly, isn't it?'

She laughed, but the laugh did not ring true.

'Yes,' Elizabeth managed to say brightly. 'It does seem silly, doesn't it. But if that's what they say, that's the way it has to be, isn't it? I'll drop it round later this morning. I've got to go out anyway. OK? Bye.'

Cold with shock and dismay, she put down the receiver. Whatever could she have done, without realizing, that was so awful that Suzanne wanted to finish their friendship? Because she didn't for a moment believe that tale about the insurance. Suzanne could hardly have got an urgent message from the company today, and if it wasn't urgent, why not just ask for it the next time she came round? In any case, Suzanne had never been a good liar, and Elizabeth knew her well enough to be certain that she was lying now.

She searched her own conscience, but it was genuinely clear. There was nothing she had thought, still less said or done, that could have upset Suzanne. They had parted yesterday, as far as she could tell, on their usual affectionate terms.

Could it be that someone was making mischief, someone jealous or malevolent, anxious to undermine their friendship? Perhaps unfairly, her mind flew to Hayley Cutler.

They had never been close. Somehow, Elizabeth was never convinced that she was entirely to be trusted, though they had all had some good times together, and Hayley had the gift of turning a gathering of four people into a party.

Remembering those good times, her eyes filled. Next to her children, her friends had been the most important thing in her life which, she sadly recognized, had become otherwise joyless. With Laura – clever, elegant Laura whom she so admired – estranged already, and Hayley suspect, she would be poor indeed without Suzanne. If it were a misunderstanding, surely they could sort it out?

But something cold and proud and bitter within her whispered that a true friend would not have listened to mischief-making, and that any approach could only result in further humiliation. The same demon prompted her to the thought that if Suzanne wanted her key back, she should retrieve her own.

Her eye went to the drawing pinned to the kitchen noticeboard, which Milla had brought home from school last week. It portrayed a rather lop-sided angel with a speech balloon which read, 'Peace on earth, goodwill to all men' in tipsy capitals. The angel's crayoned grin looked ironic now.

There had been other Christmases when things had gone more dramatically wrong – several, in fact – but she never remembered one where there had been such unease on every side. She could not precisely pinpoint its source, but it tweaked at her nerves like a persistent toothache. From some hidden suppuration poison was leaking into their lives.

She wrapped her arms about her body, rocking to and fro in that expression of misery which is as old as misery itself.

The curtains in the games room were still closed, and the air was thick with the cigars Piers had smoked last night. The light suspended above the three-quarter size billiard table had been left on, leaving the rest of the room in shadow.

Piers was oblivious to its squalor. Sitting in the big club chair by the dead ashes in the fireplace, nursing a brandy, a queasy stomach and a sore head, he heard his wife talking on the phone and scowled. No doubt she was bleating to one of her friends about how badly she was treated by her husband. He'd noticed they were distinctly cool to him nowadays.

With one exception. He grinned evilly at the thought. It was a long time since anyone had come on to him like that – in fact, if he was honest, this was a first, and he wasn't about to let scruples stand in his way.

He had felt liberated to be himself at last, in these few months since his mother died. She was a tough old bird, he reflected with a certain wary admiration, and while she might still descend from mercifully-distant Yorkshire and make him feel like the very unsatisfactory small boy she had always considered him, he had behaved, at least when she was around, with a certain circumspection.

But now, there were no controls. Lizzie couldn't say Boo! to a goose, let alone No! to her husband, and he need no longer check the bullying impulse which her perpetual cowering stirred in him.

Bullying came as naturally as breathing to Piers. His father had been a hard bastard, whom he had admired and feared in roughly equal proportions, but never loved. He had looked forward to kicking ass in his own firm when choler and rich living had carried the old boy off to an early grave, but his mother would have none of it.

'Th'art not half the man thi father was,' she said gruffly, affecting the broad old-fashioned Yorkshire she knew enraged him. 'Happen tha'll not play ducks and drakes with my grandchildren's money, and tha hast thi poor pretty wife to provide for, think on.'

And he had, as always, been unable to defy her. He had sold the business to Trucking Worldwide, and agreed to the financial safeguards her lawyers had imposed – astute enough, to be fair – and subjected himself to the constant humiliation of having been guaranteed a seat on the board without the guarantee that anyone would listen to a word he had to say.

No wonder he saw her death as liberation. And yet, and yet . . . He missed the old certainties and the luxury of safe rebellion; sometimes, in his more sober moments, he even felt frightened himself by his growing taste for violence.

He would certainly never have taken up with Hayley Cutler if there was the smallest chance that his behaviour might come under his mother's searing scrutiny. She would have laughed in earthy amusement at the notion that a woman like that could find his charm irresistible, would have suggested . . . But it had been bad enough being forced to listen to her opinions when she was alive. He wasn't about to let her start offering them from beyond the grave.

He was having to be careful, of course. Hayley was one of the group Lizzie moved around with, and he was smart enough to know that this spelled danger. A woman might be as ready for a roll in the hay as you were, then before you knew it she'd be yakking around the kitchen table to her best friend who would turn out to be your wife's best friend as well and who would see it as one of the duties of friendship to enlighten her as to who was doing what and with what and to whom.

But somehow Hayley was an outsider, never properly within the charmed circle. None of them really liked her, that was the thing, and come to that he wasn't sure how much he liked her himself, though that had nothing to do with the price of cheese. It wasn't precisely for her personality that he fancied her.

He was flattered, of course. He was far from being the only man around who had the hots for her, but she had definitely singled him out, and he was revelling in the experience. Despite the purchasing power of serious money, he had been finding life dull and disappointing, and secret assignations certainly added spice.

The brandy was beginning to kick in now, and he started to feel a sort of woozy benevolence as his stomach stopped heaving. He would have another glass, just to make sure, and then he could snooze till lunch time. Lizzie should have got the Alka-Seltzers by then.

Elizabeth's visit to Bentham's had been brief and awkward. Suzanne had done her best to seem bright and normal, but she knew she had failed. She was paralysed by the awkwardness of her position; after all, in asking for the return of her key, she was actually saying that she believed her best friend might have trashed her kitchen, and she had always been hopeless about covering things up. Elizabeth was clearly offended; she couldn't possibly blame her for asking for her own key back in exchange, and she just couldn't think of anything to say.

It had been a dreadful morning. Patrick had taken Ben off clay-pigeon shooting, and she had suffered a jealous pang at this male-bonding exercise.

She had been left to make the phone calls, and the fact that this had been her own choice did not lessen her resentment. As a person who, on the whole, was as honest with herself as anyone ever is, she recognized that unforgivably what he had forced her to face was an unwelcome truth.

Hayley's response to her request had been puzzling. She was always difficult to read, but Suzanne thought she was intrigued, rather than surprised or offended. The key had been posted through the letter box half an hour later.

Laura's reaction had been quite different. After an initial gasp of obvious dismay, she had recovered herself quickly, babbling on about the ludicrous demands insurance companies saw fit to make nowadays. She promised that one of the girls would bring it round, then rang off abruptly.

Suzanne might have known she would make a mess of it. Perhaps it would have been better if Patrick had done it after all. Then he could have taken the flak; certainly all she had achieved, despite the agonizing beforehand, was to alienate both her closest friends at once.

She put her head in her hands. Why had everything so suddenly started spinning out of control in her tightly-ordered universe? Only weeks ago, it seemed, she had been coping effortlessly with demands on every side which would have brought many another woman to her knees.

It was at work that things had started to go wrong, when the Powers That Be were misguided enough to appoint a woman surgeon. It wasn't that Suzanne was prejudiced – of course not, she judged everyone on merit – but this woman breezed in and started making ridiculous demands, oversetting procedures which had worked satisfactorily in the hospital all the time Suzanne had been theatre sister: no one had ever suggested otherwise, and three of the top men always made a point of asking for her if the operation was going to be tricky.

But the cow had given her a public dressing-down in front of her juniors, humiliating her and undermining her authority. Suzanne was upset, inevitably, and it was hardly surprising that she should make one or two trivial mistakes over the next few days.

She had no qualms at first when one of the younger male theatre nurses took over working with her *bête noire* – it was appropriate, really, since men never made such good nurses as women, though she pitied the victims of their operations – but now, to her hurt disbelief, her own surgeons were asking for him as well. Somehow, word had spread that Suzanne was difficult, not as much on the ball as she used to be.

She hadn't meant to say anything to Patrick about it, but she had been so upset that she couldn't help blurting it out.

To her surprise, he had listened sympathetically to her tale of woe. At the end of her disjointed recital, he paused, then said carefully, 'Do you want me to be absolutely, brutally honest with you, Suzanne?'

And for a moment, she had almost said yes. Almost – but she had too much to lose. She had built the edifice of Suzanne Bolton laboriously on shaky foundations, with pain and persistence over the years. His honesty was like a huge builder's ball on a chain, swinging back ready to crash its way through and bring everything tumbling down.

'No,' she said. 'I don't think I do want your analysis of what's wrong with me. You'd like that, wouldn't you? You'd get a real kick out of cutting me down to size.'

Patrick looked at her and sighed, then shrugged.

'OK, have it your own way,' he had said, and switched on the television.

So she had tried to cope on her own with her loss of self-worth. And now it looked as if she had lost herself the support system of friendship on which she was so heavily reliant.

And worst of all, here, alone, in the silence of her empty house she must confront the question she had crowded out with practical concerns until this moment.

Which one of her so-called friends could it be who had crept into her kitchen in the hours of darkness and destroyed all her precise preparations? Which of the women who had been granted this familiar access for so long had been harbouring such malice? And, still more alarmingly, if thwarted by a locked door, what might she do next?

*   *   *

93

There was a brief snatch of winter sunshine after lunch, and Laura allowed James to persuade her to come out for a walk. They drove up to the reservoir at the farthest end of the common, strode round it then began the climb to the top of the low hill beyond. They had the place to themselves, apart from a family down below at the water's edge throwing sticks for a retriever, whose joyous barks were the only sound to break the stillness.

Shading her eyes to look down at the pleasant scene, Laura drew in great gulps of the cool damp air. She had not realized how badly she needed to get out of the house, which seemed stuffy and over-heated; she had felt unable to get a proper, satisfying deep breath for the last two days.

She had put up a good show, though. James had been pleased with her and the girls relieved, as she talked and laughed and produced appropriate Christmas fare, for all the world like someone who wasn't falling apart inside. She had made constant, surreptitious rounds of the house, in fear of what else she might find – or worse still, what one of the others might find that she would be forced to explain.

But she hadn't suspected this latest horror. When Suzanne phoned her this morning to ask for her key back she knew, knew at once, that insurance had nothing to do with it. Suzanne was famously bad at the mildest social deception, and she had not been convincing. She had been kind not to confront Laura – too embarrassed, probably – but now Laura was haunted by the knowledge that her sphere of operations was wider than she had supposed. It had taken all her control to conceal from James and the girls the panic and confusion that threatened to engulf her.

They had set a brisk pace to the top of the hill and saved their breath for climbing, but now James came across to put his arm round her shoulders.

'Well done,' he said with a friendly squeeze, and she

knew he was not talking only about her effort in reaching the top. 'It's good to see that you're feeling better.'

Unreasonable rage that he had been so easily deceived rose in her, and she took a step forward out of his grasp.

'I'm not, actually,' she said, her voice cool and controlled and seeming to herself to come from a long way away. 'As a matter of fact, I'm feeling pretty dreadful.'

The comical change in his expression from complacency to wary dismay might at another time have made her laugh.

'Er – aren't you? Well, that's, that's a shame. I'm sorry. You seemed to be much brighter, I thought. Though I know, of course, that it's because you were making a big effort,' he added hastily.

She wanted to scream at him, 'Can't you see I'm disintegrating before your eyes? Can't you see *anything*?' But unless she told him her dreadful secret, what good would that do? He would look hunted, talk about stress and working too hard and seeing a doctor, all the while thinking loudly enough for her to hear that she was merely being foolish, hysterical and self-indulgent.

'Look – could we go away for a few days?' she said instead, the inspiration suddenly presenting itself to her like a gift. 'The Lake District, perhaps; fresh air and water and mountains . . .'

Her beloved Wordsworth, after all, had believed in Nature's healing powers; perhaps, far from the situation that had reduced her to this, she might find his 'tranquil restoration.' She clasped the idea to her like a talisman.

But James only looked at her with alarm. 'I'm back in the office tomorrow. You know that, Laura.'

'Take a few days off,' she urged. 'I really do need to get away for a bit, put all this behind me —'

She knew what he was going to say before he said it.

'That seems a bit extreme, don't you think? You've got another couple of weeks before you go back to school; I'm sure you'll feel much better after a good rest.'

'How can I rest here?' she cried wildly, knowing she was doing her argument no good. 'I can't even *breathe* here.'

She knew the signs of the irritation he seldom actually gave vent to, the tightening of the lips and the smoothing of his hand over his already smooth hair. He was clearly making an effort not to sound impatient.

'Laura, I know you felt your disappointment very keenly. But I wouldn't be doing you any favours if I let you get it totally out of proportion. Everyone gets rejections from time to time, and you just have to put it behind you and get on with life.'

She looked at him dumbly. How could she tell him the truth, that the pain of her rejection had long been eclipsed by the shadowy fear that was now her constant companion?

He took her silence for acceptance. 'You won't even remember how badly you felt a week from now, I promise you. And really, it would be crazy to go away at the moment. Everywhere will be booked up, and anyway, we're flat broke after Christmas. A whacking great overdraft wouldn't do anything to relieve our levels of stress.'

He laughed.

She said, 'Oh, if it's *money*, of course, that settles it,' with all the contempt she could muster and set off ahead of him down the hill, knowing she had not been entirely fair.

There was something else Wordsworth had said; something a lot less comforting.

> Suffering is permanent, obscure and dark,
> And shares the nature of infinity.

*　　*　　*

96

Struggling to match her brother Robert's longer stride, Margaret Moon returned from the Travers's party that evening in a state of seething indignation.

She might have known how it would be, of course, because it always was. People were always drawn to Robert, with his expression of cheerful tranquillity and his bow tie, and when they discovered that he was a psychologist, and a forensic psychologist at that, their fascination was often so unbridled as to be positively embarrassing. By the end of the party this evening, people were confiding in him, she was sure, the innermost secrets of their existence.

She herself had wasted an hour and a half of what was left of her life in a succession of conversations of mind-numbing triviality, and her temper had not been improved by the number of people who came up and said, 'I've just been having such an interesting conversation with your brother,' before asking her if she was going to manage to get away for a break now that the stresses of Christmas were over.

She had tried hard to remind herself that she was a priest and that they were her flock. She had tried to banish from her mind the telling image of the rich man, the camel and the needle's eye. But she needed to talk to somebody.

Not being High Church, she found the notion of the confessional uncomfortable, and in any case she wasn't ready to confess her faults. She was still at the stage of being unconvinced that the fault was hers, in any case, which was an unchristian, if human, point of view. What she wanted was to sound off, and Robert's discretion was unimpeachable.

With her own front door safely closed behind them, she burst out, 'Don't you hate it? Don't you hate all that silly superficial chat, and those sleek pampered people, and the expensive drinks and the smoked salmon that isn't even a treat any more?'

Pausing only to dislodge Pyewacket, Robert sank down in Margaret's favourite chair.

'No,' he said, having considered the matter with his usual thoroughness. 'If I'm to be honest, I rather like expensive drink and smoked salmon. So do you, of course, only you've convinced yourself that under these circumstances you shouldn't.

'But even if it is ethically correct to frown on luxuries which are taken for granted, you should have the intellectual rigour to distinguish between not liking and disapproving. You wouldn't seriously claim to like mushy peas with vinegar, despite their impeccable working-class antecedents.'

Gathering up the affronted Pyewacket, Margaret sat down in the harder chair opposite and glared at him.

'You're nit-picking, Robert. Of course I'm not hypocritical enough to suggest that I don't appreciate delicious little canapés and champagne. Most people can afford to smoke, if they're stupid enough to want to, or have a night at the pub, and if I would rather have the occasional nibble of smoked salmon or a decent bottle of wine, I haven't any hang-ups about doing it. The water at the wedding in Cana wasn't turned into cheap plonk, after all.

'But you know perfectly well what I'm really talking about – the naked materialism, the smugness . . .'

'Smugness,' he repeated, as if tasting the word. 'Smugness?'

Pyewacket, to Margaret's annoyance, jumped off her lap, crossed the room and leaped up, purring, to push his head under Robert's hand.

'Wouldn't you say they were smug? Safe in their pretty, cosy little world, no real worries . . .'

He scratched the cat expertly in the sensitive area behind his ear, and Pyewacket's purr rose to ecstatic pitch.

'I'm surprised, I must say, to hear you describe them

as smug. You've always struck me as an intelligent and sensitive woman, and it's not like you to permit prejudice to cloud your judgement.'

She snorted, but he carried on, indeflectably.

'If you want my own impression —'

'If you're going to tell me they're open-hearted models of social concern, I shall probably kick you.'

'Not that, no. But it did seem to me that the place was crackling with nervous tension. There were several people whom, if I had seen professionally, I would have assessed as being close to dysfunctional. There were some very unhealthy cross-currents in the conversations, too. Quite nasty, I thought, and claustrophobic rather than cosy. I am not, as you know, a fanciful man, but when we left I felt as if I were running for cover before the storm actually broke.'

She glared at him. 'Do me a favour! Nervous tension? Whatever have they got to be nervous about? Whether it will have to be Cava instead of champagne at their next party, and what people will say if it is? They could try just being grateful they don't have to wonder where their next meal is coming from.'

'And tell me, vicar, are you grateful to the Bishop for giving you such a nice comfortable berth without any of the problems you've had to cope with in the inner city?'

'Well, of course not,' she said crossly. 'I do have rather higher aspirations for what I want out of life than mere material comfort —'

She stopped.

'All right, Robert. All right, don't say it. Just don't say, "And they haven't?" or I shall tip that vase of jasmine over Pyewacket and he'll scratch you instead of fawning upon you in that contemptible way.'

He grinned. 'That's better. Your behaviour isn't usually

so maladaptive. Perhaps you ought to consider finding out exactly why.'

'Oh no you don't. You may be a distinguished shrink, but you're not going to start mucking about with my psyche. You may not believe in prayer and meditation, but then I don't believe in transactional analysis. I'll sort myself out in my own way.

'But come on, you can't stop there. What horrors have you uncovered in my parish which I in my blindness have ignored?'

He considered. 'It's tricky to attempt to give you chapter and verse, especially since a lot of the time I didn't even know who I was talking to. But there was one young woman – Lizzie, was it? – with a classic victim profile, and a nurse showing definite symptoms of paranoia. She seemed to be using aggression to cope with stress, which isn't the wisest method.'

'Suzanne Bolton?'

'Possibly. But in general, there was a lot of observable alienation. I found myself in one group where I was the only person who didn't have my arms folded like a barrier across my chest. And it's Christmas week; they can't take refuge in work or shopping or the school run. When things go wrong in a close community, they go very wrong, because the damage is so intimate and there's no escape.'

'Flight or fight.'

'Exactly. One of the most basic of animal instincts. And when the flight alternative isn't available, things can get primitive, and to be brutally honest, I think it's heading that way. You may find yourself with quite a job on your hands, even though it's a bit more subtle than the sort of work you've been indulging yourself with. Quite as challenging, you know, in its way.'

Margaret sighed. 'Well, I like to think you're being

alarmist, but in principle you're probably right. Do you never think it might be nice to be wrong for a change?'

'Not really, no.'

'You don't look pretty when you're smirking. But I must say I'm intrigued that you picked up an unpleasant atmosphere. I had put my own unease down to regrettable social prejudices. And yes, I shall regard them with clearer eyes.'

'Good. I think you'll find there are some very troubled souls, if you can manage to get through to them. And could I suggest that I think it might be a matter of some urgency?'

Margaret pulled a sceptical face. 'What are they going to do — nice middle-class proper people? They're hardly likely to run amuck, you know — it's not the sort of Thing One Does. But I'm certainly interested that you mentioned Elizabeth McEvoy. I had noticed that she looked pretty worn down much of the time, and that husband of hers is a horror. Perhaps I could make a start there, get to know her a little better —'

'There you are, you see? You're beginning to cheer up, now that you've got the scent of a problem. I never knew anyone so shamelessly addicted to stress. Pyewacket and I,' he stroked the furry circle of cat on his knee, 'can't understand it at all.'

She pulled a childish face at him and went to cook supper. It was true, she did feel buoyed up and encouraged by the suggestion of a challenge. Perhaps God and the Bishop (why did that seem such an unlikely conjunction?) had a task in mind for her after all, perhaps this was a community crying out for what she had to give.

She went to bed thinking about what Robert had said. He was no fool; if he had smelt trouble, then trouble somewhere there must be. But even so, she was unprepared for the ugly little surprise in the post next morning.

5

It was just before seven o'clock in the morning when the cream Series 7 BMW purred to a standstill on the road on the far side of the common. It was still dark; a damp, dreary morning with patches of mist hanging about the black mass of trees which lined the path back to the village.

The driver switched off the headlamps without putting on the courtesy light inside, and peered out through the side window across the scrubby grass. There was just light enough from the cold glare of the village streetlamps to see anything that was moving, but all was still.

Piers McEvoy was not a patient man. He swore, thumping the leather cover of the steering wheel, consulted his Rolex, flicked the switch of the radio on, then after an exclamation about the leftist rubbish being spouted by some bint who called herself a political analyst, flicked it off again. He took another impatient look out, and this time was rewarded.

A lithe figure in tracksuit and trainers was running up the path towards him, moving with a brisk, easy, athletic stride.

'About time too,' he grumbled under his breath, then pressed the button which would lower the window.

She was close enough for him to see her clearly now, long wavy hair switching from side to side, and the palest sheen of effort glistening on her skin. Her tracksuit, dark

103

violet velour, had the big ornamental zip at the neck pulled some little way down, the pale V of flesh creamy against the dark fabric.

He felt desire stirring. God, she was sexy! Incredible to find something like this lying around – or perhaps, given that he was talking about Hayley, laying around – in Stretton Noble, and even more remarkably, carrying a torch for him.

'Hi!' she called as she reached the car. 'Is it warm in there? It's damn cold out here.'

She was breathing a little faster than usual, but she certainly wasn't in the least out of breath.

'God, you're fit,' he said enviously. 'Come on, hop in, gorgeous, and I'll warm you up. You're late, and I've got to be in town at a meeting by nine.'

She pulled a face, and tried to touch a cold hand to his cheek, but he ducked away, pressing a switch to close the window.

When she opened the door, a breath of fresh damp air came in with her.

'Mmm, that's nice,' she said, snuggling into the warmth and the soft upholstery.

He was reaching across already, his mouth greedy against her cool skin, his hands running over the velvety pile of the material to the huge inviting ring at the top of the zip-fastener.

But she pulled herself free to say, 'Hey, hey, hey! Whoa, feller, whoa! It's good to know you're pleased to see me, but I passed the milkman on his rounds, and if he comes back this way we'll be the hot topic round every breakfast table in Stretton.'

He groaned, but reluctantly restored the zip to its original position and started the engine once more.

'The usual place?' he said thickly.

She nodded. 'It's much safer up by the reservoir. No one ever goes up there this early.'

The first streaks of light were appearing in the sky as he drove her back. They exchanged a long kiss, as his hands strayed intimately once more over the contours under the soft velour.

'Call me,' she said huskily. 'We've got to talk. That was good for me, Piers, that was really great, but I guess I'm getting kind of old for the back seat of cars, even the luxury models. Let's make some plans, honey. You know I'm crazy for you – wouldn't it be a lot of fun to have a bit more time together, get to know each other some more?'

He cleared his throat. 'Sounds a wonderful idea. I'll have to phone you later, though. I really can't talk about it now – if I don't make the meeting on time, someone will be ringing Liz to ask her why I'm not there.'

It was, he hoped, too dark still for her to see his expression. That was what everyone said about bloody females; you had a good thing going – and she enjoyed it as much as he did, make no mistake – and then they started trying to change it, put it on a regular footing, make it more official. Then your wife found out, and before you could say, 'What other woman?' you were in the throes of a divorce and breaking up your home and having to pay upkeep on two households instead of one.

That was the last thing he wanted. He loved his home – the furniture, the paintings, the decor, all chosen regardless of expense and paid for with his, well his father's, money – and he had no intention of changing the wife he had trained so well. She was a brilliant cook, she knew enough not to complain, and if she irritated him – well, he wasn't dumb enough to think that a different woman would be any better. In any case, he had in his time seen plenty of evidence to support the time-honoured principle that you should never marry your mistress.

Hayley closed the door with its heavy click – at least he had trained her not to slam it – and he let off the hand brake. He raised his hand in salute, sketched the obligatory kiss, and drove off without looking back.

She looked over her shoulder once, but without stopping. She ran off across the common, then into the main street once more, replacing her scowl with a smile suitable for the vicar, as she passed Miss Moon on her way back from the early morning service.

She was still jogging briskly enough, though her breathing was a bit more laboured now. One way and another, it had been quite an extensive work-out this morning.

Margaret Moon walked back home from church to her breakfast with a new sense of energy and purpose. If she had been American, like Mrs Cutler, just jogging past, she might have described this as the first day of the rest of her life. She wasn't American, of course, but just in case she felt tempted she rapidly thought of something else instead.

Her reading this morning had been peculiarly apposite – one of the suggested passages in Romans. It had contained several examples of what she privately called needle-jabs; the phrases that made you wince because they so mercilessly pointed to the shortcomings with which you were struggling at the time.

'Do not be conceited' – jab – 'Discern the will of God'– jab – 'Let your mind be remade' – jab. This morning had been a bit like sitting on a series of drawing pins, but there was no doubt about it, it got you going. And if Robert was right and there was trouble ahead, she felt that her metaphorical sleeves were now well and truly rolled up, ready for action.

She could smell the toast and coffee as she came in. Now that really was a treat; to come back from early service and find the table set and coffee ready to pour into your cup. She always returned ravenous from the Eucharist.

Robert looked very comfortable, sitting at the kitchen table reading *The Times* at its full spread while eating wholemeal toast lavishly topped with butter and Oxford marmalade without getting greasy spots all over it. Margaret had never mastered either accomplishment.

He looked up at her over his spectacles as she came in. 'Good house?'

She picked up her mail, sorting through it.

'Four, plus me. Not bad.'

He shook his head. 'You'll tell me, of course, that it's all about a relationship with God and not a performance, but I can't help thinking you could achieve some sort of compromise less recklessly wasteful of manpower – forgive me, womanpower.'

That usually stirred things up, but it was still early in the morning. She smiled blandly as she poured herself coffee and put a slice of bread into the toaster.

'I won't argue on an empty stomach. Go back to your paper, Robert.'

Robert withdrew again behind his broadsheet, and she sorted the mail as she sipped coffee and waited for her toast. There was always less than usual, of course at this time of year; two or three typewritten ones, and a delayed Christmas card from an old friend. This she opened first (she always picked the cherries out of her fruitcake, too), and enjoyed the rare treat of a gossipy letter inside.

When it came to the typewritten letters, the one she selected first, as the most interesting, was the one which looked least professional. The individual characters were faded and a little uneven, as if typed on a very old-fashioned machine. It was the sort of communication she sometimes got from elderly clergymen, who in their day had been advanced enough to type their sermons but then never got round to trading in the old Remington.

With this in her mind, she opened it, and took a moment to make sense of the words she saw there. Then she gasped, an involuntary reaction which she covered up with a cough. She didn't want to talk to Robert about it, not yet; not until she had worked out what to make of it.

She made a little production of taking out her toast, buttering it, then getting up to look for honey. She found that she was trembling, and it was difficult not to sit down heavily when she got back to her chair.

Robert was still absorbed. She spread the letter out and read it again.

It was disconcerting, how much effect venomous anonymity could have. A diseased, nauseating hostility emanated from the letter.

She cut her toast in half, but could only look at it in distaste.

Without emerging from behind the barrier of newsprint, Robert said, 'Far be it from me to intrude upon your privacy, but if you told me what came in your mail that has upset you so much, you might feel more ready to eat your breakfast.'

She looked helplessly across at the back of the newspaper.

'I give up,' she said. 'I don't know why I even try. If they'd said *you* should be burnt at the stake, I could have understood it.'

'Oh dear.' He restored *The Times* to order with one neat shake, folded it and set it aside. 'Anonymous?'

'Of course. I really shouldn't feel so shaken by it. It's very common, you know; we had sessions on the subject during training, and they kept hammering home the point that protests in this form, or any other, shouldn't be taken to heart, that they're protesting against a concept not a person. But it's still frightening.'

'Hatred always is. And that's one of its commonest manifestations, where it attaches a quite abstract notion to some hapless person, which paradoxically depersonalizes the object of hatred into a symbol of the grievance.'

'Like a racist beating up the black man next door?'

'Exactly.'

He studied the nasty little missive.

'Bad things happen to people like you,' it began. 'Call yourself a priest? You are a joke, a bad joke. You think you're different from the rest of us, special, and you go worming your way like a maggot into people's lives. They should burn you at the stake, now, like the witch you are, with your familiar, the devil-cat.'

'BURN, WITCH, BURN!'

'Ouch,' Robert said placidly. 'I did think you might be asking for trouble, calling that beast Pyewacket.'

At the mention of his name, Pyewacket, dozing in his basket, opened one eye, and Margaret laughed, a little shakily, but laughed nonetheless.

'Being an old maid, I thought misguidedly that calling him after a witch's familiar was amusing. Not very clever, I suppose. After all, the suggestion that we should all be burnt at the stake emanated originally from one of my brothers-in-Christ in a fine display of masculine Christianity.'

'Meeting prejudice with prejudice is understandable, of course, and immediately gratifying, but seldom constructive. Have you any especially rabid brothers-in-Christ?'

Margaret considered. 'Not peculiarly, as far as I know. They just specialize in being intolerably patronizing, apart from the one who is probably gay and keeps trying to line up with me against the others in a very embarrassing way.'

'And you don't see yourself as a fag-hag?'

'Robert! Wherever do you get these appalling expressions from?'

Her outrage distracted her, as it was meant to; absent-mindedly, she began to munch her toast.

'But it isn't funny, Robert. It's scaring and hideous and awful to have that level of hatred directed against you. And how can I be sure it's impersonal? Perhaps it's something I've done.'

'It's possible, certainly.'

It wasn't what she had wanted him to say. She had wanted him to dismiss it out of hand.

She said hollowly, 'Well, go on. This is pretty much your field, isn't it, looking in your crystal ball and telling the police what sort of person has committed a crime?'

'I usually have rather more to go on.'

He leaned across the breakfast table and picked up the envelope to study it.

'It's the local postmark, isn't it? Have you any particular zealots here?'

'Old Sam Briggs, I suppose, but I rather like him. He's so openly hostile that we've begun to get on quite well. I took him some shortbread on Christmas Day, and when I left he said, "Well, I won't say but what the Almighty maybe should have said females could be vicars. But think on this – He didn't." I'd be sorry if it was him.'

'Unlikely. It's an educated style and good quality paper. And . . .'

He read it through again. 'I'm much inclined to think it's a woman.'

'You're only saying that because it's more common for women to do it than men.'

'Well, not entirely. "Different from the rest of *us*", it says – you see? I would tend to read that as referring to other women. And again, "They" – not "we", notice – "should burn you at the stake"; traditionally a male activity requiring masculine force. I can't say I would go to the stake myself on that opinion, but it's a thought.'

'Hmmm.' Margaret pondered. 'Well, I suppose I just tear it up and try to forget about it. If it's prejudice, they'll get used to the idea in time; the first hundred years are the hardest.'

'Oh, I wouldn't tear it up. People always do that, and if there's an outbreak the police have nothing to go on.'

'An outbreak?' Her stomach lurched. 'Then – you don't think it's just the woman-priest thing?'

He frowned. 'No, as a matter of fact, I don't. Let me try to work out why.'

As he paused in thought, she twitched the letter back from him and read it again, with a shudder. Who was this woman – if Robert was right – who hated her so much?

'I know what it is,' her brother said suddenly. 'It doesn't to me express outrage – which was the hallmark of the priesthood debate – as much as spite. The maggot remark would be out of character for the single-issue fanatic. And if this has been sent merely to distress, picking on your particular vulnerability, you won't be the only victim. I'm only thinking aloud, remember – but you could keep that in mind as you go about your parish business.'

'Parish business!' Margaret suddenly leaped to her feet guiltily. 'Look at the time! I've got a young couple coming to talk to me about their wedding in three minutes, and I haven't even drawn back the curtains in the study yet.'

She had a busy morning with little time for reflection and she and Robert were having a cup of coffee in the sitting room after lunch when the doorbell rang. Groaning theatrically, Margaret went to answer it.

When she recognized her visitor, her face lit up with surprise and pleasure.

'Tom!' she exclaimed.

The old derelict who stood on the doorstep staggered slightly in surprise as she threw her arms round him, being unused to rapturous acclaim. It was fully six weeks since someone had made him take a bath, his clothes were ragged and stiff with weathering and old sweat, and his boots broken down and filthy; people usually requested him to move on, or move downwind, at the very least, rather than offering to embrace him. But life had taught him pragmatism, and the dirt-seamed stubbly creases of his face curved in a broad grin which displayed half-a-dozen yellowing teeth.

Margaret was ushering him inside towards the kitchen, backing off a little from the odious savours of his rich personality. In her pleasure at this relic of her past, spontaneity had perhaps prevailed over wisdom.

'Whatever are you doing in this neck of the woods, Tom?'

Shambling after her, the old man sniffed, passing the back of his half-mittens across his nose, and she noticed that the gnarled fingers which protruded were mauve with cold. But his cheerfulness was unimpaired.

'Well, you see miss, this i'nt far off me regular circuit. There's a hostel over Broadhurst way, not busy this time of year, and at Christmas most folks are happy enough to put a few leftovers the way of a deserving cause.' He winked conspiratorially.

'And when I heard you was here, and a proper vicar, like, well, I reckoned you wouldn't want an old mucker to go past your door. Might make it worth me while.'

His rheumy eyes had cased the room already, and now he rolled them suggestively at the bottle of cooking brandy on one of the kitchen shelves.

Margaret ignored the hint.

'You come here and sit down next to the heater,' she said, valiantly putting out of her head any consideration of what heat would do to the olfactory assault on her senses. 'I'll heat you up some soup, while I sort out something a bit more substantial. Unless you'd like to clean up first? You could have a bath if you like,' she offered, more in hope than expectation.

He cackled with laughter. 'Bath? Not likely, miss. Bad for your health, they are. Open me pores like that, next thing you know, there I'd be down with pneumonia. But I'll take the soup, miss, God bless you.'

He had always been a jolly old reprobate, even if he was never sober if he could help it. She wondered sometimes what his history had been before the demons of alcoholism destroyed the fabric of his life, but to ask would be a serious breach of etiquette and he had never been one who dwelt on a happier past. In the summer months he had haunted the graveyard at St John's, but clearly travelled in the winter, and she was glad to know he had a circuit of hostels which would keep him out of sheds and ditches in the most inclement weather.

As always, she relished his conversation – he was by way of being a homespun philosopher – and he ate everything she put in front of him with equally hearty enjoyment, and consented to have the disreputable holdall and the plastic bags he carried filled up as well. She did not give him money, knowing all too well where that money would go, but offered him a lift to his hostel destination.

In her tortured recollections later, she blamed herself for accepting his refusal too readily, wished fruitlessly that she

113

had, somehow or other, insisted. But scenting rich pickings in this fresh field, he had firmly declined, and she had escorted him to the door hoping only that any would-be benefactor would be wise enough not to ply him too liberally with Yuletide cheer.

A light rain was falling now, and as he stepped out again into the cold, her father's old umbrella, stuck into the stand in the hall, caught her eye.

She had meant to throw it out; it had one broken rib, but it was sturdily made in the old-fashioned way, with a solid bone handle.

'Tom!' she called after him, 'is this any use to you?'

He came back and took it from her with his gap-toothed grin, touching one finger to his brow in mock salute.

'Cheers, miss!' he said, then drawing himself up to his skinny height put his heels together, doffed his disreputable woollen bonnet and bowed. 'And the compliments of the season to you.'

Laughing, Margaret watched him execute a comic, Flanagan-and-Allen caper under the battered gamp, and then he shuffled off down the road.

'Great heavens, do my eyes deceive me? Is that really Lizzie McEvoy buying biscuits? Now I would have sworn that no one in your family would even know what a bought biscuit looks like!'

There was hardly anyone in the supermarket. It had that wearied, post-Christmas appearance, with the gaps on the shelves left by the Christmas Eve feeding frenzy as yet unfilled, and much of what remained defaced by 'Reduced' labels stuck across the improbably merry snow-scenes and the anatomically-challenged robins. It was curious that packaging which days before had looked so festive now seemed as depressing as a shrivelled party balloon.

114

Elizabeth had been stowing a box of chocolate biscuits – 'Price slashed!' – in her trolley when Patrick Bolton accosted her jocularly from behind.

She swung round, startled and defensive, and, he noted in horror, with tears in her eyes.

'Well, I do try, you know. But a person can only do so much, and there's been such a lot with Christmas and everything . . .'

'Lizzie, stop, please stop!'

He caught her hands and held them awkwardly, trying to stop the flood of self-exculpation.

'It was a joke, Lizzie, not a criticism, honestly! Stupid, I know, but truly I was only teasing you. It never occurred to me that you would think . . . For heaven's sake, you must know that no one would ever reproach you for not taking enough trouble. I thought you would laugh. Oh Lizzie, please don't cry. It makes me feel awful.'

'Sorry,' Elizabeth sniffed. She freed her hands, feeling frantically in her pockets for a handkerchief and coming up at last with a rather scruffy pink paper tissue, with which she scrubbed at her eyes.

'I'm sorry,' she said again, trying to laugh. 'What an idiot I am! I don't know what can have happened to my sense of humour. It's not you, I think it's just that I'm so tired, with Christmas and everything, you know . . .'

He glanced down at Lizzie, pretty Lizzie, so small and pale and helpless-looking. The tears were still spilling over, and he longed to do something – take a clean handkerchief and wipe them away, put his arms round her in comfort, hit whoever had brought her to this state (as if he didn't know). It was a long time since he had experienced such a surge of protectiveness; Suzanne needed about as much protection as a porcupine.

He took charge, enjoying being masterful.

'What you need is a sit down and a cup of coffee and one of those appalling sticky doughnuts they have in the café here. No, don't look at your watch. If someone has to wait for you, it'll do them good.'

'It's just that the children are with Jenny Cartwright this afternoon – oh well, I don't suppose she'll mind.'

'Good girl.'

He walked her off. Their trolleys, abandoned, nuzzled together intimately in the confectionery section.

By the time they were sitting down, she had recovered her social poise.

'Is Suzanne working today?' she asked brightly.

'Yes, and I'm doing the shopping, and we had a splendid Christmas, thank you, and yes, I got all the presents I was hoping for. It was a shame the weather was so dismal over Christmas, wasn't it, but I do think it's a little milder today, even if there was some drizzle earlier.

'Right, that's got that out of the way. Now tell me what's wrong.'

He smiled at her encouragingly. She had such a soft face, that sweet, slightly drooping mouth and her mermaid's eyes fringed with silky lashes and still misted with unshed tears.

Her sigh was so deep that it shook her slight frame.

'Oh Patrick, you're very kind. Much too kind. But I don't think I could. I think it would be . . . disloyal to tell you.'

Quite unexpectedly, he found himself seized by pure rage. This was, without doubt, Piers's doing, and if the man had walked in at that moment he would have derived considerable pleasure from smashing his habitual self-satisfied sneer right into his face.

'You could try,' he said, struggling to keep his voice

116

even. 'And eat your doughnut. It's good for you – full of E numbers.'

He was rewarded with a watery smile, and she obediently cut a small piece off the heavily-iced bun and ate it.

'You're both so kind, you and Suzanne. I don't know how either of you has the patience to put up with me. Suzanne's so good at everything; she never seems to get into the muddles I do, and now I've upset her somehow, and I don't know what I've done —'

Her eyes brimmed again, and Patrick said roughly, 'Look, Suzanne's not angry with you. She's got one or two problems and she always thinks she can handle them by herself, which is her privilege. But if that's what's getting to you —'

'No, no, it isn't, really. It's just one more horrible thing. The real problem —'

She paused, torn by some sort of conflict.

'Oh, it seems so – well, underhand, to go talking to you like this. But I don't know – perhaps it isn't true anyway, and if I don't show it to someone I shall go mad. And I can't talk to Suzanne, and I can't talk to Laura either just now.'

She dived into her capacious shoulder bag and after a few moments' scrabbling produced a white envelope, badly-typed.

Patrick took it and withdrew the letter inside. As he read it, his face contorted in disgust.

'What a filthy thing. It's a pity you ever read it. Put it in the bin where it belongs.'

'But do you think it's true?'

He paused for that fatal extra second. The suggestion that McEvoy might, given the chance, indulge in an affair was hardly what you could term a surprise allegation; Hayley Cutler was famously free with her favours, and in other company he would have observed cynically that sooner or later the muck would stick together at the bottom of the pond.

'No, I shouldn't think so for a moment,' he said heartily. 'Anyone who could do something as sick as this wouldn't worry about truth.'

Her look was direct, and reproachful.

'I know what you're really saying. And yes, I'm afraid I believe it too. The rest is probably right as well, that I deserve it for being weak and pathetic and useless, but I can't help it. That's just what I am.'

The pink tissue was being picked to shreds now.

He was ashamed of the disingenuousness of his previous reply, but could be completely honest now.

'As far as that goes, nothing could be further from the truth. Deserve it! The trouble with you is that you're far too good for him. You've been a wonderful wife and mother, and he certainly doesn't deserve you.'

They were conventional enough remarks, but his sincerity was transparent. She smiled at him through the tears that welled over once more.

'Thank you for that,' she said softly.

He could not help himself. He reached across the table to smudge the tears away with his thumb, then cupped her face with his hand to make her look at him.

'He's too stupid to realize it, but he's the luckiest man in the world,' he said, and their gaze held for a long moment before she shyly lowered her eyes and drew back.

Margaret Moon was whizzing round the supermarket, grabbing the ingredients for a quick and easy supper. Robert was going home tomorrow, but she would have to feed him tonight before the parish meeting, and after old Tom's visit there wasn't enough left in the Vicarage to satisfy a mouse of normal appetite.

118

She had just swept into the trolley half-a-dozen cartons of gourmet catfood for Pyewacket – he had gone on hunger strike to get them, after she had foolishly bought him one for a treat on a kindly impulse – when she noticed the couple in the café. They attracted her attention first by the intensity of their conversation, in a setting where most exchanges were obviously desultory. It was a moment later that she recognized them, just in time to see Patrick Bolton's tender gesture.

Oh dear, she thought, whisking into the next aisle before they could notice her noticing them. Oh dear, how difficult it was to be a priest nowadays, responsible for the souls of your flock, and yet obliged to watch them head for spiritual shipwreck without so much as firing a maroon. Someone already resented something she had said or done; this would need some serious thought.

Old Tom hummed as he lurched along the main road in the gathering darkness. There was a spring in his step now, though for some reason the pavement seemed very uneven, and he was forced to tack from side to side. Shocking, the lack of upkeep nowadays.

He wasn't feeling cold now. There was fire in his belly, and plenty more where that came from.

'God bless you, miss vicar,' he murmured. But for her, he would never have found this lovely place with all these people who were generosity itself.

'Gener-generosity itself!' he repeated aloud. 'God bless them all!'

In this benevolent mood he staggered a little further. But he wasn't as young as he used to be, and sometimes his legs got tired, very very tired. Surely one of these lovely people wouldn't mind if he borrowed somewhere to rest them, just for a minute or two. Have a bit of a picnic, maybe. Too cold now for picnics out of doors. He looked about him.

Like a dark cavern, the door to the garage he was passing gaped wide. There was a car in it, but nobody about. He was sure they wouldn't mind if he found a corner to rest these tired legs just for a little bit.

Clutching the neck of the bottle in a lover's grasp, he shambled up the path and was swallowed up in the yawning blackness beyond.

6

Missy was angry. Missy was really angry. Missy was so angry, it made a sort of fire inside her. Stupid Dumbo, who kept fighting against her when all that Missy wanted was to make things better for both of them. Dumbo's problem was that she hadn't the sense God gave little green apples, and being forced to watch helplessly while the stupid cow screwed up made her rage.

And she was very angry about the keys. She would have revenge for that. Things which had been easy before were risky now, and she mustn't be found out. Certainly not yet, before . . .

Breaking out had been a real tussle tonight. Still, at least she was able to do it now; it made her feel sorer than ever when she thought back over all the years that Dumbo had kept her imprisoned, able to do no more than peer out through the bars of the body-cage she had to live in. But she was getting stronger now, day by day, and times they were a-changin' . . . She hummed the tune softly under her breath.

Anyway, it was her time now. Her anger forgotten, she felt the familiar sense of exhilaration, more strongly than ever before, till she was quivering like an animal with its force. This was the biggest, most exciting adventure so far . . . This was the first step on the way to the real thing, the big thing. She drew a deep breath to steady herself. Nothing must go wrong tonight.

She made her preparations quickly and effectively, filling the pockets of her dark hooded coat, then putting it on and pushing her bare feet into the boots that stood beside the door. She opened it and slid into the darkness outside, testing the air for sound or movement as warily as an animal, before melting into the shadows at the back of the house.

Reaching her objective, she felt in the coat's capacious pockets. There were the newspaper balls and the sticks, the box of firelighters; swiftly and soundlessly she built up the kindling against the wooden wall of the building, then reached into an inside pocket for the plastic bottle she had tucked away there.

She squirted its contents all over the wall, and it clung there in crazy lacy patterns, lovely sticky jelly stuff with an intoxicating fuel smell. It was a big bottle; she squeezed it till it was empty, her nose wrinkling with relish as she sniffed it. But there was no time to waste.

Matches! Surely she couldn't have forgotten – but then her scrabbling fingers closed on the box in the corner of another inside pocket. She struck one, and briefly allowed herself to watch the magic of the obedient flame, as it flickered and grew.

Then she bent to her satisfying pile of kindling and touched a match to the corner of the paper. It caught immediately; swift, eager tongues leaped up, licking greedily at the fuel gel.

Just for a moment she thought she heard some sound, some movement, and her eyes narrowed as she listened, poised for instant flight. But the movement she sensed was inside the building, not outside. It could be a cat, a dog . . .

Or something else. For a second she was distracted, her eyes cold and bright and hard with interest.

She would have liked to stay to see, liked to watch the flames catch, take hold, and finally engulf the walls and roof in the searing, satisfying fire. But it was a risk she dare not take. Regretfully, with no more than a lingering glance over her shoulder, she stepped back into the shadows again and was gone.

It was some kind of sound that brought Suzanne into full consciousness – a cry from outside in the street, perhaps, or Tigger the dog chasing rabbits in his sleep downstairs. She wasn't quite sure what it was, but it was enough to rouse her from her broken and unrestful sleep. With a sort of weary exasperation she snapped on the bedside light.

These unsatisfactory nights – tossing wakefully, or half-asleep, or troubled by strange and unpleasant dreams – were of recent date. Before that, she had slept as efficiently as she did everything else: half an hour with her current novel, light off, then oblivion until five minutes before the clock-radio came on in the morning. Patrick used to joke that if he could just persuade her to sing as she woke up, they wouldn't need one.

Patrick was asleep now, with his face buried deep in his pillow. He was usually a restless sleeper, but tonight he looked provokingly comfortable. A small, genteel snore escaped him, and he twitched slightly, like Tigger.

She cast him a look of resentment, as if she felt her loss was his gain, then swung herself out of bed and put on dressing gown and slippers. Perhaps if she made herself a cup of tea she might be able to get back to sleep.

Suzanne did not like moving round the house at night. It had a different atmosphere when everyone else was asleep, and being by temperament unequivocal, she was uneasy with the ambiguity of darkness and shadows. She switched on each light as she came to it, but even so found herself glancing sharply around, as if with a swift turn of the head she might surprise a table moving stealthily, or a chair inexplicably out of place.

She crossed the hall, sensitive to the black opacity of the uncurtained window by the front door, through which she must appear spotlit on her domestic stage. She hurried to open the kitchen door.

For a horrified instant, she thought that the room itself was ablaze. It was bathed in a lurid orange glow, and she could hear the frightening crackle of flames and smell smoke without being able to identify their source. But never mind that – she must wake the others, get them outside . . .

Just then the phone began to ring. It disorientated her, and instinctively she spun round to answer it, then heard a frantic ringing on the front door bell, and her own name, and Patrick's, being shouted from outside. There were three imperatives now; it was only when a pounding on the front door was added to the shrill demand of the bell that she managed to break the paralysis of indecision.

Patrick, pale and groggy from sleep, was staggering down the stairs as she opened the front door. Ben, rubbing his eyes, had appeared on the landing. The telephone was still shrilling its summons.

It was their next-door neighbour, plump and agitated, and bundled up in an old woollen robe, who stood on the doorstep, his round kindly face contorted into an expression of tortured anxiety. He spoke his breathless message to a background of sirens, rapidly approaching.

'It's your garage, your garage! You must get out, now – that car could explode at any moment! I thought you'd never answer. Come on, come on!'

He was plucking at Suzanne's sleeve, poised ready for

flight himself. His neighbourly duty had been an unconsidered action, whose bravery was only now becoming apparent.

Idiotically, Suzanne demurred. 'The phone —'

'That's only Isabel. She was to phone after she'd rung the fire brigade, to wake you up while I came across. Come on, come on!'

Despite being so violently awakened, it was Patrick who seemed less confused. He took control.

'Ben! Downstairs, and out. Here you are – wellies and a coat. Now across the street as fast as you can, and stay there. Go *on*, Suzanne. What's the matter with you?'

As Suzanne, still looking dazed, went out, there was a wail from Ben.

'But – Tigger! I've got to get Tigger!'

'I'll fetch Tigger. Just go.'

He plunged through to the small scullery at the back where the dog slept. When he opened the door, it was painfully bright, so bright that he had to shield his eyes to see out.

Theirs was a wooden garage, old, but sturdily built, with space only for one car – Suzanne's. His own was mercifully out in the road.

Now the garage was a raging hell of flames, and through the burnt-out side he could see that the fire was beginning to lick at the metal frame of Suzanne's car, the chemicals in the paint producing extraordinary tints of turquoise and lilac.

The petrol tank was probably full; Suzanne had a habit of keeping it topped up. He grabbed the terrified animal which was cowering and whimpering in its basket, and ran outside.

The first fire engine had just arrived, with a police car in close attendance. The officers were out already, ringing the bells of houses which might be in danger as the first hose the firemen had run out filled with water. The reassuring sound of sirens in the distance told of other engines on their way.

Ben, safely on the other side of the street, was beginning to enjoy the romantic dignity of his position at the centre of this drama. Further along, a policeman, grey-haired and avuncular, was reassuring Suzanne and Patrick.

'Now don't you worry, they're good lads, these. Everything's going to be all right.'

But the end wall and the nearer side wall of the garage had burned through and the roof was balanced on the stout corner posts, which were smouldering. The front, with its old-fashioned double-doors padlocked in place, was oddly intact.

They were aiming a hose through one of the burnt-out sides, pouring gallons of foam on to the car, dowsing flames which sprang up again a moment later. Heat was shimmering on the air; the paint on the doors and windows of the house was starting to blister, and the hedge marking the edge of the property was burning strongly. But now other jets were being directed on to it and over the houses on either side, hosing down the walls and roofs to prevent the blaze from spreading.

Patrick put his arm round Suzanne's shoulders.

'Are you OK? At least someone spotted it before the house went up and we were all burned alive. I know it's distressing, love, but we just have to be thankful that whatever happens now, they've got everyone to safety. Anyway, I'm sure they're winning, and we've talked often enough about needing a new garage.'

Suzanne said nothing, standing as if still bemused, her eyes glittering hectically in the light of the flames.

* * *

126

Piers McEvoy, despite the image he tried so hard to project, was not practised in intrigue. Recognizing his lack of physical appeal, he had been too proud to expose himself to humiliating rejection, so Hayley's pursuit of him was an entirely new experience. He had been titillated by the novelty of her illicit attentions, but a lingering unease remained. And only that morning he had caught an alarming glimpse of the silken cords which could so readily slide into a noose, and like a trap-wise fox wary of suspiciously seductive carrion, he was beginning to back away.

It had been no part of his intention to become further entangled in his relationship with Hayley Cutler. But when she had phoned his office so unexpectedly that afternoon, saying that her kids were off to a rock concert and then staying over with friends . . . He had hesitated for the fatal second which allowed her to say, 'I'll get in the oysters, if you bring the champagne, and we can move on to the Southern Comfort later. Any sort of comfort you care to name, in fact.'

The low, creamy voice affected him irresistibly. What difference did it make, anyway? He could pull the plug on the whole thing any time he chose, tomorrow just as easily as today.

After that it was the easiest thing in the world to phone Lizzie and tell her he would be dining in London and back late. He didn't know whether she believed him or not, but then he didn't really care, as long as she made the right noises and didn't ask questions.

And so it came about that he was lying in Hayley's kingsize bed, under Hayley's black sheets, dozing in sated satisfaction, when they heard the sirens.

They both sat up, but it was Piers who leaped out of bed, and from the window caught a glimpse of the fire engine as it raced through the village. It was only seconds later that the siren stopped.

Piers swore. Hayley, who had sunk back on to her pile of scarlet and black pillows, raised her brows in lazy enquiry.

'For God's sake, it's a fire in the village! That means that everyone and his dog will be out on the streets, gawping. Throw me my trousers, will you?'

She made no move to help, and her lips tightened just a fraction, but her voice was caressing as she said, 'Well, honey, there are no problems, only opportunities, as they told me in business school. Why not stay a bit longer, till the fuss is over?' She patted the bed suggestively.

By then there were more sirens.

'You have got to be joking,' he said savagely, shrugging himself into his shirt and grabbing his tie from the floor. 'If it's something big, they could be here for hours. And Lizzie will be awake – how could I possibly tell her I'd been out to dinner until breakfast time?'

'Sure. And who knows? It could be your own house, even.'

Piers blanched, and swore again as he lost his balance, dragging on a sock. He thrust his feet into his shoes without tying the laces – he could attend to the finer points of his appearance once he reached his car, parked in a shady corner of the common – and snatching up his jacket hurried to the door.

A belated impulse made him stop. 'Sorry it had to end this way. That was – what can I say? – fantastic.'

'The best,' she purred as she snuggled back into the luxuriously-piled pillows. As he shut the door, he did not notice that her eyes were hard as pebbles. He did not hear her sit up and punch those same pillows in a passion of rage.

Piers had kept to the shadows of the trees and shrubs which overhung the pavement when he arrived, but with lights popping on in houses all over the place, he dared not risk that now. The alleyway leading to the common turned and ran along the backs of the houses; there was a fence at the bottom of Hayley's garden which was awkwardly high and would do nothing for his city suit, but the alternatives were worse. Swearing and sweating, he heaved himself over it and reached his car without mishap. He sat there for a moment, thankfully, regaining his breath, then drove slowly home.

Elizabeth was sound asleep when he went in, her hand tucked under her cheek like a child's, but Paula tapped on the door a minute later. She had been wakened by the fire engines and was too excited about the fire to notice her father's uncharacteristically dishevelled appearance. With a finger to his lips, he warned her not to wake up her mother, and gave his whispered agreement that she could go along for two minutes to see what was happening.

He came out in his pyjamas when he heard her return ten minutes later.

'It's the Boltons' garage,' she said in a breathless whisper. 'They've got loads of fire engines and police cars and everything.'

He was startled. 'The Boltons'? Nobody hurt, though?'

She shook her head. 'It's just the garage and Mrs Bolton's car, that's all. Ben said the car might blow up and we could all be wiped out, but I don't believe him. The flames were brilliant, though.'

She sounded wistful, but didn't try to argue about going back to bed.

He switched off the bedside light and slid quietly into bed himself. That had been a near thing! It just showed, these risks were simply unacceptable, and the resolution he had made that morning took firmer root.

* * *

129

Wakened by the sirens, Margaret Moon had left the vicarage in haste, with an unarticulated sense that it formed some part of her duty to be where trouble was. Now, she was regretting her failure to subject impulse to the discipline of scrutiny. She found herself contemplating a row of backs, dramatically silhouetted against the swirling flames and the spotlights from the fire engines, and feeling awkwardly redundant. It was her vocation to help, but all she was doing at the moment was gaping vulgarly at someone else's disaster, no better than the despicable voyeurs who clutter the motorways after a pile-up.

And could she, she wondered with her usual painful honesty, be quite certain that it was pastoral duty and not prurience which had prompted her impulsive action? She felt uncomfortable and foolish, unable now to walk away without making an even more elaborate statement.

There was a sudden shower of sparks, prompting a collective 'oooh!' from the crowd, like spectators at a fireworks display. As the heads swivelled, Margaret noticed that Suzanne now stood a little apart, her shoulders hunched as she looked bleakly straight ahead.

Margaret touched her arm.

'Mrs Bolton – Suzanne – are you all right? You're looking very chilled; can't I take you off somewhere to keep warm while the experts deal with all this?'

The woman turned. She was shivering so violently that her teeth were chattering, though probably as much with shock as cold, and for a moment she stared at Margaret as if she barely knew her. The strain showed nakedly in her face, until she straightened her shoulders and pinned on her social smile.

'Oh Margaret, it's you! I'm so sorry, the light dazzled me for a moment.' Her voice was much too bright. 'No, honestly, I'm absolutely fine, just a little bit shaken, obviously. It's awfully kind of you to offer, though.'

It was amazing how it all came out, Margaret reflected, as if at the touch of a button – the middle-class response. Suzanne had managed to make all the right noises, the ones which allowed people to make the socially appropriate offers of help in the comfortable certainty that they would not be embarrassingly accepted. That left everyone with their self-esteem intact – she, strong and self-sufficient, they kind and concerned – which worked splendidly unless the strength and self-sufficiency were as illusory as the kindness and concern. Margaret had long ago learned to free herself from the tyranny of this sort of convention.

'I know you feel obliged to say that, and I admire your bravery. But from experience I also know that women have a dreadful tendency to go on saying they're fine, in case they inconvenience somebody else.'

Suzanne, who had half-turned away, stopped. When she turned back, her lip was trembling.

'I don't want to cry,' she whispered.

'Of course you don't, not in front of all these people,' Margaret said briskly. This was not the moment for debilitating sympathy. 'What you need to do is promise yourself a good bawl later, to get it out of your system. I promise to stand by with the man-sized tissues, and to keep you supplied with tea laced with brandy – it's my secret weapon against the bad moments of life.'

Suzanne managed a weak smile, but there was bitterness in it. 'Most of my moments seem to be bad these days. This is just a rather spectacular example.'

'It's that, certainly. But look, I really think they're getting it under control.'

And indeed, as she spoke, it became apparent that the

131

flames were dying down. Hissing, spitting and steaming, the blaze subsided.

Its final extinction was almost shocking in its abruptness, the fiery brilliance transformed in minutes to a charred and sodden greyness. The roof had not fallen in, the petrol tank had not exploded, the houses on either side were safe. Destruction limited, disaster averted. All in a day's work.

They would play the hoses on the timbers for a bit longer, of course, because smouldering wood could all too easily reignite, and rake out the rubble and set a watch, but the show was over.

'I really thought the whole thing was going to go up,' Margaret heard one man say, in a tone that was almost aggrieved at the anti-climax; yawning and shivering, people were starting to disperse.

Ben, still clutching Tigger, now sound asleep in his arms, went to huddle against his mother.

'Time we got you back to bed, young man,' Patrick was saying when the fire chief and one of the policemen came across.

'I think it's safe enough for you to go back to the house now, sir. Perhaps you could give us the key to the garage doors, and we'll try to get the car pushed out, just in case.'

'Still no idea how it started?' Patrick asked, but the fire chief shook his head.

'We haven't had a chance to look yet. But we'll find out, I can promise you that.'

The policeman, the sort of fresh-faced lad who made everyone else feel old, added, 'We'll need statements from you, of course, but it'll be time enough in the morning. Unless there's anything you want to tell us now, I'd just make the most of what's left of the night, if I were you.'

'But the men!' Suzanne exclaimed. 'They've worked so hard, I must make some tea for them.'

Margaret could see what it had cost her to make the gesture; that she accepted Margaret's offer of help without polite protest was eloquent proof of her exhaustion. Patrick took Ben and went to fetch the key; they followed more slowly.

From the front, the garage looked oddly normal, with the double door still padlocked in place, but the side and back walls were almost demolished, and the outside of the car was burned and blackened. Firemen were using their huge boots to kick out charred timber and were pulling away loose struts, raking the hotter embers outside. They were calling cheerfully to one another, happy at the successful conclusion to the night's work.

Margaret glanced at the detritus as they passed, picking their way carefully along the path which was awash with foam, water and soggy ash. It had clearly been a garage of exemplary tidiness, and she contemplated, wincing, her own garage clutter being similarly exposed to public view. It was probably the sort of thing your mother should warn you about, like wearing clean underwear in case you were knocked down.

There was nothing to shame the Boltons here. A barbecue, grill slightly twisted; a garden lounger now melted plastic and warped metal; a ruined lawnmower and an old umbrella reduced to a skeleton of spokes and a blackened bone handle . . .

She stopped. It felt as if everything stopped: heart, lungs, brain, even time itself as she recognized the innocent domestic object, its handle familiar even under the coating of soot.

Her father's old umbrella, which had stood in her own hall until this very afternoon. Until she had given it to the old friend who had come to her vicarage for his beggar's due.

She opened her mouth to speak, but before she could frame the words, there was a hoarse, chilling cry from the fireman who had just opened the implacably pad-locked doors.

'Smoke inhalation,' they said, then added, 'most probably,' which didn't help when you had caught sight of the charred, blackened, twisted shape which had been the man you had warmed and nourished and laughed with only that afternoon, a man who had been drunken and destitute, yet blessed with a serene acceptance of his disordered life and an uncomplicated zest for chance-come food and warmth.

Suzanne was in the bathroom, retching. Patrick had hustled Ben upstairs, mercifully before he had noticed anything further amiss. Margaret, ashen-faced, had sat down abruptly at the kitchen table when she realized that her legs had turned to rubber. Her lungs felt raw with the smell of smoke; was she imagining that it held a heavier stench than that of charred wood and blistered paint? She tried not to think about it.

After that, everything changed. The firemen who had been so cheerily clearing up were removed from what had now become the scene of the crime; other vans arrived with plastic sheeting and arc lights, and the stolid, reassuring uniformed officers had been replaced by tough-looking young men in jeans and casual jackets. A policewoman in plain clothes, introducing herself as Jackie, was finding her way about the unfamiliar kitchen with the air of one who was no stranger to this duty, setting out mugs and making tea.

With Ben safely asleep, Patrick came downstairs and brought out the brandy. Suzanne, face the colour of putty and with reddened eyes, sat shaking at the table as he clamped her hands round the glass and forced her to take a sip.

'I killed him,' she kept repeating. 'I killed him. I locked the door last night, I locked him in, and I killed him.'

'You always lock the door,' Patrick said flatly. 'You do it every day. 'It's not an unreasonable thing for you to do. It's not your fault that some poor stupid bastard chose to doss down in our garage the night it went on fire.'

Margaret looked up. 'Do they know yet what started it?' she asked the policewoman. 'Could it have been an accident?'

The girl's face was sombre. 'I don't think they know yet. But I have to say it seems unlikely.'

'Kids doing it for some sort of stupid lark?'

At Patrick's suggestion, Jackie shrugged. 'Could be. Have you had problems with vandals lately?'

'Not that I've heard of,' Margaret said. 'And usually the church and the churchyard are seen as easy targets. The youngsters round here don't seem the type.'

She got an old-fashioned look in reply.

'There's no such thing. Come down to the station on a Saturday night – the place is stiff with parents explaining that their child isn't the type. You never know when perfectly normal kids are going to break out, but usually they leave pretty clear traces.'

As she spoke, the door opened and a tall man with greying fair hair came in. He was wearing a shirt and tie and a Barbour jacket; his neatness seemed incongruous in the circumstances, and the smear of soot on his face added a further touch of unreality.

'Detective Inspector Vezey.' He spoke without any other attempt at social overture. 'I gather that someone here thinks they know the victim?'

'Yes, I do,' Margaret said, then felt obliged to qualify the

135

statement. 'At least, I recognized the burnt umbrella – it has a very distinctive handle – as one I gave this afternoon to a down-and-out called Tom. He was a regular at the church where I used to work, and – and he came here because he knew this was where I was.' Her voice wobbled and she stopped, biting her lip.

The detective's eyes were light brown and cold, and under their momentary sharp focus she felt that he could read the pain and the sense of responsibility she was struggling with as if it were written across her forehead.

But he made no comment, simply saying, 'I'll take a brief statement from you then. Constable!'

He snapped his fingers; the look Jackie gave him was wary, but a notebook and pencil appeared in her hands as if by magic.

When Margaret gave her name, he eyed her keenly once more. She had never been the sort of woman men undressed with their eyes, but under his gaze she felt stripped to bone rather than flesh. She did not enjoy the experience; she raised her chin and met his eyes robustly.

'Moon,' he said. 'An unusual name. Are you related to Robert Moon? You're physically very like him.'

I've never heard of him in my life before: the tempting response rose to her lips.

'My brother,' she said.

He evinced no surprise. 'I've worked with him. He's a useful man. Still in Bath, is he?'

'Oh no, in bed by now, I should think.'

With horrified embarrassment, she heard her own voice make the puerile joke. What could have possessed her? It must be shock, and if she allowed herself to laugh she knew she wouldn't be able to stop.

Determinedly not looking at anyone, she hurried on, overriding the quiver in her voice.

'I'm sorry, I was confused for a moment. What I meant was, he's staying with me at the moment in the Vicarage.'

'The Vicarage?' That surprised him into reaction. 'Right. I'll make time to see him tomorrow. Warn him to expect me. Now, if you can just tell me . . .'

It didn't take long. Vezey processed Margaret's meagre information in a matter of minutes; in not much more, he established that Suzanne had parked her car shortly after four, that she had left the garage door open in case she might want to go out again, and that she had locked the door at nine o'clock, when she had let the dog out. He remained impassive when she said, her voice trembling once more, that she wondered if it might have been a cry for help that wakened her.

His manner gave her no encouragement to elaborate or to dwell upon events. When he had finished, he said, 'We won't need you again before the morning. I suggest you get some sleep. Jackie, you can come with me.'

Jackie had been clearing mugs and glasses; with an apologetic glance she abandoned her task and followed him out.

Patrick got to his feet. 'Do you suppose he'll lock us up if we don't do as we're told? I'm certainly much too cowed to argue. Margaret, do you want me to walk you home?'

'Good gracious, no. The place is alive with policemen. I'll be safer than I would be on any normal night.'

At the door, Patrick said good-night and headed upstairs, while Suzanne, looking worn and fragile, held it open.

'Taking the blame,' Margaret said with what conviction she could muster, 'is an indulgence you simply must not permit yourself. I'm saying this to myself as much as you, because if he hadn't come to see me, this wouldn't have happened. But we might just as logically blame a stone if he'd fallen and cracked his skull on it. Or Tom himself, for that matter; he chose to trespass in your garage. He wasn't to know there would be a fire, but then neither were you. Try to sleep.'

'You've been very kind,' Suzanne said. 'I'll try.'

She shut the door, but through the uncurtained window at the side of the front door Margaret saw her stand motionless, her hands covering her face.

With fingers that were shaking and clumsy, Hayley Cutler fumbled the brass bolts, fitted only that day, into place on her back door, as if she could keep out by these physical means the darkness she felt surrounded her.

She had not immediately followed Piers out to see the fire. She had taken a bath first, running it as hot as she could stand and tipping in lavish quantities of the costly bath oil which had been her Christmas present to herself.

So she had arrived late on the scene, after the crowd had dispersed. A young policeman, looking shaken himself, told her the gruesome story.

Hayley had fled home, driven by irrational terror: irrational, because she knew how many police were within earshot of even a muffled scream.

Fear was stalking her close. When Suzanne had asked for the return of her key, Hayley realized instantly what lay behind the request; it had seemed, at the time, comforting that she herself was not the only target.

Yet someone had struck again at Suzanne – at her garage, like a warning – and an innocent dosser had been, they seemed to think, an accidental fatality of vandalism.

Perhaps he was. But in her heart she did not think so.

The walls of the cottage were thick and the windows had shutters which she had never used. Now she went to unfold them; thick with dust, they creaked and loose plaster fell out, but she felt safer once the bars were swung across.

She had forgotten to switch off the coffee machine, and the red light glowed invitingly. She poured some into a mug, wrapping her hands round its comforting warmth. It might keep her awake, but then she wouldn't be able to sleep anyway.

The conclusion seemed inescapable. Denied entry to Suzanne's house, someone had reacted in this hideous way. Might her bolts and bars attract similar revenge?

Most horribly of all, that gave the stalking monster a human face. Only four people had keys; she was one and Suzanne, the present victim, was the other. There were only two people left; Laura Ferrars and Elizabeth McEvoy.

She had known them for years. She had talked with them, laughed with them, looked into their eyes and seen no shadow of the insane malevolence this suggested. Their husbands, of course, might have used the keys they held, but who knew better than she that Piers had had nothing to do with it? And James – well, it was impossible to imagine James creeping around at night – it would ruffle his hair! She smiled at the thought, but the smile was short-lived.

She even considered Patrick, briefly. He was a tough, cold sort of character – at least, he never came on to her the way other men did – and if it had been her garage he'd be right up there on her list. There had been an added chill factor lately, notably towards Piers as well. Maybe he had figured they had a thing going, and he obviously had a weakness for sweet St Lizzie . . . But it was hardly a reason for starting a fire which might have killed him as well as his wife and child.

No, the case against the men just didn't hold up.

The letter and the apple she had found impaled had alerted her to the existence of hatred, and tonight, alone in the house, she was very, very frightened. At best, the fire had been the work of someone supremely indifferent to the safety of others. At worst . . .

She took another gulp of her coffee and shivered. For who could tell whether or not the malignity who had done this had known that the old man was there?

7

'I will turn their mourning to joy: I will comfort them, and give them gladness for sorrow.'

Holy Innocents Day: this was the prescribed introductory sentence. It was undeniably apposite, but in the light of last night's events seemed offensively pat. This morning Margaret found herself seriously out of tune with God, and she had always had problems with the Book of Jeremiah anyway, with its suggestion that a new set of wives and children could painlessly replace those so arbitrarily removed.

Tom had been an innocent, in his way, stripped by his addiction of all the sophisticated cushioning that protects prosperous mankind from the rawness of existence. The latter part of his life, at least, had been spent in what previous ages had seen as the beggar's office: that of offering others occasion for the exercise of charity. He had been harmless, as harmless as the sparrow to which you might flick crumbs out of your plenty. Could she really believe, today, that not one fell outside the Creator's knowledge and design?

Perhaps it was a lesson about eternal values set against temporal ones, but this morning she didn't feel philosophical, she felt flayed and tired and headachy, and for all the point there was in this service, she might just as well have stayed in bed with an aspirin.

Generally, she liked the morning services on Saints' Days. There might be two or three devout souls; on occasions, she had read the service for herself with the sense of acting for others as the link which kept unbroken a chain of prayer stretching back across the centuries.

Today, she could not rise above a theologically childish resentment that an all-powerful God could not have seen to it that poor old Tom had chosen the garage next door instead.

Still, she had a job to do, and this was one of the mornings when she did it because that was how she earned her living. She hadn't always enjoyed going to the bank either.

She found and marked the readings, being only further irritated to discover her own rebellion echoed in the first one, about Rachel who had also refused to be comforted.

Her preparations made, she went as usual to kneel in prayer, but finding it impossible to open her mind to God, relieved her feelings with a tirade about waste and futility – spiritually immature, perhaps, but satisfying.

There were three people there this morning. Clearly, last night's accident was not yet common knowledge, or there would have been a larger congregation, some in genuine prayer for the tragedy and some to discover whatever gossip might be going. It was a tradition which, if not officially sanctioned, was certainly time-hallowed.

Elizabeth McEvoy was there, unusually. She was a faithful Sunday worshipper, but Margaret had never seen her there on a weekday. Presumably Suzanne had phoned to tell her what had happened.

Elizabeth spent a little time after the service kneeling in prayer, and was the last to leave the church. Looking at her drawn face, Margaret said, 'I'm so glad you came this morning. I hope it helped.'

Elizabeth looked confused, as if the remark were unexpected. 'Well . . .'

'I know. Nothing helps much, does it? Something like last night just leaves you feeling sick.'

This time there was no mistaking the other woman's surprise, or even shock.

'Oh, dear God! Is it all over the village? I suppose he was with Hayley Cutler – I could swear I recognized her perfume on the shirt he was wearing last night.'

Margaret had suffered agonies of gaucherie as a teenager, but it was many years since she had felt so helplessly embarrassed.

Her face flaming, she stammered, 'Oh – oh no, you misunderstand me! I wasn't talking about your husband at all.'

As if blushing were contagious, Elizabeth too turned a painful colour. She opened her mouth as if to speak, but no words came.

'You obviously haven't heard,' Margaret said hastily. 'I assumed you would know – the fire at the Boltons' —'

'Oh yes, of course.' She struggled to regain her composure. 'But – but that was just the garage, wasn't it? Paula said they had got it under control last night.'

'Well yes, but unfortunately an old tramp had taken refuge there —'

Her embarrassment forgotten, Elizabeth listened in horror, her eyes filling with ready tears.

'How – how perfectly horrible! Poor Suzanne – I'll phone her whenever I get home. And – and about the other thing —'

She paused, and Margaret was wise enough to say nothing.

'I've blurted it out to you now, so where you're concerned I haven't any face to save. And they always say, don't they, that there's no such thing as a mistake in these circumstances. Perhaps I really wanted someone to know. Sometimes I feel it's destroying me, that I shall go mad if I go on and on, acting as if everything is all right. My whole life is such a wretched mess; whatever I do is wrong —'

'Wrong for whom?' Margaret interjected crisply. 'Wrong for you? Wrong for your children? Or just wrong for your husband?'

Elizabeth stared at her, as if this were entirely a new idea.

'He wouldn't like me talking to you – to anybody.'

'I don't think that's specially relevant, do you? I'm always at the end of a phone.'

'You're very kind. I'll think about it. I'd better go now. I felt I needed to come, but I didn't tell anyone I was going out.'

As Margaret went back to the vestry, she paused for a moment in front of the altar. She wasn't yet prepared to surrender her larger grievance, but in fairness she had to admit that getting out of bed this morning hadn't been as pointless as it seemed.

When she got back to the vicarage at half past eight, there was a car parked outside. She was no expert on marques, but it was large and black and somehow brutal-looking, and she sighed.

It was an unwelcome sight. Muttering darkly, she let herself in and followed the voices through to the kitchen.

Robert, looking uncharacteristically grave, was seated at the little round kitchen table, facing her as she opened the door. She recognized the man with his back to her as Vezey, the detective who had questioned her the night before. He did not get up as she came in.

Robert did, to pull forward another chair, though the table was not really designed for three.

'Margaret, you've met Rod Vezey, I gather.'

'Yes, last night. Good morning, inspector.'

'Yes,' he said, glancing at her briefly before transferring the powerful focus of his attention back to Robert. 'So that's the current state of play. Anything you can make of it?'

Margaret pointedly lifted the empty coffee pot and made a business of refilling the kettle and noisily setting out a cup, saucer and plate for herself.

With his elbows on the table, Robert made a steeple of his fingers, and contemplated them.

'Profile of a pyromaniac,' he said slowly. 'Well, putting it simplistically, it's revenge for lack of love, of human warmth. There's something very trite about psychological symbolism, isn't there? Conscious symbolism is always considerably more subtle – but I digress!

'They're more commonly male than female, though that's based on old research: women are achieving equality in all sorts of unexpected areas these days. Often the parents have been either physically or emotionally absent.'

'Personality?'

Robert considered the other man's question.

'Liable to be anxious and self-punishing; when anxiety for one reason or another gets out of control, rage takes over. The fire may be an undirected explosion of fury, or an act of direct revenge against someone in particular. But I don't suppose that's really taken you much further.

'Is there any hard evidence?'

'Not much. They can tell it wasn't a gang of kids, for instance – no trampling on the soft ground round about, apart from the firemen, of course, and the regulation boot is nothing if not distinctive. But there's concrete right round

145

the garage, so anyone could have walked across it and left no trace.'

As Margaret came back to the table with the coffee pot, Vezey wordlessly held out his cup to be refilled. Offer it up, Margaret's better self urged, but she could only suppose that offering God seething resentment controlled by the conventions of hospitality put her on a par with Pyewacket hopefully presenting her with a particularly mangled mouse.

Noticing his sister's expression, Robert hurried on.

'How much have they been able to establish about the way the fire was started?'

'Very neat. Set just as you'd set a fire in the hearth, with paper and sticks. The end wall had been sprayed with that gel stuff they use on barbecues – lethal. I'd take it off the market, if I had my way. We found the bottle – with smudges rather than prints, unfortunately – but it could come from any one of a dozen shops. There was one like it in the Bolton's garage: there's probably one in half the sheds in Stretton Noble. It's real barbecue belt round here.'

There was a sneer in his voice, and Margaret discovered, to her own surprise, that she felt defensive.

'Eating out of doors is hardly a crime,' she said tartly.

Both men looked at her, Robert in mild surprise at her tone, and Vezey, she thought, with the air of one addressed by a kitchen chair; interested in the phenomenon but far from sanguine about the quality of its contribution.

'I didn't say it was,' he said.

Before Margaret could speak again, Robert interposed.

'And the victim? Is it possible it was murder rather than accident?'

Vezey gave the question his careful consideration, but the downturn of his mouth expressed scepticism.

'The mechanics would be far too elaborate. And there's no mystery about him; he was Tom Porter, well known to the local force. Travels round various different circuits in the course of a year, so as not to use up the good will. Done it for years. We lift him every so often when someone complains.

'He goes in to the city during the summer months – where you encountered him, Miss Moon – and he knows all the hostels where he can con a bed in winter. They reckon he would have been making his way to the hostel near Broadhurst, but we found an empty bottle of vodka beside him. Presumably some dogooder was misguided enough to give him cash in hand as a Christmas box.'

The sneer was back, but Margaret managed not to leap into a denial of responsibility. 'So at least he would know very little about what happened?'

There was no compassion in his face. 'Who knows?' he said, rising abruptly.

'Work that up into a profile for me, Robert, will you? I'll contact the force in Bath – say I need you here for a few days.'

He walked out without farewell, and they heard the front door slam behind him.

Margaret counted to ten. 'Would you like me to invite you to stay with me for a little longer?' she asked sweetly.

Robert grinned. 'He's quite something, isn't he?'

'Does that sort of rudeness come naturally, or has he been specially trained?'

'He's focused,' Robert said placidly. 'He's superbly effective – just doesn't waste energy on the peripheral things.'

'Like common politeness.' Margaret refilled their coffee cups, but as curiosity overcame her indignation, asked, 'What will he do now?'

147

Robert shrugged. 'Arrange door-to-door enquiries. Talk to the scene-of-crime officers and the fire scientists. Chase up the path lab for a full report on the body – they'll drag their feet, because charred bodies ... Well, it's understandable.'

Shuddering, Margaret agreed.

'Then he'll have to get back to his desk and deal with the other ninety-three cases he's got sitting there. Everything else doesn't stop, you know; this is just one more case.'

'And do you think you can point him to any short cuts?'

'Mmmm. One or two fairly obvious things, I suppose. The neatness of the fire-laying – that's extremely interesting. Usually it's a case of dowsing with petrol and flinging a match.

'This suggests someone in the habit of setting domestic fires. Could be male or female, but it does have implications about social class. They don't put open fires into council houses any more, so setting one is almost a forgotten art. Having an open fire is rapidly becoming another middle-class affectation. And the barbecue fuel – that's interesting too. Such a very domestic substance to use, wouldn't you say? Most male fire-raisers would, as I said, automatically think of petrol, or possibly paraffin, if its handy.

'Of course, you know as well as I do that it's not an exact science. I have to follow hunches, and the skill lies in analysing whether the hunch is soundly rooted in a subconscious synthesis of legitimate information, or whether it's something the little green men from Mars whispered in passing. It'll be easier once they get me a précis of the evidence and I have something to get my teeth into.'

'Have a guess.'

He sighed. 'Now you want a crystal-ball answer again, which wouldn't matter if it weren't for the fact that Vezey will too. If I had to make a wild guess, I'd say the perpetrator was middle-class and female.'

'Like the letter-writer?'

'Sorry, you've lost me.'

'The anonymous letter-writer. Female, you said, and educated.' Female, educated and hostile towards me, she thought, but did not say.

'I'd forgotten all about that. How extraordinary! I should have mentioned that to Vezey; it's certainly the sort of thing that could be connected. You've still got it, haven't you? They just might manage to lift some prints. I'll take it along and try to catch him after breakfast. Unless you would like the fun of telling him yourself?'

Margaret pulled a face. 'I have better things to do. I promised I'd visit Suzanne Bolton this morning.'

Then, trying to reassure herself, she added, 'At least he seems satisfied that it was an accident. It would be awful to think we had a murderer in our midst.'

When Robert fixed upon her that look of detached curiosity, she always felt like a laboratory rat demonstrating some unusual aspect of animal behaviour.

'How very extraordinary that you should find that reassuring,' he said. 'You mean, you would rather have a pyromaniac on the loose, setting random buildings ablaze with no concern for safety, than a murderer with a specific and probably quite logical reason for killing one particular person?'

'Who says it would be a logical murderer?' she protested, for form's sake. But in truth, despite what she had seen last night, she had not until now understood the terrifying subtext to the blaze. Last night she had seen the extinguishing of the fire as the end of the crisis, not the beginning.

Looking back in the light of later events, she could pinpoint this moment as the first time she experienced the cold trickle of fear between her shoulder blades. She shivered involuntarily.

Then she laughed. The winter sun was shining brightly, showing up the windows which were badly in need of cleaning. The homeliness of the kitchen, with its cheerful yellow walls and its comfortable domestic smells of toast and coffee made her reaction seem melodramatic.

'Robert, you are the limit,' she said. 'I thought you would have grown out of trying to wind me up, and I would certainly have thought I was much too old to let you.'

Laura didn't know what to do.

James had come back from collecting the morning paper as usual, full of the events of last night as recounted to him in graphic detail by the newsagent. She listened, then burst into tears of horror, a reaction which, in the circumstances as he saw them, he clearly considered extreme behaviour. He took himself off for the London train promptly and with obvious relief, leaving the girls still in bed and Laura sitting at the breakfast table trying to control her panic and consider the situation more dispassionately.

She couldn't have done this. Surely she couldn't! Surely she would remember something about it, or have wakened James going out – but then she had to admit that it had been her complaint when the children were small and noisy that a brass band marching through the bedroom wouldn't have roused James.

Her resentment against him grew. If he had done as she had asked – as she had begged – and taken them all away yesterday, she would not be sitting here this morning, wondering if she were going mad.

And perhaps, a chilling voice inside her whispered,

Suzanne's garage would still be intact, and an old man would be shuffling on to his next begging round, hungover perhaps but otherwise unharmed.

The feeling of suffocation she had experienced before came over her again, and she took gulping breaths, trying to get more oxygen into her lungs. She began to feel very strange, light-headed . . .

Hyperventilating, she thought, I'm hyperventilating. I've told hysterical girls that often enough. With a supreme effort of will, she calmed her breathing, regained control of herself. She was a sensible, highly-intelligent woman – at least, she had been. If she still was, what would she do?

She clung to the thought. Putting a good face on it was, after all, second nature, and she thought the thing through. She would go and see Suzanne, of course. She would take along a neighbourly present – a quiche, perhaps, or a frozen stew that she could just pop in the microwave for supper – and she would put things back on a normal footing.

She had probably been over-sensitive. It was probably quite true that the insurance company wanted the keys called in; they made all sorts of demands nowadays, and probably Suzanne had asked everyone else for theirs as well.

She forced herself to be cheered by this reflection, and jumped up to busy herself in making her preparations, so that she didn't have time to analyse it too closely. She left a note for the girls and set off.

The activity, and the shroud of plastic sheeting enclosing the Boltons' garage, took her by surprise, as if she had previously contrived to blot out the stark reality of what had happened. There were tapes cordoning off one side of the drive, and a knot of men stood in earnest conference. It made her feel strange and uncomfortable; she turned her mind instead to Suzanne's need for her solace and support.

As she rang the doorbell, she heard Suzanne's voice, talking on the telephone, obviously. She heard the 'ping' of the receiver going down, and a moment later Suzanne opened the door.

'Sorry,' she said dully. 'I was just arranging with the insurance to have a replacement car delivered today.'

They were all in the habit of the friendly peck on the cheek in greeting; under stress, you might hurl yourself at your friend for a supportive hug. Suzanne did neither.

Laura's brave smile faltered. 'I – we were so upset to hear what had happened. Er – I brought you this.'

She held out the package, over-wrapped in foil, and Suzanne took it.

'Thank you. Everyone's been very kind. Do you want to come through to the kitchen?'

She stepped aside. Laura hesitated briefly, then went in.

The kitchen, to anyone who knew Suzanne, was eloquent proof of her shaken state. There were cereal packets and a bottle of milk sitting on the kitchen table; unwashed mugs and bowls were lined up on the draining-board and the surface by the toaster was defaced with unwiped crumbs.

Suzanne clearly wasn't seeing it. She was pale, with deep olive shadows round her eyes, and her hair, normally so neat and springy, was lank and flattened to her head. She was dressed smartly as always, in neat black trousers and a soft white wool sweater, but this had been worn before and had a smudge of dirt on the sleeve.

Laura felt brief shock, as if some part of the other's personality had been eroded. Unthinkingly, she stretched out her hand.

'Oh Suzanne, you poor thing —'

There was no doubt about it; she shrank away. Then, as if embarrassed by the stricken look on Laura's face, she tried to laugh.

'Sorry, I'm just terribly twitchy today. I think I'm probably still in shock. I can't describe how awful it's all been.'

But Laura noticed she moved to the far side of the kitchen table, as if Suzanne were trying to keep a physical barrier between them. She was beginning to feel light-headed again, and her only wish was to get out of there, get out of this terrible situation before one of them felt forced to confront it directly.

'I think you should be in bed, you know,' she said. 'You can't have got any sleep at all last night, so I'm just going to go away again. Is Patrick still sleeping?'

'I told him to go in to work today. He dropped Ben off at the Cartwrights.'

They were walking through the hall as she spoke, Suzanne a little ahead. As if struck by a sudden thought, she spun round.

'But he might easily come back very early,' she added.

Oh, my God! She's afraid that if I think she's on her own, I might come back and do something worse! Laura would never know how she managed to keep her voice steady, reply with the appropriate concern, 'Are you sure you'll be all right on your own till then?'

Suzanne's voice rose. 'Yes, of course! In any case, Margaret Moon may well look in, and Mrs Burden's been in already. Jenny Cartwright's going to bring Ben back later – I'll hardly have a minute to myself.'

Laura was outside now, grateful for the coolness of the air on her face.

'Lizzie will be along to see you too, no doubt.'

Suzanne took a step back inside the door. 'Oh – probably,'

she said, then closed it. Laura heard the safety-chain being slid along its groove.

She wasn't aware of walking out of the garden and along the road. Everything about her seemed remote and insubstantial, and she was only recalled to herself when she heard someone saying, 'Hello, Mrs Ferrars.'

It was the vicar in a grey coat and neat dove-grey shirt with the clerical collar at her neck.

'Have you just been in to see Suzanne? I'm on my way over there. How is she this morning?'

Laura stumbled on her words. 'Oh – well – all, all right, I think. That is, as all right as she would be. Given what's happened.'

'Yes, naturally.'

The vicar was looking at her, very directly. Behind the spectacles, her eyes were as clear and steady as a child's; indeed, the whites, like a child's, were clear and almost bluish. They were eyes that could look through you, see into your very soul.

'And no doubt she'd be glad to see *you*,' she said.

Laura muttered something, and incontinently fled. The sarcastic tone in the vicar's remark was pointed. The vicar knew, as Suzanne did, what she was doing; perhaps they believed she was doing it consciously and deliberately. They were only waiting for proof, and then . . .

Inside the tent of plastic sheeting, it was now uncomfortably humid. Underfoot, the damp ash still held some residual heat; the sun, the arc lights and the body-warmth of the half-dozen men in white boiler-suits raised the temperature and intensified the acrid smell. The men's breath condensed on the cold polythene, dripping back down in a sort of acid rain.

'Just as well we don't have a pine forest in here,' one said to Rodney Vezey, who had just come in; he regretted the mild jest as the inspector's eyes surveyed him expressionlessly before he turned away.

They were sifting the ash now in great sieves, a thankless task which would probably leave them no nearer any solution to the crime. There was no reason to suppose that its perpetrator had set foot inside the garage, but it might yield a picture of Tom Porter's last moments.

Vezey was listening now to the man in charge.

'Well, sir, as far as we can tell, he was sleeping on the garden lounger – tucked himself up in a few rags he most likely had in that holdall.'

He pointed to a mess of burnt webbing and plastic on the floor. An empty vodka bottle, blackened and cracked by the heat, was lying on its side with the metal cap discarbed nearby.

'It would take a bit to rouse him, with the skinful he had. But something must have – the heat, or the smoke making him cough – because he got to the door there, where they found him.'

The doors, unyielding last night, stood open now.

Vezey nodded curtly, then went back outside again, filling his lungs gratefully with the chill fresh air. He returned to his previous station, leaning up against the blackened brick of a garden wall in the corner where the pale sun provided a little warmth.

Apart from instinctively thrusting his hands further into his jacket pockets, he paid no attention to the cold. Once you had served your time as a copper on the beat, you knew enough to wear good thick-soled shoes and then forget it.

From his vantage point he had observed the comings and goings of women to the house with a flicker of contempt. They reminded him of his mother, and that wasn't a compliment.

She had just their sort of cool civility, which seemed to have no other purpose than to keep people in their place at a safe distance, and she had made no exception for her only child. Messy things, children, with uncomfortable needs, so you had as little to do with them as possible. You paid someone else to care – and sacked them if you thought they weren't caring in precisely the way you had in mind – and you considered that you had purchased freedom from responsibility.

He had only once – in some teenage desperation that seemed faintly comic now – approached her with a plea for help. She had been appalled.

'My dear Rodney! Didn't you talk to your housemaster? No, I suppose you wouldn't. Well, there's a wonderful chap who specializes in teen problems; I'll fix up an appointment for you right away.'

'Don't bother,' he had muttered, and went out and got drunk instead. The resultant hangover had been surprisingly effective as distraction therapy.

His determined disregard for social forms had begun as a punishment for his mother, then became rebellion, then habit. Now, having discovered its effectiveness, it was a principle. Time was increasingly a scarce commodity and he chose to bestow it only upon those who could be useful to him.

Robert Moon was a useful man, carrying remarkably little baggage for a psychologist. Most of them only took it up because they were basket-cases themselves.

He had been commendably prompt in coming along with his preliminary ideas and the anonymous letter, so that Vezey had been able to add pertinent questions to the list his cohorts had been primed to work their way through.

People were always reluctant to admit to receiving hate-mail; even in cases where the content was harmless enough, to attract hatred is in itself somehow shaming. If you could suggest an epidemic, evidence was more likely to be forthcoming.

The sun was a little stronger now. He tipped his head back, savouring the warmth on his face as he contemplated the meagre evidence.

'Start every case, my son, by statin' the bleedin' obvious,' his first detective-sergeant had instructed him, and it was a discipline which had proved itself over the years.

The fire-raiser was someone who could get out at night: someone who lived alone, or who had a partner who was in collusion – unlikely, when you were talking about arson – or who slept soundly. Someone, perhaps, with access to sleeping pills, who could make sure they did? That probably meant half the village: insomnia was the mark of those not exhausted by hard physical labour.

They could check whether anyone had bought barbecue lighting gel lately. At this time of year it would be a purchase unusual enough to attract attention. But the chances were it had been opportunistic, with a bottle beside the barbecue in every shed.

Middle-class and female, Moon had suggested tentatively, with a positive maze of conditional hedging. Not the clientele you normally found down the nick. But then, as he himself could testify, that sort of life style was no guarantee of emotional security.

And then there was the old boy, Tom – though in fact, despite the descriptions, he hadn't been that old. Early fifties, the local sergeant reckoned, and he allowed himself a brief spasm of pity for the poor bastard. On the other hand, he couldn't think an extended life span would have proved happy or rewarding. With increasing age and abuse would come the string of infections, the confusion of mind, the ultimate death in a hostel if he was lucky, a ditch if he wasn't. If the smoke had got to him first, it would have been – bearable. If not . . .

He never permitted himself to think about things like that. They got in the way.

He had dismissed the possibility that it might be murder, but now meticulously he put the idea to the test.

Could one of the almsgivers have plied him with vodka and told him he could get in to the garage? For a moment he toyed with the seductive notion that Tom might have been party to some scandalous incident in the vicar's past which she had killed him to suppress, then regretfully discarded it. She, or anyone else, would have had to be sure that the doors would be left open, which happened only occasionally.

Suzanne Bolton herself? She could have told the man he could bunk down in the garage, but she had been out all day and in all evening, having brought the boy back with her in the car. No, that didn't look like a runner.

Insurance fraud was the next thing to consider, of course. If Suzanne – just by chance, naturally – had happened to have left her car out last night, he'd have had the lighted matches under her fingernails by now, but he had yet to find the householder who would set fire to a garage next to the house containing a relatively new car with a full petrol tank.

But someone had. You might have no reason to suspect the presence of a vagrant, but you would know that the car was there. It could be malevolence, recklessness or idiocy, but whichever it might be, it was an alarming situation. They needed to get this one under lock and key as soon as possible. Panic would spread like measles in a place like this, and they were probably all intimate friends of the Chief Constable.

He contemplated the thought morosely, then went back inside to see how the investigation was progressing.

*   *   *

After her visit to Suzanne, Margaret Moon headed towards the church once more. She had some organizing to do; she had decided that, as they had done at St John's Marketgate, she would hold a Watchnight Service on New Year's Eve. It was always very popular with the young, though the authorities tended to frown on the idea because of the danger of rowdyism. The Bishop, apparently, had raised his eyebrows – a salient feature – but Margaret was of the opinion that a higher authority even than he might find a spot of youthful exuberance a great deal more excusable than polite apathy.

But it was not her grand design for the spiritual welfare of her parish that was preoccupying her as she walked along in the fragile winter sunshine. She was very much exercised over Suzanne's story of the keys, confided it seemed almost against her will, and then only on the promise of strict secrecy.

Obviously, no one needed a key to approach the garage. But Suzanne was convinced that this was the latest, terrifying development in a pattern of persecution against herself, by one of her friends.

Margaret sighed. She had, of course, urged Suzanne to tell the police immediately, but the woman had become almost hysterical at the suggestion.

'How can I?' she cried wildly. 'How can I tell the police that I suspect my *best friends*? I don't know which one it is; it's difficult enough already, and the police would go and accuse them all, and then I'd have nobody left, nobody!'

And her husband didn't count, Margaret thought sadly, remembering the scene in the supermarket, but she said only, 'I'm sure the police would be tactful,' though she wasn't altogether convinced of that herself.

The other woman shook her head frantically. 'You won't tell them, will you? You promised!'

'No, I won't,' she said heavily. 'I promised, though I wish you hadn't asked me to.'

'I'm – I'm sorting it out myself.' Suzanne turned away, fiddling with the twisted flex of her toaster. 'Taking precautions. Just till I know, OK?'

And there Margaret had to leave it. Perhaps it would all come out when the police got round to questioning Patrick, who also apparently knew but hadn't made a direct connection.

Well, perhaps there was none. Perhaps Suzanne was exaggerating. She was certainly overwrought.

But then her mind went to her meeting with Laura Ferrars. That had been very strange. Mrs Ferrars had always appeared a calm and collected person, as you would expect from a woman in her position. It was natural, no doubt, to be upset about the fire – they all were – but not to be able to reply to a casual social remark was surely out of character. 'No doubt she'd be glad to see you': that was all Margaret had said, wasn't it? Hardly what you could call contentious.

Piers McEvoy and James Ferrars would have had access to the keys too, of course, but Suzanne had been forthright in dismissing them. And given Robert's analysis as well, her gut reaction was probably right.

So who could it be? Laura Ferrars, who had always seemed so level-headed, until today? Elizabeth McEvoy, who had troubles enough, without seeking for more? Hayley Cutler?

She held that thought. The woman was apparently both immoral and unscrupulous, and it was tempting to assume her guilt. But somehow . . .

If only she could discuss it all with Robert! But she

had promised, and though the confidence had not been made under the seal of the confessional, she was bound by professional ethics.

She was most unhappy about it, though. Margaret sighed again as she turned in under the lych gate.

8

'Sir —'

Rod Vezey was coming out of the tent of plastic when the voice hailed him, and he looked up. Jackie Boyd, the young DC who, with her short spiky red hair had the look of a fledgling bird, was waiting there, standing uncomfortably as if ready to take flight. Her obvious unease irritated him.

'Speak up, Boyd, if you've got something to say.'

She flinched, but said sturdily enough, 'They want you round the back. There's some sort of footprint – not very good. . .'

Behind the concrete apron round the garage was a fringe of long grass by the fence dividing the garden from one of the little pathways so common in Stretton Noble. This one was gravelled, with more rough grass growing up the shallow bank.

'Here, sir.' One of the detectives was pointing to an area by the fence.

'Someone's been through here – see?'

The long, lush blades were flattened in the spot where someone would have had to set their foot to cross from the gravel of the path to the concrete of the garden if they were to squeeze through the fence.

The grass had not held what could be termed a footprint, but there was the blurred outline of a shoe or boot.

Vezey studied it attentively. 'Small,' he said.

'That's right, sir. We'll get photos and exact measurements, but it looks as if it's a pretty small chap. A kid, even.'

'Or a woman.'

'Suppose so. Not usual, you'd have to say.'

'Any idea of the type of footwear?'

'We'll let the lab boys do their stuff. But don't hold your breath.'

He turned, looking for his sergeant, a bullet-headed young man called Dave Smethurst.

'Dave! Get a group combing that area – both directions, on all fours if that's what it takes. See if you can figure where our friend came from to get on to the path.'

Smethurst nodded. 'Sir. But I've walked it already, and most of the houses have a gate and a neat little path. A fence like this is the exception.'

'Do it anyway.'

At least it was evidence. He liked physical evidence; you could make something of it.

Then an unwelcome thought struck him. There was a child in this house, and children were famously reluctant to take the long way round.

Suzanne Bolton, her face tear-stained, opened the kitchen window when he tapped.

'Well, of course he does,' she said in answer to his question. 'If it's the quickest way to go.'

'When was the last time he did it?'

She looked bemused. 'I haven't the slightest idea. You'll have to ask him – he's at the Cartwrights'. Yesterday, perhaps?'

'But not last night, or this morning?'

'Not that I know of.'

He turned away. Perhaps the lab boys would know how

long it took bruised grass to spring up again. They knew the most extraordinary things, but it wasn't the sort of evidence the Crown Prosecution Service liked. This was what he termed 'thumb-and-two-fingers' evidence, the sort they held out at metaphorical arm's length with a pained expression.

Still, it was another straw in the wind. Moon's off-the-wall hunches had an uncanny way of proving to be right.

Andy Cutler kicked the stand out from under his motorbike to park it in the driveway outside the Briar Patch, and got out a chain and padlock from the pockets of his leathers. The bike had an engine immobilizer, but it was the joy of his life and he was taking no chances. As he bent to fix it, the helmet he had tucked under his arm fell and rolled across the pavement to land at the feet of a woman who was walking by.

She stooped to pick it up, and he recognized her: Miss Moon, the vicar. He thanked her politely as she handed it back to him.

'That's a nice bike,' she said. 'It's a Harley-Davidson, isn't it?'

He stared, astonished. Old dames like her not only didn't know the makes of bikes, they tended to freak out if they so much as saw one. His pale olive skin flushed with the pride of ownership, and he could not help looking fondly at the machine.

'Cost enough,' he said gruffly.

'What did you do to earn it?' She actually sounded interested.

'That was five years of Saturdays and school holidays working in the supermarket.'

He paused, but she was still paying attention, not glazing over like most wrinklies once they'd asked what they thought was a suitable question.

'Other kids say I'm lucky to have it, but they spent their Saturday mornings in bed.'

'It can't have been what you might call exciting either. What are you doing now?'

He looked at her vicar's shirt and collar; suspicion seized him and he withdrew.

'There's no need to chat me up, you know, just because you think it's your job. I'm not into God-bothering.'

She didn't take offence. She smiled and said, 'I'll let you know when I start the sales pitch. Just at the moment, I think you're an interesting person, and I'd like to know more about you.'

'Not much to know, really.' It came out off-hand, because he had felt bad about being ungracious, so he hurried on. 'Foundation course in computing at the local college. It's pretty naff, but the syllabus is OK. I want to go on and do electronics at university, but Hayley – Mum – says she can't afford it.'

'Wouldn't you get a grant?'

He shot her a sideways look. 'She *says* she can't afford it. She's always had money for whatever she wants. It just doesn't stretch to serious handouts to us.'

'To be fair to your mother, a lot of people find money's hard to come by these days.'

For a second he was prepared to go along with the diplomatic whitewash, but the lure of being listened to was too strong.

'She says the business is going down the tube,' he burst out, 'but she's said that before. And then surprise surprise some new boyfriend turns up and bales her out.'

He paused again, but the vicar didn't look shocked and he went on, 'Still, this time she's been in a serious bad mood for days, so maybe she has got problems. She got a huge bunch of flowers today – roses and things – and she looked really pleased till she read the card, and then she freaked out. She tore it up and started pulling the flowers to bits and threw them all over the place. Then she stormed out and shut herself in her room. We cleared it up OK, me and Martha, but – it's a bit heavy, I suppose. We really don't know what to do.'

'Do you,' suggested Margaret gently, 'have grandparents?'

'Yeah, sure. Grandad and Sarah. They live in Brighton.'

That wasn't such a dumb idea. Grandad was pretty old, but Hayley still paid attention to what he said.

'I could go round and see her, of course, if you thought it might help.'

He looked awkward. 'Well, maybe not. She isn't exactly into that kind of thing. But I could phone Grandad, maybe; get them to come and see her. Though if he comes I'll have to cut my hair and lose the earring if he's not going to have a coronary and make things worse.'

'Oh, what a shame!'

To his further amazement, the vicar was looking at his ponytail and silver skull earring with what seemed to be genuine approval.

'I do think it's a splendid hairstyle – neat, becoming, and at the same time rebellious. All the things a young man's hairstyle should be.'

'You're a funny sort of vicar,' was all he could think of to say.

She laughed at him. 'If you mean vicars are usually male and boring and stuffy I'll take it as a compliment. But it's a bit sad if you feel I've got to be conventional. Jesus certainly wasn't; he was notorious for having a pretty rackety set of friends.'

He felt thrown off balance, yet at the same time intrigued.

'I've never heard anyone put it quite like that before.'

167

'Do me a favour? Come along to my youth club when I get it going. I badly need some street cred, if it's not to be composed of intensely respectable teenagers. And if you think respectable adults are boring, try talking to a teenager who was born aged fifty.'

'You didn't warn me you were starting the sales pitch.'

She grinned, and when she did she suddenly looked a lot younger.

'OK, so it was an ambush. Think about it, will you?'

'I might.'

Unlike every other adult of his acquaintance, she didn't labour the point.

'Good,' she said briskly. 'And now I must go. I've got a lot to do today.'

He noticed then that she was looking quite tired, very tired in fact. Then she was gone.

He turned back towards the house, and his spirits, which had lifted, sank again.

When Margaret arrived home that afternoon, Minnie Groak had Robert backed against the wall at the far end of the kitchen. He looked afraid to move, like the victim of a knife-throwing act in the circus, as she shot questions at him, her sharp black eyes brilliant with curiosity.

Margaret's heart sank. She had told Minnie not to come in Christmas week, but after last night naturally Minnie would be round, rootling like a pig for whatever truffle of gossip she might unearth.

Minnie came to 'oblige' at the vicarage for two hours every week. This was not an arrangement of Margaret's making; Minnie was a trial inherited from the previous incumbent.

'But I don't need a cleaner!' Margaret had protested to

John Anselm when he broached the subject. 'I live alone, I don't have obsessive standards and I can keep a doll's house like this perfectly well on twenty minutes a day.'

'Well, that's a mercy,' he said, the corners of his mouth twitching. 'Minnie doesn't come to clean. Oh, she always gets the Hoover out, but in much the same way as they carry in the Mace to the House of Commons, without any expectation that it will be used.'

She stared at him. 'Then what on earth —'

He held up his hand. 'Ah. Minnie is your channel to and from what most of your well-heeled parishioners would probably term the sub-stratum of the village. That's the small local industry of people who go to the big houses to clean, rather than to attend drinks parties, the ones who rarely come to church and if they do shuffle past crab-wise while you are being sidetracked by the "Nice, morning, vicar," brigade.

'Minnie Groak knows about everyone and everything that goes on in this place. If anyone is in trouble, I'll hear about it; if I want to make a point I can be sure it will be circulated in the right quarter. Of course, it's a bit like keeping a Venus flytrap as a pet; she has a sordid appetite which must be fed, but there's plenty of harmless stuff that will keep her happy.'

'So you pay her to come and gossip?'

He sighed. 'I suppose so, yes. It's dirty work, my dear, but keeping one's hands clean is a luxury which in our business you can't afford.'

The dreadful thing was, Margaret had begun to appreciate his argument. Reaching the have-nots in Stretton Noble was a serious problem, and she had not yet discovered a better way of making contact. Acceptance of the situation was not, however, enjoyment, and she had looked forward to the week's respite.

'Minnie! I didn't expect to see you,' she said now with false brightness as she entered the kitchen. 'Have you had a good Christmas?'

At the prospect of a more promising quarry, Minnie turned and Robert, with impressive agility, dodged about her; greeting Margaret with the enigmatic words, 'MacGregor! the grandest of them all' he shot towards the kitchen door and freedom, muttering lines whose source Margaret registered vaguely as being 'The Relief of Lucknow', a childhood favourite.

Minnie always arrived for work wearing a man's raincoat, long, shabby and drooping. When she took it off, the impression remained; her slouching posture, her long thin arms and the grey drabness of her skin and clothing made it look as if she too might be suspended from a peg and ignored.

Only her eyes and the loose, talkative mouth told a different story. As she switched her attention to Margaret, the floodgates opened.

'Well, that was a nice to-do last night, wasn't it? What this place is coming to, God only knows – oops, sorry, vicar, but then, He does, I expect – and none of us able to sleep easy in our beds at night.'

She sniffed, portentously. 'Not but what we might have expected something, what with all the comings and goings this last bit. You might say it's a judgment, but then it's not them as deserves it that suffers, mostly. Still, that's life, isn't it?'

'Comings and goings?' Margaret said feebly, finding herself as usual mesmerized against her will.

Minnie's rubbery lips curved in relish. 'You know me, Miss Moon, never one to gossip,' she said virtuously. 'But being the vicar, it's only right you should know.

'There's some funny doings, that I can tell you, with

all that lot; thick as thieves, they are, the Boltons and the McEvoys – she's a poor soul, of course – and the Ferrars and that Mizz Cutler – no better than she should be, she isn't. Sacked poor Tracy Weekes who did for her, didn't she, just before Christmas – fine Christian time to do it, I said to Trace – and told her she was having to cut down. Well, according to Tracy there wasn't much cutting down anywhere else, the drinks or the posh clothes. And just try asking my fine lady what it's like up the reservoir of a morning – or of an evening, or any time she can get it —'

'Minnie!' Margaret protested.

'Oh, don't go thinking I'm telling you what anyone else couldn't tell you. That Mr McEvoy, of course —'

'I'm so sorry to hear about Tracy losing her job.' Margaret at last managed to find her voice. 'Is she all right, or is there anything I can do?'

Cut off in full flow, Minnie subsided sulkily. 'Oh, Tracy!' she dismissed her. 'That one's just as happy signing on. Doesn't know the meaning of hard work, she doesn't.'

Ignoring the Hoover standing in silent reproach at her side, Minnie changed tack.

'But you've been round talking to Mrs Bolton. Poor thing, all that happening. A dead man right on your doorstep; not very nice, that isn't. All right, is she?'

'Yes, fine,' Margaret said faintly. This was worse than usual, much worse; she felt too much sickened by this evidence of local prurience to pay her dues. 'She's being very brave. Now, Minnie, if I could leave you to do the kitchen, I've got a lot to get on with.'

Minnie bridled. She had expected a better return on her investment of effort in coming today.

'That's right, you go and shut yourself up, vicar,' she said spitefully. 'Better not to be about these days, not once

171

it gets dark anyway, so I won't be staying late. There's queer goings-on, no doubt of it; people have seen shadows moving when they shouldn't be, and there's nothing to say that old man's going to be the last.'

Margaret had reached the door, but she turned. 'What do you mean, Minnie? Do you know something? If you do, you should go to the police.'

Minnie's eyes, dull and opaque now, surveyed her malevolently. 'Me? How would I know? Nobody ever tells me anything.'

With which pointed remark she switched on the Hoover and fell to pushing it to and fro across the carpet tiles with a fine show of industry, ignoring the whistle indicating that the bag was already full.

Elizabeth McEvoy had no wish to go to the Golf Club Christmas Dance. It seemed so tasteless, somehow, but that consideration wouldn't deter Piers. Nor could she tell him bluntly that the thought of dancing with him, held close with his hands moving insolently over her body, made her feel sick. He would mock as over-reaction her reluctance to go out, though in her fragile emotional state, she felt tears come to her eyes at the thought of abandoning her children. He certainly wouldn't agonize over precious, delicate, vulnerable flesh. But wood burned too, and porcelain would crack and glass would shatter; he might fear for his own treasures, if she could hint at the threat from a faceless terror with a compulsion to incinerate, destroy . . .

'Do you think it's wise to go out?' she said. 'It might be our turn next, and it would be awful if anything happened to the house.'

Piers's eyes did flicker with brief concern round the room with its exquisite furniture – the Louis Quinze commode, the

William Kent mirror – and its lovingly-amassed paintings and porcelain. Then he snorted.

'We've got a baby-sitter, haven't we? And there's a smoke-detector in the hall, after all. She's no mental giant but even she would surely notice if flames began licking round the legs of her chair. In any case, the village must be stiff with flat-feet; who's going to try anything now?'

'They don't think it's murder. Patrick said they were all gone by five o'clock,' she argued, but not hopefully.

Patrick had phoned to say that they were calling off tonight. Suzanne was still upset, they were all suffering from lack of sleep and all that anyone wanted was an early night.

They had not spoken since their meeting in the supermarket. With some constraint, Elizabeth said, 'Poor Suzanne. It must have been awful, for all of you.'

Patrick sighed. 'Yes, poor Suzanne. She's not like her usual self at all. Perhaps it's an improvement.'

He laughed. Elizabeth didn't.

'Joke,' he said. 'It was a joke. I think.'

Then his voice softened. 'And you, Lizzie? How are you? Are you all right?'

'Oh, I'm fine, just fine,' she tried to say brightly, but the genuine concern in his voice was her undoing, and her voice wobbled.

'Oh, Lizzie–' He broke off, and she could hear the harsh edge of frustration. 'I can't bear it that you're upset, and not to be able to do anything, to have no right —'

She cut him short. 'Patrick, there's nothing you or anyone else can do. I'm just so worried by all this.'

'Aren't we all?' he said grimly. 'To be honest, I'm not sure how I would cope with another night like last night, and Suzanne would simply fall apart.'

'But surely you've had your turn?'

'Who knows? The police certainly don't.'

She asked briefly about the progress of the enquiry, then rang off. She had problems enough at the moment without adding guilt about possible disloyalty.

But even hearing that the Boltons had scratched did not discourage Piers, and Elizabeth went off reluctantly to give the children their supper and change.

When she appeared, dutifully strapless in black chiffon, he had a large whisky at his elbow. It seemed unlikely it was his first; he downed it in two gulps then rose, his colour high and his eyes glittering.

'Come on, Lizzie, let's party! Boogie the night away – or at least until the band packs it in at one o'clock. Oh, and do you think you could possibly, just for me, rearrange those martyred features into some semblance of a smile? It won't bother me if your face curdles the cream on the trifle, but other people may find it hard to get into the party mood with you playing the part of chief mute at a Victorian funeral.'

Hayley Cutler studied herself in the mirror in her bedroom with her eyes half-closed in rigorous self-appraisal.

She had chosen to wear poison-green satin, cut low to expose her magnificent cleavage, and her hair was piled in a topknot from which wispy tendrils fell. She had taken a lot of trouble with her make-up; concealer to banish the smudges round her eyes, blusher on the cheekbones to draw attention away from the lines of strain about her mouth.

Yes, she looked good. And there was no doubt about it, anger did give an added sparkle to your eyes. She had always had a temper; she knew it to be a good servant and a bad master, but sometimes the demarcation lines weren't too clear.

She just had to change her plan of campaign, that was

all. 'When the horse is dead, you get off and walk,' as the Chinese proverb had it, and Hayley had never wasted energy in those circumstances by applying the whip. She had had enough of feeling persecuted and scared; now, with other things on her mind, she was coming out fighting.

When she arrived at the Golf Club, the McEvoys, the Joneses and the Ferrars were already there – Laura looking dreadful – and Hayley made her way across the crowded room towards them. Was she alone in feeling bitterly amused by the hypocrisy as they exchanged social kisses all round?

On every side, Stretton Noble's home-grown sensation was the topic of conversation. The police had started house-to-house enquiries, and in the nearest group a matron, her horsy face pink with indignation, was proclaiming, 'So I just said to him, "Officer, if you devoted your energies to combing the council estate at Newtown instead of interrogating People Like Us, your endeavours might be crowned with success and we could all sleep safely in our beds."'

So it was easy enough for Hayley to introduce her topic of choice.

'The police came to check me out today, can you believe that? And I'd a couple of things I wanted to discuss, but forget it! All they would talk about was some evidence that someone climbed my back fence on to the path. Well, I told them it wasn't me, but they just looked at me with fish eyes and wrote it all down. Then they sent round the inspector – the graduate from the pit-bull charm school, summa cum laude – to see what he could screw out of me, you should pardon the expression. And do you know – call me hypersensitive – I kind of got the impression it was us girls they were homing in on! Isn't that something? It was lucky I could tell him I had an alibi, wasn't it?'

She ran her neat little pointed tongue round her lacquered lips and smiled directly at Piers, who had half-turned and was now standing very still, his prominent eyes fixed on her.

'Oh, I haven't had to disclose it yet, but it's my little insurance policy. Just in case.'

The frisson within the group had been almost visible. Laura seemed paler than ever; others stared into their drinks and shifted their feet awkwardly.

It was Anthea Jones who broke the silence with desperate vivacity.

'Oh gosh, I hope they don't ask Richard to alibi me. He's always so exhausted he crashes out – unless he's on call, of course . . .'

Piers turned his back and began to order another round of drinks.

Satisfied with the effect she had produced, Hayley reached for a peanut from a dish on the bar. With a jolt, she realized that Elizabeth was staring at her.

Sweet, simple St Lizzie, she had always styled her acidly. But now she found herself dropping her eyes and turning hastily away, as if that searing gaze might brand the red 'A' for adulteress on to her forehead.

Margaret Moon was deeply asleep when the relentless double ring of the telephone summoned her, dragging her up through layers of sleep that seemed dense as water, and bringing her gasping awake. She hated night phone-calls; they left her heart racing and her hands shaking so that she could hardly pick up the instrument. All too often they heralded disaster or sudden death.

The room was dark, apart from the disembodied luminous figures of the clock which showed 2.14.

The person at the other end of the line was crying. The voice was female, but so distorted as to be unrecognizable.

'I have – I have to talk,' it said. 'I have to talk to someone. During the daytime, it's not so bad; I can pretend it's all a bad dream, none of it's true. But I know she's done it, I know she has, it's terrible. And she's so strong at night, I can't stop her. I can't fight much longer. You have to help me . . .'

Sleep fled. Margaret said carefully, 'Of course I will. What do you want me to do? Try to stop crying, and tell me what the matter is.'

There were more sobs, and a silence. Then the hoarse voice said chillingly, 'Can you – can you do – exorcism?'

'Exorcism?' In the darkness, Margaret felt the hairs on her neck stand up, and groped for the switch on her bedside lamp, even though the darkness it could dispel was only physical.

'I can't think of anything else to do. It's my last hope.'

She had never heard such desolation, such inconsolable despair. Margaret could feel herself being drawn into the icy hell of terror and hopelessness. Her fingers went instinctively to the little silver cross she always wore about her neck, and clung to it. She managed to say, as if calmly, 'We can talk about it. Tell me who you are. Do I know you?'

'Yes, but –' It had dwindled to a whisper now. 'I can't – I'm trying, but I can't any more . . .'

Into the unnerving silence that followed, Margaret called urgently, 'Are you still there? Can you hear me? Hello? Hello?'

'Oh, butt out, you silly old bag!'

It was a high-pitched voice, like a child's, but hard and bright, and it trailed off into a foolish, artificial giggle.

The contrast was so bizarre that Margaret wondered if

she could be still asleep and dreaming. But the second voice was going on.

'Call yourself a priest? Well, that's a joke! Everyone thinks you're a joke, a joke, a joke. But don't try any of your magic on me, you old witch, or I'll fix you all. Dumbo too. I'd wipe her out tomorrow, stupid cow, only —'

'Only what?' Even in her confusion, Margaret recognized where she had encountered those sentiments before, and strained to identify the speaker. But there was no clue in that strange falsetto.

'Only nothing, nothing, nothing. Just wait and you'll see. I've lots more nasty surprises. I'm clever, you see, clever, clever.'

'I'm sure you are, very clever.' She made her voice soothing, as if she were speaking to a child. 'But could I speak to your friend again? She sounded unhappy.'

For some reason this was amusing. The strange laughter continued for some time, then stopped abruptly.

'No. Dumbo's gone.'

'And who are you?'

There was a long, long pause. Then the voice said, 'I'm Missy. That's who I am.'

'And have you done something, Missy? Something – bad?'

There was a gasp that was almost a cry, then the receiver was banged violently down.

Margaret set down her own receiver. She was shivering with – what? She hardly knew how to define it. Shock, fear?

The omnipotence of a loving God was the bedrock of Margaret's belief, allowing her to be robustly sceptical of exorcism and all its spiritual implications. But this – this soul-terror of someone believing herself to be in the grip of the Powers of Darkness! It was like a chill

178

finger of frost reaching out to blight the sunny garden of her faith.

It took a minute for her common sense to reassert itself. She was shivering because she was cold, she told herself, and what she needed was a fresh hottie and a hot drink. Wearily she dragged herself downstairs to the kitchen, where she switched on the electric heater and warmed her hands.

She had tried to be quiet so as not to wake her brother, but she could not disguise her relief when a few minutes later the door opened and Robert appeared looking offensively alert and fresh in a smart grey-silk dressing gown.

'The phone woke me. Not more trouble, I hope?'

'The next time I'm rude to you,' Margaret said, trying to make light of her unease, 'remind me how pleased I was to see you at this moment.'

'Don't think I won't.' He eyed her shrewdly. 'Sit down before you fall down and tell me about it while I make tea or something. Or Horlicks? Do you still take six spoonfuls?'

She had barely begun her story when he stopped her.

'What about the last recorded number service?'

She shook her head. 'We don't have it here yet. Nothing's ever that simple.'

'Oh well, it would have felt a bit like cheating,' Robert said philosophically, setting the mugs down and joining her at the table. 'Now, start again.'

She found it hard to stay cool and objective, and it was a very imperfect account. However, under his skilful questioning more detail emerged; he persuaded her to define the accent, the vocabulary and the nuances of expression while these were still fresh in her mind.

'Female, middle-class and educated,' he said, making little effort not to sound smug.

She was still too distressed to be irritated. 'Yes. And the

same phrases as in the letter. She didn't mention burning at the stake this time, but —'

She broke off. She still felt cold, and wrapped her hands round the mug as she went on. 'But Robert, the first woman – Dumbo – who talked about exorcism. I know it sounds melodramatic, but I believed her. She sounded – possessed.'

Robert had fetched a packet of digestive biscuits. He chose one and munched it with maddening deliberation.

'Well, it's not surprising she was convincing. It's probably what she believes. The suggestion of exorcism is not without precedent.'

She stared at him as he flicked a crumb from the collar of his dressing gown.

'Do you mean–' she began, then said crossly, 'Oh really, it's too much. This is where I'm expected to say, "Wonderful, Holmes!" and look astonished and impressed. Shall I just send them round with the handcuffs?'

'Oh, good gracious no, much as it would gratify me to astonish you. I haven't the slightest idea who she is, but I think I can tell you what's wrong with her. Everything you've told me points to the operation of dual personality.

'Your first speaker – Dumbo – is probably the personality everyone sees. She's likely to be in ignorance of Missy's actions, except when these leave physical traces. But she clearly suspects something now, and fights to keep the "demon" at bay. Hence the belief that she's possessed, which actually is quite a useful way of describing the situation.

'Missy, however, may well be able to see what Dumbo does, characteristically with considerable impatience. She'll struggle for control, and to mould Dumbo's life to her requirements, which probably represent the uninhibited side of an inhibited nature. She'll be aggressive, even crude.'

Forgetting her distress in fascination, Margaret said, 'I've heard of multiple personalities, of course. But what starts it?'

Robert shrugged. 'Did I somehow forget to mention to you that psychology is not an exact science? Received wisdom is that it's a hysterical dissociation with its roots in trauma, frequently some childhood trauma so great the child can't bear it, and as it were "creates" a less sensitive alter ego to bear it instead. It might be sexual abuse, or unresolved bereavement, or any one of a dozen other causes. If the situation stabilizes, the second personality may lie dormant for years – even forever – but under stress the psyche may fragment again, seeking the same resolution to its problem.

'The danger here is that the alter ego has no moral development. It's like a wilful child interested only in its own gratification.'

'Someone who might set a garage on fire with a car inside, if it suited them?'

'With a person inside, if it suited them.'

The kitchen was hot now, too hot, and the rational, scientific explanation seemed little less horrifying than the supernatural one. The blackness outside the windows seemed to mock the brave, silly illusion of security created by electric light and bright colours.

'I'm going to bed,' Margaret said abruptly, and Robert rose too.

'Get some sleep and don't worry about it,' he said. 'Vezey may be uncouth, but he's a first-class policeman. I'll process this for him, and he'll get it wrapped up quicker than you can say bell, book and candle.'

She managed a smile. 'Always the little ray of sunshine,' she said, and went to bed.

*　　*　　*

Having set down the receiver with a smash, Missy backed away from the telephone as if it were alive and deadly.

That was dangerous, dangerous. Just like before, stupid bloody Dumbo had dropped them in it. That woman somehow knew too much, and she had said ... had said ...

Her throat was constricting in a funny way, but she couldn't cry. Missy had no tears. Missy had used them all up long ago.

But she was afraid. She, Missy, clever Missy, had been lured into saying too much. It would be disastrous if they were discovered now, and there was no saying what Dumbo might do, once she got Missy back in her cage again. She hadn't got the sense God gave little green apples.

No, it was all up to Missy. She must do what was best for both of them, since for some stupid reason she couldn't get rid of Dumbo. They were joined as horribly as Siamese twins, sharing all the vital organs, and if anything happened to Dumbo ...

But Missy never thought about these things. Missy did things, instead, and now she knew just what she had to do.

Not that it was easy. She had to make do with what she could find, because Dumbo wouldn't buy any of the things Missy really wanted: lovely, smelly paraffin; thick gloopy petrol in a can ... And Dumbo was strong during the day, very strong.

Sighing, she tiptoed through the quiet house to the coal-cellar. There wasn't any more barbecue gel; firelighters would have to do.

In the flimsy modern box that was the Vicarage there was no light, no sound.

In the guest room at the back of the house, above the

kitchen, Robert slumbered with his accustomed tranquillity, his sheet neatly turned down and his pillow unrumpled. Margaret, in her bedroom at the front, had collapsed into a stupor of physical and emotional exhaustion.

Neither of them heard the sitting-room window break, or smelled the first wisps of smoke as they seeped through the floorboards. Only Pyewacket, snug on his cushion in the chair in the kitchen, raised his head, wrinkled his patrician nose, sneezed, then shot swiftly out of the cat-flap in the kitchen door.

It was only when the smoke-detector in the kitchen started pulsing its shrill alarm that Margaret at last blearily opened her eyes. The air was thick with acrid fumes and her eyes began to smart and stream.

Dazed and disorientated, she struggled through the smoky hell to where she thought the door might be. She fought the blackness, lashing out as if it were a circling foe, waiting for her to weaken, but her lungs were starting to labour in a desperate attempt to draw oxygen from the foul air. She could not get her breath; she staggered, and as she fell surrendered to the lurking dark which rushed in to engulf her.

9

<hr />

Rod Vezey put his head in his hands and groaned.

'A nutter,' he said. 'Oh dear God! Are you really telling me that we are going to have to question women – middle-class, I-know-my-rights-and-may-I-just-have-your-number-before-we-start-officer women – when the one we want won't even know when she's lying?'

He was seated at a desk in the shabby office of the sergeant whose patch included Stretton Noble, in the nearby small town of Burdley. Flimsy, garish paper-chains were looped incongruously from the corners of the room to the white plastic central lampshade, and below an improbable tinsel tassel dangled to swing in the dusty current of air from the radiator. It was half past nine, but as yet full daylight had not penetrated the dirty ribbed glass in the window.

Opposite him, Robert Moon looked like a man whose self-image has been severely compromized. Wearing a hand-knitted fisherman's sweater and baggy cord trousers borrowed from Ted Brancombe, he appeared dishevelled and unkempt; he had not shaved, and without his usual expression of cheerful composure he looked much older, the lines of age and exhaustion clearly marked. He seemed unable to sit still; he changed his position in the chair, fiddled with paperclips, got up to untangle a twisted sash cord at

185

one of the windows. He was clearly exercising tight control, but every so often his fingers beat a betraying tattoo of frustration.

With an obvious effort, he forced himself to give Vezey's question his usual measured response.

'Yes, I think that is entirely possible. Well, yes and no, perhaps. From what Margaret told me before–' He broke off, then continued, 'the woman knows that something is going on – something alarming and evil which she is powerless to prevent – though she can only guess at what it is, and certainly will have no precise knowledge of how it happened. She's obviously going to be in a very overwrought state.'

'Unlike every other woman in the place, you mean?' Vezey groaned again. 'Have you any idea how many of them there are in Stretton Noble who meet your specifications?'

'A fair few, I daresay.'

He spoke tersely, with the air of one deliberately distancing himself from a problem which is not his concern. Standing by the window, his fingers again drummed out his irritation on the sill.

Vezey got to his feet. 'I'd better get on. I've got a briefing to give in ten minutes, and they won't be happy when they hear it's a kid-gloves job.'

'You mean, they prefer it when they can beat them up round the back of the station, no questions asked?'

It was such an entirely uncharacteristic remark that Vezey turned round to stare at him. The tension in the atmosphere had become so marked that even a lifetime's dedication to dismissing the inconvenient emotions of others did not equip him to ignore it.

He said, awkwardly and against his better judgment, 'How is she – your sister?'

Robert swung round, his eyes glittering.

186

'I thought you'd never ask. Oh, she's fine, given that someone tried to kill her and very nearly succeeded. Of course, we won't be sure her eyes are unharmed until they take the pads off today, and her throat's so raw that she can't really speak. It was the formaldehyde, you see, in the fabric of an old sofa, and the fumes came up through the floorboards straight into her bedroom. Nasty stuff, but they don't *think* her liver and kidneys have been damaged, so that's all right, isn't it?'

'And you're blaming us? Somehow we should have stopped it? You know better than that, Robert.'

The opposition and the appeal to his common sense triggered the response he needed to make.

'Blame you?' he exploded. 'You knew there was a pyromaniac loose in a small village, but you all went home at tea time. Of course I blame you. But I blame myself a lot more.'

Wisely, Vezey did not mention manpower or priorities. 'You got her out,' he said.

'Only just. It was minutes before the smoke alarm got through to me.'

'You can hardly blame yourself for sleeping heavily.'

'Oh, can't I?' He smiled mirthlessly. 'You must know very little about psychology. Didn't they make you take classes in it?'

'I'm not going to let you pick a quarrel with me, Robert, no matter what you say.' Vezey crossed to the door. 'I've got a lot to do —'

'You certainly have. In my professional capacity, I must warn you: this is only the beginning. Perhaps the first killing wasn't planned, but the fact of poor old Tom's death would breach a barrier in her mind. With the attempted murder last night she's crossed the Rubicon. It may not be fire next time – though it may be, who knows? – but case histories often chart fire-raising as part of the progression towards direct violence.'

'It's got top priority now. I've been taken off my other cases and we're throwing everything into it.'

'There's a proverb I'm trying to remember – something about stable doors —'

At the sneer, Vezey's lips tightened. He turned to the door and opened it, but said only, with obvious restraint, 'I understand that you are distressed. I can only assure you we are doing all we can. And now, if you will excuse me . . .'

Moon had twisted the sash cord into a tight knot: he flung it at the window which it hit with a thud.

Then his shoulders sagged.

'I'm sorry, Rod,' he said tiredly, rubbing his hand across his face. 'I know that was unfair. I just can't see things straight this morning.'

Vezey closed the door again, though his hand still rested on the handle.

'It's a funny thing, family,' Robert went on. 'We all lead our own, very separate lives. I see Margaret, what – twice, three times a year? But almost my first memory is being told it was my job to look after her. And I was there, in the room next door to her, when she nearly died.

'I want whoever did this put away, Rod. I can dress it up in fancy clothing, if you like, and I can even make it sound quite professional and caring: it's just as important for herself that she be stopped as it is for the safety of society, blah, blah, blah. I can spout that sort of claptrap indefinitely.

'But what I actually want is for this person – this damaged, frail, vulnerable person who probably has every psychological excuse in the book – to be punished for what she did to my sister.'

Rod Vezey was not given to flights of fancy, but he had a brief, vivid picture of a small stout schoolboy in shorts and spectacles valiantly standing between his smaller stout sister and the vicissitudes of childhood. Not much had changed.

Sancta simplicitas! He, who for his own preservation had excised any trace of the sacred simplicity of family feeling, knew a pang of acute regret.

He said, with uncharacteristic gentleness, 'I didn't cut all the psychology classes. You don't need me to tell you that yours is a perfectly healthy reaction.

'Go back to the Brancombes', have something to eat, then get some sleep. Thinking is your best contribution to this investigation, and you're too tired to think straight. I'll be in touch.'

Jean Brancombe had neat, rounded ears, small quick hands, russet-grey hair and large, anxious brown eyes. With the imagined addition of a tail and whiskers, her resemblance to a fieldmouse would be complete.

She tended to dart about restlessly, powered by short bursts of energy, her little fine-boned body quivering with the exertion, and her demands upon herself were relentless. While Ted, her husband, had what amounted to a genius for placidity, she existed in a state of permanent nervous exhaustion.

The family Christmas – twenty-two of them round a festal board groaning under the weight of lightly-disguised cholesterol – usually left her almost prostrate, and Ted normally forbade further excitements for a month.

But the events of the week had made rest impossible and her driven scurrying became more and more frantic. She had started getting up at night in her dressing gown and wellington boots to prowl round the barns, so temptingly

189

full of combustible hay and straw, until Ted discovered what she was up to.

'I'm putting my foot down,' he said, and Jean, as she always did when Ted put his foot down, complied. But he couldn't stop her lying awake, twitching at every sound, from the movement of cattle in the fields to the unexplained crackle of a twig in the shrubbery under their bedroom window.

And now this. She had gathered Robert up, of course, with her usual warm-heartedness; it was actually a relief to have somewhere to direct her nervous energy.

After frying him a lavish breakfast she had made the pastry for the steak-and-kidney pie for lunch and popped the meat, along with the rice pudding (half-milk, half-cream, with flakes of butter on the top to make a nice thick skin) into the bottom oven of the Raeburn. Now she was ready to trot along to the vicarage – she never seemed able just to walk – to get some things to take to poor Margaret.

It was drizzling and miserable, but a little crowd had gathered to view the aftermath of the latest village drama. There were about ten adults and half-a-dozen children watching the activity as if it were a side show; Jean knew most of them and paid the petty coinage of meaningless exclamation as she worked her way purposefully through their ranks.

Apart from the blackened, broken window on the ground floor and the smoke-streaks up the wall, the house looked surprisingly normal. There were men in the garden; one crouching on the path below the window, two in earnest discussion, another taking measurements and writing them down in a fat black notebook.

At the garden gate, a uniformed constable stood guard. He looked down at her, his youthful complexion turning pink as he almost visibly wrapped himself in the dignity of office, striving to project authority towards someone who had more than once caught him scrumping apples in her orchard.

'Good gracious, Tommy Compton, is that you under that cap?'

One of the children sniggered, but Jean, oblivious, twittered on happily.

'Well! Your mother told me you'd gone and joined the police force, but this is the first time I've seen you in all your glory. Let me look at you – yes, very smart! And they do always say poachers make the best gamekeepers, don't they?'

A volley of stifled giggles came from the children, now listening with undisguised glee, and the young man's face proclaimed an even deeper shade of embarrassment.

Jean tidied him to one side.

'Now I'm just popping in to sort out some things to take to Miss Moon in hospital, all right?'

He opened his mouth, but before he could find his voice she was hurrying up the path. He shut it again hastily, aware of his young tormentors and reluctant to afford them more amusement by futile protest. There would be other, less inhibited lines of defence if these were deemed necessary.

But Jean encountered no further opposition. Apart from the area of fire damage, the house would not hold useful evidence, and the detective in charge was quite prepared to accede to her request.

'Her cleaner's upstairs already, starting to clear up,' he said, and was startled to be put aside with a force totally unexpected from one of such small stature and nervous appearance.

'Is she, indeed!' said Jean, and with the light of battle in her eyes shot up the stairs.

Minnie Groak jumped guiltily as, entirely without warning, the bedroom door was flung open. She had just settled down to a comfortable and luxurious rummage through Miss Moon's bedroom drawers. She had been saving the best till last, but now realized the folly of her strategy; anyone might have guessed at the Boots' cosmetics and the Marks and Spencer's knickers, but now she would never know what riches her trawl through the vicar's correspondence files in her study might have yielded.

'And just what do you think you're doing here, Minnie Groak?'

Mrs Brancombe stood in the doorway like a small avenging angel, the flaming sword all but visible as she prepared to expel the other woman from her anticipated paradise.

Minnie's eyes fell. She was afraid of direct confrontation, an uneasiness rooted in her schooldays when, caught out in some pernicious piece of tale-bearing, she had suffered condign punishment. There was a whine in her voice when she spoke.

'I'm sure I don't know why you should go asking me like that, Mrs Brancombe. I came here out of the goodness of my heart, and who else should come and sort things out for the poor lady, I should like to know?'

Jean eyed the open drawers pointedly, but retreated from direct accusation.

'Well, Minnie, if you really want to be helpful you could get a bucket of water and a scrubbing brush and start cleaning the kitchen walls and floor; there's a lot of hard work needed down there.'

Minnie smirked triumphantly.

'Well I would of, naturally, only the policeman said I might be in the way. But I could go and clean out her study —'

But Jean's blood was up, and she had no hesitation in quashing this attempt to snatch victory from the jaws of defeat.

'I think Miss Moon would prefer to do that herself. If you really want to do your Christian duty, the church needs a bit of cleaning and tidying for Sunday. It's my day, but I have to get some things Miss Moon needs in hospital. I'll give you the key. Be sure to lock up after you, and someone will be round to get it back from you tomorrow.'

Routed, Minnie accepted it meekly and Jean supervised her departure. Now she must see to it that the police never admitted that wretched woman again.

Margaret had forgotten how much afraid she had been of the dark as a child, forgotten over the comfortable adult years when darkness was a benison before the greater blessing of sleep. She had forgotten how thickly-peopled with demons that darkness had been.

As she lay now, blinded as yet only by the benign, soothing pads they had bound across her eyes, she discovered that the demons had never been truly vanquished. Beneath the shell of her stated optimism they gnawed like rats at the soft underbelly of her fear.

Last night she had made all the right noises while the hospital staff repeatedly sluiced her streaming, burning eyes and made her sip some liquid which did something to alleviate the raw agony of her throat. They were, they had said, practically sure there would be no permanent damage, but then they would say that, wouldn't they, and practically wasn't quite sufficient reassurance when you were lying with nothing to do except consider the worst-case scenario.

She made an effort to control her thoughts. This was just a more dramatic example of 3 a.m. despair, and there were few people who didn't know all about that. But then, perhaps if you were – blind (she forced herself to shape the word) daylight never came to reduce the Giants Despair of darkness to human scale.

There was no means of knowing how long she had been lying awake, or what time it was. She could have slept for one hour or ten; it could be daylight or the middle of the night. She could be alone, or someone could be watching her in silence. And how could she tell who it was, whether it was a nurse, or a friend, or the fiend who had tried to kill her last night, returned? It was all she could do not to scream.

Minnie was fuming as she pushed through the group still hanging about the gate, ignoring the eager questions of a couple of women she knew. If Jean Brancombe thought that she, Minnie, was going to go and do her chores for her, she had another think coming. Still . . . She fingered the key in her pocket speculatively.

You never knew what might be kept in the church. Miss Moon quite often saw people in the little vestry, and if the key let her in there . . .

Well, she didn't mind doing a bit of dusting, after all. Not if it was going to help out. She was a fool to herself, she knew that, and she would get no thanks for it. But then, she should be used to that after all this time. Blessed is she who expecteth nothing, for she shall not be disappointed, as her mother always said.

She had begun to feel positively virtuous by the time she arrived at the church.

It was the key to the side door that she had been given, and she went round by the little path, shielded from the road by the low branches of two ancient yew trees.

There was a parcel lying on the doorstep. It was fairly small, wrapped in brown paper; taped on to the front was a piece of paper with the direction, 'Rev. Margaret Moon, Vicar, St Mary's Church', printed on it. Minnie picked it up, opened the door and went in.

She paused as the chilly stillness of the empty church struck her almost like a blow, but only briefly. With the parcel in her hand she headed straight for the vestry door. She had every excuse now; obviously she must place this parcel on Miss Moon's desk. She had the key ready in her hand, large, solid and old-fashioned.

There was no point in even trying it. She could see that the lock on the vestry door was small, neat and modern, a thoroughly efficient mortice lock, to thwart modern thieves who knew all about the value of ecclesiastical plate.

Thwarted herself, Minnie sat down on the nearest pew with a sense of injustice. Here she was trying to be helpful and people treated her as if she wasn't to be trusted. Jean Brancombe could have given her the key to the vestry and then she could have put the parcel in and dusted the room a bit for poor Miss Moon.

She cast a disparaging look around, at the flowers up by the altar, dropping their petals and wilting. One of the carved saints from his niche seemed to be giving her a hard stare, and she stared insolently back. If they thought that after an insult like this she was going to clean their stupid church, they were out of luck. Stuff the lot of them!

She was still holding the parcel, and now looked at it again with automatic curiosity. She shook it, tentatively, then felt the edges. A book, by the feel of it; not much interest in that. Probably just someone returning one they had borrowed.

Minnie turned it over idly. There was writing on the back, she noticed suddenly, near the bottom of the left-hand side: a small, neat, distinctive script.

'Pray for us sinners,' it read, 'now and at the hour of our death.'

Her eyes narrowed in sudden interest, and she looked at the package hungrily.

After all, it could be urgent, couldn't it? There could be a message inside that Miss Moon needed to get at once, and with the poor lady in hospital, Minnie saw her own duty clear.

Delicately she slid her finger under the sealing tape and prised it off.

Margaret had not been aware of falling asleep again, but she awoke to a cheerful nurse asking her to sit up so that she could remove the bandages.

There was no time to agonize. First there was weak light, then strong, and then she was blinking blearily in a world she had almost managed to convince herself she would never see again. Her eyes were watering, she explained defensively to the nurse in what remained of her voice, only because of their sudden exposure to light.

'Of course,' the nurse agreed sympathetically and found tissues so that she could give her nose a good blow. Promising some of the ice cream and jelly they kept for tonsils patients, she left Margaret to appreciate the riches of normal existence.

She groped for her glasses on the bedside table and put them on, and the fuzzy outlines of the room jumped into vivid focus. Her eyes were smarting, her throat felt as if someone had taken sandpaper to it, and now she considered it, she was probably homeless as well. But she could see, and she was hungry; to these blessings were added the sight of Robert coming in at the door.

'Goodness,' she grated. 'You do look peculiar!'

The strain which had been etched so markedly on his face eased.

'You have no idea how happy I am that you are able to

tell me that, even though it shows an appalling disrespect for Jean's handiwork and Ted's taste.

'But don't try to talk. It's obviously painful, and anyway you wouldn't wish to deprive me of the only opportunity I may ever have to talk uninterrupted while you are in the room. I'll let you tell me if there's anything special you want, but keep it brief.'

The nurse brought in a tray as Margaret squawked, 'Information!' then obediently subsided to address herself to soup, milk, and the promised jelly and ice cream with a good appetite.

'Well, the house first of all —'

Catching sight of her frown, he checked himself. 'Oh, Pyewacket, I suppose. I can't think why you need to ask. He saved his own elegant skin via the cat-flap of course, and is now being so pampered by Jean that he may never deign to return.'

She thought about laughing, but deciding that might be too ambitious smiled instead.

'The house isn't as bad as you might think, though I'm afraid one end of the sitting room is pretty much a write-off. You've lost quite a few books and a couple of paintings and of course that old suite, but that was what caused the trouble with the fumes anyway. There's some smoke damage, but Jean Brancombe's been round there and had all the windows open, and she says that once the clothes and the curtains have been to the dry-cleaners and the carpets have been professionally cleaned – she's arranging all that – there won't be much damaged beyond repair except the mattresses. And your insurance will take care of all that.'

Margaret nodded, making impatient 'get-on-with-it' signals with her hands.

'The police work? Well, there's not much to say, unfortunately. The sitting-room window was broken, fireflighters were laid along the window ledge inside by the curtains, so that they caught, then fell on to the armchair – and the rest you know. There are no footprints except a smudge of mud that might or might not have something to do with it.

'They'll be taking fingerprints from you and me – oh, and the dreaded Minnie Groak, I suppose – for elimination purposes, though they don't think they have anything meaningful.

'They're questioning all the women who fit the profile, which as you can imagine is causing no end of fuss. Vezey says there have been four complaints to the Chief Constable already, two alleging that nothing is being done and two complaining about harassment.

'Is there anything you can suggest yourself? I'll get you a pen and paper so you can write it down.'

He failed to register Margaret's hesitation. Then she shook her head. 'Oh, I don't need paper,' she said hoarsely. 'I won't talk much, but my throat's quite bearable now it isn't so dry.'

'Well, don't overdo it,' he said, not noticing her evasion. 'I don't know when they'll let you out, but Jean's got your bed made up already, and is killing me with kindness. And you're under police protection, too, for the next bit; there's a nice chap out there, having a wonderful time chatting up the prettier nurses. So we should be safe enough, unless my coronary artery furs over as a result of Jean's cooking in the next couple of days. Ted's continued survival is a mystery to me.'

Minnie Groak lived with her mother in a maisonette at the council end of the small housing estate which also included the vicarage.

Mrs Groak was as grossly fat as Minnie was spare and

angular. She had muddy grey eyes, paler than Minnie's, and thinning iron-grey hair gathered into a wispy knot at the back and splayed in greasy strands across her flat skull.

She sat habitually in an old moquette armchair close to the fire, like some bloated spider crouched balefully in the corner of her web. Persistent local rumour had it that the inoffensive long-departed Mr Groak, after performing his duty in providing her with a daughter to minister to her old age, had been eaten.

She didn't get about much these days, but longer years than Minnie had yet served in minding other people's business had whetted rather than sated her appetite for gossip. She had to feed it mainly on Minnie's doggy-bags of information from the feast in the outside world, and today she was expecting some particularly rich pickings. Not only was there the detail of the fire at the vicarage and the police activity there, but Minnie had said she would take the chance to give the place a good sort-out while the vicar was in hospital. Mrs Groak knew precisely what *that* meant.

She actually licked her lips when she heard Minnie's key in the lock, Minnie's voice calling, 'That's me, Mum, I'm home.'

Minnie had been hugely excited when she got the parcel open. 'My Diary', the book had said on the front in worn gold letters on faded blue suede. It held the promise of a voyeuristic feast, and a sensual shiver of delight ran through her.

She did not think of blackmail, though she would have readily accepted that the effort of keeping secrets deserved reward. Her excitement was at once both purer and more sordid than that; that of infiltrating another person's mind, preying on their inmost thoughts. The victim of a dreary life, she had only vicarious interest to infuse it with the colour and spice she craved. Access to a personal diary was riches beyond any expectation, and she opened the book with almost the feeling of incredulous awe with which she might have checked a winning sequence of lottery numbers.

But when, with fitting reverence, she turned the first page and discovered that what lay in her twitching grasp was a *kiddie's* diary, her disappointment and disgust were such that she could have torn the miserable thing up on the spot.

It was only self-preservation that stopped her. There was no name, no message inside, but what if Miss Moon had been warned to expect it, told that someone would be leaving it on the doorstep of the church? It wouldn't take long for that Jean Brancombe to come round accusing her; she almost managed to feel aggrieved at the thought.

So what was she going to do with it now? Now she was worried – Minnie was a worrier – and all for nothing. What with that, and being chased out of the vicarage, it had been a bad morning. She had hoped there would be such a nice lot of 'news', as she liked to call it, to chew over with Mum today.

She grabbed the silly book and its wrappings together with anxious haste and shoved them into the raffia shopping-basket she always carried, arranging her unworn pinnie neatly across the top. With a final baleful glance round the church with its dead flowers and dusty surfaces, she left.

Mrs Groak, with a piercing look at her flustered daughter, took the little book greedily into her hands. She rubbed up the flattened suede, smoothed out the pages with her spatulate fingers with their purplish ridged nails.

The pages were stiff, almost brittle with age now, particularly the ones at the end which had been so oddly blackened with a thick layer of crayon. There were bobbles and blisters on some of the pages too, though it did not cross her mind that these were the stigmata of ancient tears.

She read slowly and with total concentration the first entries in that childish hand. '1st January, 1967: Today we went to the panto. I wore my new dress. It was funny. Even Daddy laghed.' '3rd January: Today I rode my pony. Macroni cheese for tea.'

She turned the empty pages over too, almost as slowly, until she reached the poignant entry, 'Mommy died on this day and I wish I could be dead too.'

Without comment, Mrs Groak read on, stroking the paper smooth and flat, turned the black pages in the same manner, then closed the book.

Minnie had watched her with open impatience. 'Well? What do you think, then, Mum? What should I do with it?'

Mrs Groak pursed her rubbery lips, so like her daughter's, and considered the matter.

'It's funny, that book is,' she said at last. 'Funny.'

'What, I know it's funny! Doesn't take much to see that, does it? What I want to know is, what am I going to do with it now?'

But Mrs Groak never left a topic till she had sucked it as dry as one of the fly carcasses discarded in the corner of a spider's web.

'That there's someone who's lost her mother when she was a little thing. Took it badly, she did.' She remarked on the phenomenon without pity.

'Yes, but —'

'Maybe taking it badly still. Maybe that's why she wants to show the vicar, so vicar can help her. Tell her her mother's gone to a better place, maybe. That's what they tell people, if they're daft enough to believe it.'

Minnie was not entirely convinced by this analysis.

'Doesn't seem likely, not after all these years. Seems a funny thing.'

'That's what I said.'

'But what am I going to do with it now? No use to me, that book isn't. And there's them that goes around just looking to cause trouble.'

'Shouldn't rightly have opened it then, should you? Not for something like this, I mean,' she added unreasonably.

With a feeling of injury, Minnie pointed out that but for the drawback that she hadn't known the contents beforehand, she would indeed have adopted this wiser plan. She suggested, not very hopefully, that she might just throw the nasty thing away.

Mrs Groak sucked her teeth. 'Can't do that, my girl. Not by what you've told me. You can wrap it up again, same as it was, can't you?'

'Paper's torn.' Minnie looked gloomily at the flimsy wrapping which in spite of caution had ripped under her attack. 'I can put on a new wrapper – just gets thrown away anyway, it does. But what am I going to do with it then?'

'Well, can't post it, can you? That Betty Bailey who does the post in the shop snoops into everything.'

'What if I take it back to the church, right where I found it? Nobody'd know then.'

'Have to be careful, you would – see nobody saw you putting it back. But I reckon that'd be best. You get that done right away whenever it's dark my girl, before someone finds out and stirs up trouble.'

So Minnie Groak wrapped up the pathetic little testament once more, addressed it with a blotchy ballpoint in her illiterate capitals and putting on her long raincoat set off once the lights had come on and a damp January dusk had set in.

But to her dismay, as she walked down the main

street, raffia basket in her hand, she passed not one but two police patrols – bobbies on the beat, a sight not seen in Stretton Noble these ten years. As she neared the church, she could see two of them chatting under the lamp right outside the lych gate. They fell silent as she approached, so she marched straight on, feeling nonetheless as if they might be able to see right through the sides of the basket to the illicit package within.

Beyond the church, she turned up an alleyway into a back lane and stood, hand on bony chest, feeling her heart pounding. That did give her a turn, all right! And what was she to do now?

She daren't go past the church again, that was for sure. She daren't leave it till morning either, in case someone started asking awkward questions.

Minnie had been walking without conscious direction and instinctively had taken the turn for home. Just ahead of her now lay the vicarage, deserted at the moment with no lights and no one about. If she popped it through the letter box, chances were no one would be any the wiser. Anyone might have seen it lying on the step and brought it round to the house, anyone.

She dodged the fluttering police tape that had been strung across the gateway, and carried out her plan without mishap. She returned home feeling thoroughly ill-used; seldom had she expended so much effort for so little worthwhile result, and she still felt shaky when she thought about the policemen.

It gave her another nasty turn when two more turned up on the Groak doorstep next morning to take her fingerprints. It was, they explained, purely for the purposes of elimination and they would not be kept permanently, but even so after submitting to their ministrations Minnie's guilty conscience left her, as she put it, 'just a bag of nerves' without even the spirit to go along to the shop to find out what was happening today.

10

It had been a quiet night, Rod Vezey reflected thankfully as he yawned a jaw-breaking yawn at his desk on Saturday morning. There had been saturation policing, but no one had anything to report which seemed, either to them at the time or to him reading their reports now, in the least suspicious. Perhaps the firebug was exhausted too. He certainly was, having gone to bed late, risen early and slept badly in between, expecting at any moment that the phone would ring summoning him to yet another disaster. He had trained himself long ago not to need much sleep, but he felt jaded today, lacking the clarity of mind he wanted.

In some ways, of course, the lack of activity was a disappointment, since success based on pure detection was rare. Most of the time, in policework, the way the job had been done told you who had done it, because they had done it that way so often before. There was the small problem of proof, but at least you knew where to start.

Apart from that, you had your informers, unsavoury but vital, and then the villians unlucky enough or inept enough to be caught in the act. That must cover fully ninety-nine per cent of cases solved.

This, unfortunately, looked like coming into the one per cent category. And after wading through last night's ration of turgid prose ('At 01.14 I was proceeding along Letham

Lane': did none of them just walk?) he couldn't see that they were any further forward. It would have been nice if one of those expensive police patrols could just have picked her up as she struck the next match.

He sighed. That was the trouble with high-profile policing; criminals went to ground and kept their heads down till it stopped. He cherished no illusions that she might have got something out of her system. Robert's warning hadn't told him anything he didn't know already; this one wouldn't stop until somebody stopped her, or she went so barking mad that they were pointing at her in the streets. She might pause, though, pause for days, weeks or months, and the budget wouldn't stand for more than another night or two at this level, especially since Miss Moon – thank God! – seemed to be recovering satisfactorily. One accidental death and two cases of arson did not justify the open-ended commitment of unlimited police resources, even if middle-class Stretton Noble was shrieking its collective head off.

Fortunately Cooper, the Chief Constable ('Our 'Enery' to his men) was one of the few human members of the species he had ever come across, but even 'Enery had wanted a direct report, and had finished the conversation by saying, more or less humorously, 'All I ask, Vezey, is that you come up with something to get them all off my back. Yesterday I even had my ear bent by some ancient colonel who had my old Dad as his RSM about forty years ago.'

So that didn't make things any easier, and once the Press got over their Christmas hangovers and realized that this was a juicy one, it would be worse still. He got up from his desk to make himself another cup of the strong black instant coffee that they claimed did terrible things to you, but without which he would be entirely unable to function.

It was like watching a shadow show behind a screen. He had had this sensation before while working with Robert

Moon; he could let you see what was taking place, but was powerless to hand you the evidence that would rip the screen and expose the reality behind it.

He could see the woman he was looking for, could see her stress, her anxiety, her pain. He could see her desperately striking back at a world that must be punished for – what? Some failure of love, Robert had said, but how many lucky adults could say that this did not feature at some important part of their lives?

Ruffling through the disorder of papers on his desk, he picked out his interview with Margaret Moon in hospital the previous day, grimacing in remembered frustration. Why were things never straightforward?

Vezey had gone reluctantly; he did not like hospitals. He walked along the aseptic corridors feeling chilled, as always, by the contrast between their professional tone of relentless optimism and the miasma of human suffering.

Miss Moon, however, was sitting up in bed when he arrived, looking, despite her ordeal, surprisingly calm and cheerful for someone whose eyes were still the colour of raw steak and whose voice was strained and clearly painful.

He had promised he would keep it short and she was able, under his questioning, to describe the voices she had heard and the differences between them, though not, unfortunately, with any sense of recognition.

'Well, I know now of course that they were the same person,' she added carefully, 'but it honestly didn't occur to me at the time.'

'Good.' Vezey had made a particular note of that; it was the sole glimpse they had of the other persona and suggested a noticeable difference between them. It was, at least, a chink into which the lever of questioning could be inserted.

'Now – she thought of phoning you when she was in this

desperate state. Do you think this was purely because you were the vicar and could carry out this exorcism she wanted, or because she had some previous direct contact with you?'

Margaret shut her eyes for a moment in concentrated thought, almost as if she were replaying the conversation in her head.

'Well, it's certainly someone I know – Dumbo said "Yes" when I asked her. But "direct contact"?' She considered it, then said positively, 'Nothing was said either way, I'm sure of that. But if you're asking my impression . . .'

He nodded. 'Anything.'

'It is my definite feeling that from the way she began the conversation she had been in recent contact. She didn't say, "Is that the vicar?" or "Is it all right if I talk to you?" as most people would, she just started straight in.'

'Right. So let's start with your contacts on that day.'

Margaret coughed, with evident discomfort, and took a soothing drink from the glass at her bedside.

'Yesterday there was Suzanne Bolton, of course. I spent a long time with her. A couple of her neighbours – I can't remember the names – came in as I was leaving, and I exchanged a few words with them, and with Laura Ferrars earlier, on the way to Suzanne's. Oh, and Elizabeth McEvoy at the church. Old Miss Christie was at church as well, I talked to her briefly —'

'Not relevant at the moment,' he interrupted brusquely. 'Save your voice. We're sticking to the original profile meantime. Those women – close friends, aren't they, all about the same age? And the American, Mrs Cutler, too? You weren't speaking to her?'

Margaret shook her head. 'No. I passed her as she came back from jogging the day before, but she certainly hasn't sought me out. But —'

She broke off.

'Go on,' he urged.

'Oh, nothing, really.' She was clearly not in the habit of prevaricating, and colour began to show in her cheeks. She coughed again, making a business out of taking another sip from her glass, but he was not deceived.

He hesitated. He did not want to upset her, not least for fear of incurring her brother's wrath.

He said, keeping his tone as light as possible, 'Now, why do I feel there's something you're not telling me?'

Over the rim of the glass, her eyes behind the spectacles were rounded in anguish, and she went pinker than ever.

The penny dropped. 'Oh, good grief,' he said in exasperation. 'We're on sacred ground here – seal of the confessional, and all that, aren't we?'

'Well, not exactly,' she said, but she would not meet his eyes.

'A professional confidence, then? Do you know who's doing this?'

'Oh, no, no – nothing like that . . .'

'But a useful piece of information, nonetheless. Oh, for goodness' sake, Miss Moon, someone tried to kill you last night. Don't you think, even if you feel that you have higher duties than your civic ones, that you might tell me from self-preservation?'

'Least of all from that,' she said coldly. Now she looked directly at him, eyes guarded and mouth firmly shut.

He hammered his fist on his knee in frustration.

'So tonight, when someone else dies because you haven't pointed me in the right direction, you will feel quite justified because you kept a promise of silence to someone who had no moral right to ask it of you?'

She bit her lip, and emboldened he went on.

'It's a question of time, you see. Your brother says – and I don't need to tell you that he's very astute – that this one's going to strike again. I need every short-cut I can find, if we're to get there first.'

'Oh, I know all that. I'm not stupid,' she croaked impatiently. 'But you're asking something I can't do.'

She sat back against her pillows, battered perhaps, but still sturdily unyielding. He wondered if anyone had ever felt driven to shake her until her teeth rattled in her head, but that was hardly a productive thought.

He ran his hand through his hair in a gesture of impatience. 'Look –' he began forcefully, then stopped. There was no chance of bludgeoning his way through. He would have to try another tack.

'Supposing,' he said carefully, 'supposing I suggested to you the direction in which I am planning to move. Would you feel capable, without compromising your integrity, of telling me whether, in the light of this information which you cannot give me, I am wasting my time?'

She considered what he had said. Then, 'Yes,' she said positively.

He gave a sigh of relief. 'Thank God for that. Right.' He ran his hand across his chin in thought.

'These four – Bolton, Ferrars, McEvoy, Cutler. Do you consider that is a line worth following up?'

'Yes,' she said, not happily but without hesitation.

He rose. 'Thank you: I hope I haven't tired you too much.'

It was infuriating that she wouldn't give him the information direct, he thought as he scanned his notes again, but at least he had prised out confirmation for the area he had defined. He hadn't time for detail at the moment anyway.

The other notes he had dug out related to his interviews with the women they had discussed. These had not been easy. He had taken along with him the chirpy WDC Boyd, who at the end of the gruelling round had said forthrightly, 'Thank goodness that's over. Right bunch of neurotics they are, and with nice homes and lots of money, what have they got to be neurotic about, I should like to know?'

Vezey's lips twitched. 'That's what we would all like to know, Jackie. It was rather what I thought the interviews were about.'

'Oh.' For a moment she took it as a rebuff, then recognized it as one of Sir's rare jokes, and grinned.

The enterprise had been, he acknowledged, a fishing expedition as much as anything else. He had wanted a good look at the four women he had placed in the frame: surely the one who made last night's frantic phone-call must be showing visible signs of strain?

Well, if she was one of the four, she certainly was. Each of them in her own way was showing signs of severe strain, which left him back at square one.

They had gone to the Briar Patch first. It was his second interview with Hayley Cutler, of course; he had been abrupt with her before, and had no time to waste if he were to get round the rest of the women today, so she had in a sense the right to be irritated, snapping his head off when he asked if she had suffered any particularly traumatic stress in her childhood.

'Stress?' she had spat at him. '*Stress?* Shee-it, my childhood was nothing *but* stress. You want I should fill you in on a couple of calm periods?'

'Or could we, maybe, talk about what's happening right now, instead of in the distant past?'

He had had more than he could take of that sort of attitude. Too many people had been bending his ear with their views on the inadequacy of the police investigation, so he had stalled her with promises of another visit, and left.

Laura Ferrars, so icily cool that she looked as if she might

211

splinter into pieces at any moment, had denied any stress at all. She contrived to imply that people like her had, as they were entitled to expect, perfectly satisfactory childhoods, and that such a question was grossly impertinent. It was an obvious defence mechanism, but there wasn't a lot he could do to get behind it.

With Elizabeth McEvoy he had been forced to proceed much more gently. Whenever he had appeared, she had begged to be reassured that the police wouldn't let it happen again.

'It's the children,' she had said, her eyes brimming. 'I'm so frightened for the children.'

One of them was ill, a little girl who came trailing into the room sniffling and coughing pitifully, and demanding to be taken on her mother's knee.

Stifling his irritation he had made meaningless comforting noises. A distressed subject was no use to him, but even once she was calmer he had no reward for his patience. Questioned about her childhood, she was vague, more concerned with the child on her lap; it had been, she seemed to think, much as others were.

Mrs Bolton, the last on their list, had been by turns lachrymose, belligerent and downright obstructive. No, she had not had a particularly happy childhood, but it wasn't something she was prepared to discuss. She had terminated the conversation firmly with a ringing denunciation of the police as amateur psychologists.

All of them, without exception, had looked at him as if it were he who was mad when he asked if any of them had noticed any friend who spoke oddly or differently at times.

No, it had not been a successful series of interviews. All it had established was that all of them were reluctant in one way or another to go into detail about their childhoods.

Perhaps anyone would be; he sure as hell wouldn't care to have someone raking through his memories of that uncomfortable part of his life.

And getting information from other sources on that sort of subject was seriously delicate; he'd have to be pretty sure of his ground before 'Enery started getting more phone-calls complaining about harassment.

He groaned, and reached for another half-pound of paper from the table at his side.

It was, thought Patrick, as if Suzanne had suddenly gone stone-deaf, or he had lost his voice. Or perhaps it was more like dreaming, when you talked and talked at people but found you were inaudible and invisible too.

'We have to send him away,' she repeated. 'We have to get Ben out of here. If we don't, we could be signing his death warrant. We have to live with this – this nightmare, but he doesn't. Would your parents take him, do you think? I know they're not very fit, but surely they wouldn't mind when it's a matter of life and death?'

He tried again. 'Suzanne, please! Look, I've fitted another three smoke-detectors, and it wasn't easy. I had to go to that shop over at Darnham before I found one that hadn't been completely cleaned out. And there's the security lighting. The place lights up like Harrods' frontage now every time a cat so much as tiptoes across the garden.'

'Would your parents have him, do you think?'

He sighed, running his hand helplessly through his hair.

'Well, yes, I suppose they would. But Ben won't want to leave his friends, and with the best will in the world my parents would find it hard to amuse him. They lead a very quiet life since Father's coronary, as you well know. And as I said before, I think you're simply over-reacting.'

'That's settled, then. Will you phone them or shall I?'

Patrick conceded defeat. 'I'd better do it,' he said grimly. 'Mother's bound to get into a flap, and I can't think you would be the person to calm her down.'

He wasn't either, as it transpired. His mother, a highly-strung lady now under continual tension about her husband's health, reacted badly to the suggestion that only Ben should be fleeing. She wanted her own son removed to safety with almost as much insistence as Suzanne had shown, and Patrick found that telling himself she meant well and had had a difficult time lately didn't stop him feeling irritated, it merely made him feel guilty for wanting to yell at her at the top of his voice. Perhaps he too was more strained than he was allowing himself to admit; everywhere you went these days, people seemed to be twitching.

He had felt tired before he even set off on the two-hour drive, beside a sullen Ben, who had protested to his mother but found that he too seemed to be dream-talking. Having to leave Tigger behind had been the worst part.

'But if it's so dangerous, it's dangerous for Tigger too! And he's only small, perhaps Granny wouldn't notice him much. I don't want anything to happen to Tigger,' he had wailed.

Perhaps it wasn't entirely tactful to be so worried about Tigger when he obviously had no qualms about leaving Suzanne; her lips tightened and she remained implacable as she swiftly packed a depressingly large suitcase for him.

'He won't be away that long,' Patrick protested. 'The police will pick someone up any minute. You could hardly move for policemen in the village last night, apparently.'

But she had ignored that, like everything else.

Patrick deposited Ben at his parents' house, had a cup of tea and did his best to reassure his mother, then extricated himself from her still-anxious clutches for the long dreary drive home, with nothing to take his mind off his problems.

He was seriously worried about Suzanne. She was behaving as if she were heading for some sort of breakdown, but supposing she – they – did manage to hold things together, what was their future? Even after this awful business had been cleared up, was there the slightest chance they could return to the sort of loving relationship they had once had? It all seemed a very long time ago now: he had practically forgotten what the girl he had fallen in love with had been like. She was certainly unrecognizable in the hard, bitter shrew he seemed to be married to now.

There had been so many quarrels, so many hurtful words hurled in temper. People might talk about saying in anger things you didn't mean; in his now-extensive experience of the state, you meant them all right. It was just that in a saner moment you would realize that they should never be said. Once spoken the words might be withdrawn – perhaps – but they would be entered indelibly in the black book of resentment that every unhappy couple keeps as meticulously as a ledger: occasion, date and reciprocal insult.

And that was an attitude that fed on itself and grew until it smothered love and changed the tone of everyday life. Could they change it back? Did he – and this was the shameful heart of the matter – even *want* to change it?

About him the traffic was slow. There was a hold-up on the motorway with roadworks, and when he fiddled impatiently with the radio, looking for distraction, all he could find were tired-sounding carols and dogged, desperate good cheer. He snapped it off and sat drumming his fingers on the wheel.

Outside, it was cold and grey, with a hint that fog might descend later, and as he inched along the windows began to steam up. Within his personal mental cocoon he felt detached from reality, insulated briefly from the problems behind and the pressures ahead, both imposed and self-induced.

He had made a genuine effort to put her out of his mind. It was disloyal, it was pointless, it was wrong. But here, in this strange little pocket of disconnected time, he permitted himself to pretend it didn't count. Just till the traffic moved off, he promised himself. Just these few minutes of the dangerous indulgence of thinking about her.

Lizzie. Elizabeth. He murmured the name luxuriously aloud, and her face swam up before his eyes, her face as he had seen it across the unromantic plastic of the table in the supermarket café: her lips quivering and the tears spilling over from her sea-grey eyes, so soft, so vulnerable. All he had wanted to do was to take her in his arms and protect her from the world, and in particular from her slob of a husband. Patrick liked to think that he was as civilized as the next man, and it shocked him to discover that at some deep and primitive level what he wanted to do was punch that smug, freckled face until the man screamed for mercy.

It was a very long time since Suzanne had made him feel like a man instead of a peculiarly inept and irritating child.

The traffic was picking up speed now. He changed gear and accelerated. He changed gear mentally as well. There was, as he had told himself a thousand times, no point in torturing himself with thoughts of Lizzie. Like most over-indulgences, you paid with later pain. They were both trapped; by duty, by children and by long habit. He didn't even know if she thought of him in any way other than as a kind friend. Like the lanes of the motorway running ahead under the sweep of the headlights, the future looked grey, dreary and featureless.

Home at last, he parked the car in the driveway behind

Suzanne's hired replacement, outside the ruined garage. It was six o'clock; a wasted Saturday. As he got out of the car, three of the new security lights came on, making him jump.

As if that were an awaited signal, the front door swung open and Suzanne stood there, wearing her coat and carrying the hold-all she always took to hospital with her.

'Oh, there you are, Patrick! You're terribly late – I expected you ages ago.'

Put on the defensive, he said, 'Well, the motorway was horrendous. And I could hardly just dump Ben on the doorstep and get back in the car, you know. But what —'

She cut across him. 'You'll have to move the car. I can't think why you didn't park it in the road, as usual. There's no way I can get mine out with yours there.'

'You're surely not going to the hospital!'

In the harsh light he could see her high colour. Her eyes were hard and bright and she was clasping her bag so tightly that her knuckles gleamed white.

He strove for tact. 'You're still very tired and shocked. I thought you'd warned them you wouldn't be back for a day or two? You really don't look well enough to cope with a night-shift.'

He thought he caught the gleam of tears in her eyes, but all she said fiercely was, 'Life has to go on. There are patients who need me, you know, and I'm a trained nurse. Your training gives you the discipline to put other things out of your mind.'

Patrick opened his mouth to speak, thought the better of it, shrugged, then got back into his car and reversed it out into the street.

Suzanne followed him, then put down her window as he passed her on his way back.

'You will test all the alarms to make sure they're working, won't you? And if you hear anything, be sure and phone the police.'

And will I call the fire brigade if the house goes on fire, he thought of asking, but decided against such provocation.

'Don't overdo it,' he said instead. 'And drive carefully. It's going to be foggy tonight.'

He raised his hand in farewell but she drove off without looking at him, and feeling foolish he lowered his hand and went into the silent house.

It was blazing with light. All the curtains had been drawn, but in each room every light was on; the reading lights as well as the overhead light in the sitting room, the light over the mirror in the bathroom, even the hob light on the kitchen cooker. What fiends of darkness could she be trying to hold at bay?

The thought made him deeply uncomfortable. He went through the house, Tigger bounding enthusiastically round him as he switched them off. Was this really within the bounds of normal behaviour, or was Suzanne . . . He shied away from articulating that fear.

He certainly pitied the people she would be dealing with tonight at the hospital. She was probably more in need of medical help than they were. He decided to have a quiet word with Richard Jones the next time he saw him.

Tigger was still dancing round his feet; he couldn't have been fed, though Suzanne normally did it before she went out at night. He opened a tin of dogfood and scooped it into the little dog's bowl; Tigger wolfed it gratefully, his whole body waggling in the brief ecstasy of eating.

Patrick was tired and hungry himself. He mixed a gin and tonic, sipping it as he checked in the oven and fridge to see whether Suzanne had left something for him. Once, there would have been a place laid at the kitchen table, a casserole in the oven or a plate to put in the microwave; it was the sort of thing on which she had prided herself. Now there wasn't even a note to say what she wanted him to use from the freezer, and if he took the wrong thing – and somehow he inevitably would – there would be more tight-lipped patience to endure.

He took another sip of his drink. There was a long evening stretching ahead, and he hardly needed to look to see if there was anything on the box. At this time of year it was a diet of films you had seen three times already and re-runs of sitcoms which had been only slightly funny the first time round. And Suzanne was clearly expecting him to be on fire-watch all evening; he was only surprised she hadn't left buckets of water everywhere as well.

He set his glass down rebelliously. He wasn't going to let her dictate to him; she hadn't even bothered to make a meal for him, when she had been at home all day while he spent five hours on a tedious expedition pandering to her neurosis. He picked up his car keys again and went out.

11

It was such a relief to get out of hospital. Hospital was, Margaret Moon reflected, the last place anyone would choose to be ill in. This morning she had been roused from sound sleep to breakfast at 6.30: after that, every time she had fallen into a comfortable doze, she had been wakened by noise, visitors or a nurse taking her temperature or giving her another eyewash.

Now she sank into the deep soft cushions of the Brancombes' sofa, under the crocheted comforter Jean had insisted on, and looked round the big farm-house sitting room with a sigh of content.

There were no signs of Christmas past in the tidy room, apart from a neat pile of cards waiting to be checked off on the Christmas card list beside them. It was Jean's practice to clear the house the day after Boxing Day: it just made her nervous, she said, sitting there waiting for pine needles to fall on the carpet, and the housework took twice as long when you had to take all the cards down each day to chase the dust from your polished surfaces, and then set them all up again.

It was eight o'clock. They had been sumptuously fed, and Robert had left after supper for another consultation with Rod Vezey. Ted had gone out to check on the cows, and Jean had insisted on popping along to the vicarage

221

with a list of things Margaret might need for the next few days, until her home should be habitable again.

Pyewacket lay on the hearthrug, purring his satisfaction at his first experience of an open fire, and the only other sound in the room was the muted roar of the log blaze and the occasional crackle as a dry twig caught. Survival, sight restored and the kindness of friends; she was a lucky woman. Tomorrow she would have to deal with all the problems of the aftermath of fire and the details of her losses, but following St Matthew's sage advice about the sufficiency of each day's troubles, she put such considerations out of her mind and closed her eyes in unarticulated thankfulness. She was drifting agreeably between sleep and wakefulness when Jean returned.

'I've put your clothes up in your room, dear,' she said. 'Here are the books you wanted, and I picked up the post while I was there.

'And do you know, we've got such a nice young man outside? He says he's been detailed to keep an eye on the house, with you being here. I tell you, I'll get the first sound night's sleep I've had since this whole dreadful business began.'

'I'm glad I'm able to be of some service to you, even if it's only by proxy,' Margaret said, taking the books and the pile of mail from her. 'You look worn out, and I feel so guilty that Robert and I have billeted ourselves on you too.'

Ted, his rounds finished, had come into the room behind his wife, and put his arm round her shoulders.

'Ah, Margaret, when you've known Jean as long as I have you'll realize that this is her chosen state. Never happy unless she's overworking and has something to worry about. And if she hasn't got a big worry, she can always find a little one to be going on with.'

222

'Well, if it was left to you, Ted, the world would run down and stop,' his wife retorted, pulling a face at him. The look they exchanged was one of perfect understanding.

This was one of the occasions when Margaret felt a pang of regret over her single state. It was a rare occurrence: too often long-married couples made her wonder if they shared the nature of St Aldegonde, reputed to delight in marriages and public executions.

She turned to sorting through her correspondence. There wasn't much: one or two late Christmas cards, a couple of circulars and nothing, she noted with relief, addressed using an old-fashioned typewriter. Then she came to a parcel underneath, untidily-wrapped and directed in uneven, ill-formed capitals. It had not come by post. She looked at it with a rising sense of unease.

Ted noticed her change of expression. 'Something wrong, Margaret?'

'I don't know,' she said slowly. 'It's just–' Overcoming a feeling of reluctance, she forced herself to open it, then stared in some bewilderment at the little blue book.

'It's a child's diary,' she said. 'A diary from 1967. Who in the world could be sending me that?'

She shook it, expecting a note to fall out, then searched through the wrappings for any clue. Finding none, she opened the book under the Brancombes' interested eyes.

'1st January: Today we went to the panto. I wore my new dress.' Oh, and she couldn't spell 'laugh' – look. Daddy obviously wasn't easily amused!

'What age is she, I wonder? There are a few other spelling mistakes, but it's very neat in general.'

She came to the blank pages. 'Now she's given up. That always happened to me. I never seemed to have anything to confide to my diary in February, and after that the relationship became one of embarrassment. But see, here we are again. Oh – oh, good gracious. How dreadfully, dreadfully sad. Look.'

The other two bent over her shoulder and read the stark entry announcing the child's mother's death. They read on, through all the details of that hideous Christmas, the news of her brother's death, all told with childish simplicity and unreliable spelling. When they came to the pages of final despair – black, black, black – there were tears in Margaret's eyes and Jean was openly weeping.

Ted cleared his throat. 'Poor little thing,' he said, and blew his nose loudly in a red-spotted handkerchief.

'It's her, of course,' Margaret said softly. 'This is Missy, and this is what caused it all. It was just too much for her to cope with and she blotted it out, created someone who could cope with it for her, just as Robert said. And now something else has happened, something that is too much for her in adult life, and her creation has returned to haunt her. To haunt us all.'

'We've got to help her.' Jean was twisting her hankie in her fingers. 'We've got to do something.'

'It's certainly a cry for help,' Margaret said. 'But the trouble is, it's a very imperfect one. She told me on the phone she was in desperate distress; she's explained to me why, now. But she hasn't said who.'

'Perhaps she's going to. Perhaps that's the next step,' Jean suggested. 'It's too much to expect her to trust you all at once, but given time —'

Ted stared at them. 'We give this to the police,' he said. 'Now. This minute.'

'But —'

'You can't —'

The two pairs of eyes fixed on him held identical expressions of accusatory horror, and Ted flushed.

'Look, I'm not being heartless. That's the most tragic

thing I've ever seen. But you're not just talking about a woman with problems, you're talking about a woman who's gone mad. I don't suppose that's what they call it – Robert would have some fancy technical name, I've no doubt – but that's what she is. At this very moment she may be planning to burn down another house. You were lucky on Thursday night, Margaret, you know that. Someone else may not be so lucky.'

The women exchanged glances.

Margaret said slowly, 'I'm a priest, Ted; she's addressed the parcel to me as the vicar. It's – it's a problem I've had a lot of difficulty with already. How do I balance up the dangers against the betrayal of trust?'

Ted snorted, but it was Jean who said, slowly, as if she were thinking aloud, 'But – are you sure it would be a betrayal? She doesn't ask you to keep it a secret, after all, does she? Perhaps she sent this to you, hoping that you would do just that – take it to the police, so that they could stop her before she did anything worse.'

Torn, Margaret stroked the soft cover, trying to feel her way through to the ethical decision. She could think of objections to both courses of action, but there was no doubt which was the more sensible. And where moral issues were concerned, common sense was often the best, and indeed the only guide you had.

She sighed. 'All right, Ted,' she agreed reluctantly. 'I think you'll get Robert at the police station in Burdley. That would be the best thing.'

Ted came back from the phone saying, 'They'll be here in twenty minutes. And Robert says not to touch it – fingerprints.'

'Oops,' said Margaret, looking down at the book which she was still holding protectively between her hands, as if somehow that might shelter its owner. 'Oh well, they've taken my prints already, so they'll be able to eliminate them, no doubt. In any case, how could I have known what was in it unless I'd touched it – silly man.'

However, she tipped it neatly on to the wrapper then slid both off her knees on to a coffee table without touching them again, while Jean scurried off to the kitchen to set up a tray with tea and enough cakes to supply the complete operational strength of Burdley division.

When Robert arrived, Vezey was with him, as well as a silent young man, also in plain clothes, whom Vezey addressed as Dave.

Vezey, taking large tweezers out of his pocket, lifted the book on to a convenient surface, and with Robert looking on opened it, held it flat with the end of a pencil and turned the pages by the same method. He made no comment, but when they had finished he clicked his fingers and Dave produced two large plastic bags. The book was dropped into one and the wrapper into another; the bags were sealed and labelled.

'Thank you,' Vezey said curtly. 'We'll go back and get on with that right away. I'd like you too, Robert, if you don't mind.'

'But you'll stay and have some tea,' Jean protested, her hospitable soul outraged. 'It's on a tray, all ready . . .'

'You're very kind. But we've got no time to waste. There's another long night still ahead of us.'

They went out, and the chill that struck the room was not solely from the cold damp air that came in through the open front door.

Laura Ferrars said, 'I think we should put this house on the market and move away from here.'

She and James were alone together in the sitting room having coffee after supper. She made the dramatic statement

226

with a strange, dream-like lack of emphasis, but James, for once shocked out of his usual cool detachment, positively jumped with surprise.

'What did you say?'

'The house. That we should sell it. You don't really want me to repeat it, you heard me perfectly well. It's just that you don't want to believe I said it.'

'It's not that I don't want to believe it. It's that I *can't* believe it. We've lived in this house for fifteen years; it was your dream house, remember? Space for the girls to have their own rooms, this little sitting room as well as the big one —'

'Oh, there's nothing especially wrong with the *house*.' Laura's voice quavered as she dismissed fifteen years of meticulous planning, decorating and furnishing. 'It's where it is, here, in this place, this awful, awful place.'

This was, paradoxically, helpful. James believed he understood: the Boltons' fire had been very upsetting, and now of course everyone was running around panicking because of the attack on poor Margaret Moon. And yes, theoretically, they could be next – anyone could be next – but that didn't make it likely, and this sort of hysteria certainly wasn't constructive. It wasn't like Laura to behave in such an extreme manner, but then she had been behaving very oddly ever since her disappointment over the job.

He said soothingly, 'Look, this unpleasantness is all temporary. With the effort the police are putting in now, they're bound to find whoever it is before long, and things will return to normal. My dear, it's perfectly natural you should be upset, but I have to say I think you're getting it just a little out of proportion.'

'Is it the money?' Laura said, her voice rising. 'We'd get a really good price for this house, so you wouldn't lose out at all on the money side. Which, of course is all you really care about, isn't it?'

James was moved to protest.

'That's utter nonsense, Laura, and you know it. I'm simply stunned by what you seem to be saying. You love this house, or so you've always said, and all our friends are here —'

'Friends? What friends are these?'

'Laura, perhaps I'm being stupid,' he said with the maddening assurance of one who considers the suggestion unfeasible, 'but this is a conversation I am entirely failing to understand. We've been friends with the Boltons and the McEvoys for years, and Hayley too, of course, and the Cartwrights and the Joneses and —'

'These are not *friends*. They're acquaintances of long standing. And even you can hardly be insensitive enough to describe Piers McEvoy as my friend. It's his fault I'm in the state I'm in now. He's – he's an insect. If I could rub him out with my foot, I would.

'I need to get away, James. I can't be responsible for what will happen if you make me stay here. Something terrible. I need a new life, real friends – friends I can trust, who trust me —'

Once again, James believed he had seen the light. The girls had had a spat, that was it, and it was true enough that Piers had been a complete sod over that appointment.

He said kindly, 'You know as well as I do, my dear, that making friends doesn't happen like that —'

'Do I? How do you know what I know?' Her eyes were dangerous, too bright. 'And don't call me "my dear". It's what you call your bloody maiden aunt, "my dear".'

There was a frantic note in her voice, and he was starting to be seriously alarmed. 'Laura —'

'Oh, shut up! "My dear" – that's just your mark, isn't

it? Where's the excitement, where's the passion in that? Where's the passion in our marriage, come to that?

'What's happened to us, James? Where did they go, the people we used to be? When did the dream disappear?'

She was almost shouting now, and he shushed her nervously. The girls, mercifully, were out, but the way she was going on the people next door would be able to hear her.

'Oh, don't shush me, James! Can't you hear what I'm saying? Can't you understand how wrong, how dreadfully wrong things are –' She caught her breath on a furious sob. 'But you don't want to know, do you? The only passion you have left is a passion for monotony!'

For a moment anger flared. Just for a moment, he was tempted to shout back, to detail at the top of his voice his own dissatisfactions. He too had had his painful accommodations to make, like giving up the precarious criminal bar to be a commercial solicitor when the girls were born. She had never acknowledged that sacrifice, or perhaps he had never made his wretchedness evident. Perhaps by then it had already become easier to pretend that everything was absolutely fine. But it was certainly too late now – years too late – and control was a habit long-established.

With heightened colour he rose from the armchair at the opposite side of the fireplace. With what he felt to be a certain dignity, he said, 'I'm sorry you're so distraught. Clearly this is something we have to talk about when you are feeling calmer, but there is absolutely no point in prolonging this discussion now, and I have no intention of doing so.'

He left the room and heard, with a sense of unreality, the crash of some piece of crockery hitting the back of the door he had just shut, then a wail and a tempest of frenzied sobbing from his wife.

He put his hand to his brow and found that he was sweating. He felt completely, uncharacteristically, at a loss. What should he do now?

Get out of the house until she calmed down, suggested itself as the only answer. It was probably the time of the month; she was often pretty touchy around then. She'd have a good cry, take a couple of aspirins, go to bed and feel better in the morning.

The golf club came to mind as the obvious haven. He was not usually what is termed a 'clubbable man' but tonight the thought of male company was very attractive. There were women members too, of course – it performed the social function of a country club – but the ambience was distinctly masculine and the women tended to be unobtrusive. Just at the moment that was a very soothing thought.

The fog was starting to close in and James drove with even more than his usual caution up the hill to the car park where there was already a good number of cars. The club, he surmised, would be providing a convenient excuse for people to catch up with the latest developments in the Stretton Noble crime wave. The local store, he had noticed when he passed earlier, appeared to be performing the same service for its different clientele.

The hum of talk, as he entered the main bar, seemed to have a fevered pitch. Normally a local sensation would be greeted with a sort of discreet relish, but this tense atmosphere was something different. After all, it could be your home tonight. No wonder Laura was being – difficult.

Patrick Bolton was there, eating on a stool up at the bar and chatting to Jonnie Marsden, a pleasant, quiet man with a business in Burdley. James went to join them.

'Evening Jonnie, Patrick. Ready for another of those? My shout.'

He bought the drinks and joined them, and only then noticed Piers McEvoy at the far end of the long bar, slotting back the Scotch as usual in a group of other men. There was a lot of noise down that end, as there always was when Piers was about. He was open-handed with his rounds, running up a tab which he paid off without question at the end of the evening. It assured him, James reflected cynically, of an audience at least of the more dedicated bar-flies, if no one else.

Piers looked across from his conversation and made a beckoning gesture: James and Patrick both raised a hand in greeting, but made no move to join the other man. He turned back to the group about him with a shrug, and a moment later there was a loud gust of laughter.

The conversation at James's end of the bar was considerably quieter. He found himself mentioning, in general terms of course, Laura's incomprehensible outburst, and found Patrick eager to talk about Suzanne. Evelyn, Jonnie's wife, had wanted them to take turns at staying awake on fire-watch, and they all agreed that the situation was enough to get anyone going. Jonnie confessed to having gone out and bought three industrial-sized fire-extinguishers which were now looking entirely out of place in his small modern bungalow. The three men laughed comfortably, and Patrick ordered another round of drinks.

It was, perhaps, half an hour later that James noticed Hayley Cutler come into the bar. She was by herself; she smiled perfunctorily and waved towards them, but did not come over. The bar was even busier now, but when next James looked she was talking to Piers, drawing him slightly apart.

Piers, unmistakably, was not pleased, but he ordered drinks for them both and went to sit with her at a table in the far corner. James was intrigued now; it would not do to be caught staring, but out of the corner of his eye he was able to see that an acrimonious conversation was taking place. There were no raised voices, but Hayley was pressing some point, leaning forward and gesticulating, while Piers's position in his chair – leaning well back from her with his arms crossed and a thunderous expression on his face – was as clearly repelling her submission as if James had been able to hear the short, contemptuous sentence which was his reply.

Hayley drew back, her face turning an ugly muddy red, and for a moment did not move. Then she leaned forward, called him something which, probably fortunately, James could not hear, then got up and strode out, her eyes hard as flint and her jaw set as if it were cast in bronze.

Piers glared at her departing back, his pale prominent eyes bulging even more in what looked like an effort not to shout at her. He took out his handkerchief and mopped his brow and the back of his neck with a pudgy hand that did not seem quite steady. He reached for the glass in front of him which still contained most of a double, and downed it in one. Then he got up and came over to James and Patrick.

'Come on, you two,' he said with a show of his customary jocular manner. 'You've been tucked away at the fairies' end of the bar all night – come and join the chaps!'

Jonnie Marsden, a blameless family man, looked embarrassed and as Piers lingered drifted quietly away.

'What about some bridge?' Piers suggested. 'I'm just in the mood to make a night of it.'

'Not for me,' Patrick said, slipping off the bar stool. 'I'm getting back.'

'James, then?'

James hesitated. He wouldn't exactly choose to spend a long evening in Piers's company, but then the prospect of returning home before Laura had gone to bed was unappealing, to say the least.

'Well, just a few rubbers, then.'

'Excellent fellow! Come and we'll find another pair of like minds, and I'll get the drinks in.'

It was eleven thirty when Patrick went out into the car park, jingling his keys in his hand as he walked. The temptation had been served up to him on a platter, frilled and garnished by Piers's obvious indifference to his nervous wife, left alone at home. Patrick should resist it, he knew that. But would he? He had heard mermaids singing, and like Eliot's Prufrock he was doubtful. But in his heart, his trousers were rolled already, and his fingers sticky with peach juice.

He started the engine and drove slowly from the car park. The fog was becoming smoggy, and the headlamps reflected back off the surrounding soupy grey. He dipped them; he could see the road in front more clearly now, but the damp dirty blanket closed in about the windows of the car in an echo of that isolation he had experienced this afternoon.

Left or right at the bottom of the road? Left for home, a nightcap perhaps, and the late film on television, or right . . . ?

He clicked on the right-hand indicator. After all, he tried to convince himself, he was only paying a neighbourly call to see that Lizzie was all right, because her bastard of a husband didn't care.

The house looked quiet and peaceful enough. The children must be in bed, for the only room lights showing were behind the curtains in the drawing room. He parked his car in the road outside, walked up the path and rang the bell.

When Elizabeth opened the door, she had been crying. She had wiped the tears away, tried to put on a public face, but the heavy swollen lids and the quiver at the corner of her delicate mouth gave her away.

He had planned it all. He would say, cheerfully, 'Just called in on the way back from the Club. Piers looked settled in for a long session, so I thought that I'd just check that you were OK.'

But her pathetic attempt at a welcoming smile was his undoing.

'Oh Lizzie, sweet Lizzie,' he said, and held out his arms.

She threw herself into them and clung to him as if he were the only solid rock in a sea of troubles that threatened to engulf her.

They had done no more than talk, mostly, and they were sitting with comparative decorum on the sofa, with Lizzie's hand lovingly imprisoned in Patrick's clasp. They heard no warning sound, no footfall on the thick pile of the hall carpet: with a movement that was purest instinct, when the sitting-room door burst open they leaped guiltily, foolishly apart.

There in the doorway stood Suzanne. She was in her nurse's uniform, but some of the buttons were undone, and her hair was wild as if she had been running her hands through the thick, strong curls.

'Am I to be left with nothing, nothing?' she cried. 'I try, God knows I try. Sometimes I think I will kill myself, I try so hard. My son has grown away from me, I'm not strong enough even to do a single night's work, and now it's the oldest story in the book, my husband's car parked outside the house of my best friend. It's so banal it's embarrassing. Couldn't you come up with something just a fraction more interesting, Patrick? Or even something just slightly less devastatingly hurtful? Isn't it enough that I've been stripped naked – am I to be flayed as well?'

Her sudden intrusion, the sobbing, hysterical onslaught, seemed almost to have paralysed them. After a long moment Patrick struggled to his feet.

'Suzanne, I know what this looks like, but —'

'Oh, spare me the crap. It's bad enough, God knows, without the lies and the clichés.'

Elizabeth found her voice. 'Patrick only came in to see if I was all right, Suzanne. I was pathetic and stupid and burst into tears, and he was kind. It's my fault; he's done nothing.'

'No,' Patrick protested. 'It wasn't your fault, Lizzie. It was my choice to come here. And —'

Suzanne stood watching them, white-faced, her eyes glittering as she followed these exchanges with turns of the head like the spectator at a curious tennis match. But suddenly she yelled, 'Oh, it's not Lizzie's fault, of course. Nothing's ever *Lizzie's* fault. Dear, sweet, helpless Lizzie!'

And then she was upon her, with a banshee scream. She had the advantage of surprise; taken unawares, Lizzie was still sitting at the end of the sofa which slid backwards under the impact of Suzanne's weight. A little table toppled; a dainty Limoges snuffbox smashed on the parquet floor.

Patrick grabbed Suzanne from behind, pulling her up and away and imprisoning her flailing arms, but not before she had raked her nails savagely down the side of Elizabeth's face.

Patrick gasped as he saw the scratches, now filling with blood. Suzanne, too, stopped struggling, as if the sight of what she had done had knocked the fight out of her.

He was too shocked to feel anything except bewildered dismay.

'Suzanne, are you out of your mind?'

Her body sagged against him and he took the risk of releasing her from smothering restraint, while still holding himself ready to spring at any threatening movement.

But she was quiet now. Suzanne looked from him to her handiwork on the other woman's face, and her eyes fell. She walked away to the door calmly enough.

When she reached it, she turned.

'I'm sorry, Lizzie,' she said, her voice sounding eerily normal. 'It shouldn't have been you, it should have been that bastard there. At least my nails are clean. Wash it with antiseptic and it'll heal in a day or two.'

She went out. Patrick, sick and shaken, made to take Lizzie in his arms again.

'My darling, your poor face —'

Elizabeth was still sitting at the end of the sofa, pushed back as Suzanne had left it. Her eyes were wide, as if contemplating a horror too deep for tears. She was struggling desperately for control.

'No, no, please. Don't touch me, Patrick. Please, just go now.'

'But Piers – how will you explain it? Will he be all right?'

She drew a shuddering sigh, and got out a foolishly small handkerchief to dab ineffectively at the scratches.

'Oh, Piers,' she said, with a travesty of a smile. 'No, I don't suppose he will be. He won't be pleased about the Limoges, apart from anything else. But I'll cope. I'll think of something. And it certainly won't help if you're here.'

'No. No, I don't suppose it will.'

'I'm not worth all this, Patrick. And Suzanne needs you, you know she does.'

He didn't want to hear her say that. He would be the judge when it came to the question of her worth to him, but she was right about Suzanne, and Suzanne was his wife.

Patrick looked with hopeless yearning at the woman he had been permitted to love for such a short time, at the disordered room, and worst of all at her disfigured face. He had done this to her, as surely as if he had used the nails on his own hand which had caressed her so lovingly before.

'What will you do?' Conceding her point, he was still reluctant to leave her.

'I'll go to bed. He won't be back until after I'm asleep anyway. But go now, Patrick, please go.'

She had been magnificent, but her voice was rising and even he could see that he was making matters worse rather than better. He took an irresolute step towards her, but her shrinking was obvious.

'Don't worry, I'm going. I'm sorry, Lizzie, more sorry than I can possibly say. Don't get up: I'll see myself out.'

With a heavy heart he left her, sitting on the sofa still, but now with her head bent so that the light of the table lamp fell on it, creating a nimbus out of her fair hair.

12

The streetlamps were pale fuzzy haloes of dead light tonight, and in the main road a car inching along was no more than a grey shape defined by the trapped beams of its futile headlights as they failed to penetrate the gloom.

The fog was growing denser, the yellowish polluted fog of the Thames Valley, thickening in eddies and swirls until it seemed almost viscous. It enfolded buildings, trees, figures, as if the air itself were becoming as solid as the objects it shrouded. PC Tom Compton was not as a rule a fanciful man, but as he trod his lonely beat he almost turned to see if a bow wave was forming as he breached the opacity ahead.

Compton was not happy. He was accustomed to the comfort and security of a police car, dry and warm, with the familiar crackle of radio voices from headquarters and other nearby cars, and his partner for company in the slack times and support if things hotted up. Even when he had been on a foot patrol, there had always been two of them; tonight he was on his own, with not a soul about. Well, probably not. He glanced over his shoulder nervously.

He was in radio contact, of course, but tonight the strategy was to cover the village with as many officers in as many places as possible, particularly now that visibility was reduced to only a few paces.

And that idea was a loser for a start. There wasn't an

icecube's chance in hell that he would see anything, unless he tripped over the fire-raiser – a woman, they seemed to think – squatting over the next blaze warming her hands. Someone could be within three feet of him, ahead or behind, and he wouldn't even know.

He shivered. As a mere PC he wasn't, of course, privy to the discussions of the great men who flaunted a 'D' before the 'C' in their police title – PCs to them were a lower form of life – but the rumour was all round the station that the woman they were looking for was a nutter. It wasn't a comfortable thought.

Compton turned on to a back lane which ran behind some of the smarter houses, with the trees of the common dripping eerily on the other side. With sight being so little use to him his hearing seemed much more acute and he found himself becoming aware of all sorts of little sounds in that heavy greyness, muffled and distorted by the blanket of the fog. There were rustles too, and the snapping of twigs in among the light undergrowth and the bushes. Was that one of the foxes, scavengers of dustbins, which were so common here, or was it someone moving lightly and furtively among the trees? Perhaps it was an ordinary citizen perfectly legitimately taking his dog on its late-night walk. Perhaps it wasn't.

There was a thick fur of moisture on the pile of his clothes now, and it was condensing on his brows and eyelashes too. He knuckled his eyes as if that might restore clear vision and peered into the damp darkness, shining his torch which dazzled but shed no light. It was probably no more than imagination which made him think he sensed the stir of someone's passing on the thickened air.

Rod Vezey, when he reached Burdley, was high; high with a sort of nervous jubilation. He strode through the little police station, Moon and Smethurst trotting in his wake, with such purposeful haste that he created a stir.

'Well, well! Do you reckon Wonderboy has had a break-through, then?' the constable manning the front desk asked the sergeant.

He, dislodged from his office and grudgingly back on the desk too, sniffed.

'About bloody time too, if you ask me,' he said bitterly.

In sublime indifference, the usurper shut behind him the door of his annexed territory and said, in an unconscious echo of the man outside, 'Well, it's about time we got a break, isn't it? All I ask is that it hasn't come too late. It's an evil night out there.'

He stood in the centre of the little room, frowning his concentration, then gave his orders.

'Dave. Get across to headquarters with these bags now. Take it as quickly as you can – siren if you must – but for God's sake don't kill anyone, even yourself. I'll phone ahead and get a print man waiting for you. That probably won't tell us much, since I'd be astonished if our friend here has form, but we can't get down to analysing the thing until fingerprints have finished with it. And once they've finished, I want full photocopies faxed here asap. We must be in a position to act first thing in the morning.'

'OK, guv.' Smethurst took the plastic bags and left.

'Robert, I want you to sit down now and dredge up all you can remember of what the diary said. Write it down. I'm just going through to see if anything's come in from the patrols. And switch on the kettle, would you?'

Leaving Moon sitting down at the desk and reaching for paper, he went through to the other small office which had been transformed into a primitive ops room. Two PCs and a woman sergeant were running it, manning hastily-installed radio equipment and telephone lines. One man was talking quietly into the speaker of his headset, but they all looked up when Vezey entered.

'Anything to report, sergeant?'

She pulled a face. 'Nothing interesting that I can see, sir.' She hesitated; his own state of high tension was obvious.

'Er – has something else come up?' she could not resist asking, though she was not sure it was wise.

He gave his brief, mirthless grin and stretched out his hand with a seesaw motion.

'It's just possible. Keep me in touch, if anything comes in,' he said, and vanished again.

When he returned, Moon was methodically covering a sheet of paper with his neat, precise handwriting.

'Nearly there,' he said without looking up. 'It's not very accurate, but I think I've got the gist. There are probably things you can add that you've remembered and I haven't.'

'I'll have it photocopied whenever you finish, and then we can both have a look at it.'

Vezey got out the mugs and coffee. 'Milk and sugar?'

Moon had finished by the time the coffee was ready, and they sat with their copies on either side of the desk. Vezey was able to add one or two points; it was certainly not wholly accurate, but there was enough information to be useful.

'What does this do to your profile – that's the first point, isn't it? Anything that helps to fill it out?'

Moon scanned it again. 'Curiously enough, I'm not sure that in psychological terms it's added a great deal to what we had already surmised. It's mainly confirmatory, in fact. But it's interesting to see the connection with Christmas; that's probably always been a tricky time for Missy. Most women seem to get themselves to the verge of collapse by the time the turkey reaches the table, and in her mind it would be inextricably linked with stress already. If a crisis of some sort arose at this time, she would be particularly vulnerable.

'But I must say, it's fascinating to have chapter and verse. I'd like to write this one up; I can't think of a case where there is such a clear description of the factors contributing to dual personality.'

'Let's cut the theoretical crap, shall we, and get down to the investigation?'

Moon blinked but said nothing, only surveying him owlishly over his spectacles, and Vezey had the grace to look abashed.

'Oh – sorry, Robert. But it's just – oh, I don't know. It seems as if while we're groping along in a mental fog, anything could be happening in the fog out there, anything.'

They both glanced automatically at the impenetrable blankness outside the uncurtained window.

Vezey persisted. 'Well, what do you reckon?'

'In practical terms? There, of course, you know as well as I do what questions to ask tomorrow. It's all down here.'

Moon tapped the copy on his knee with his pen. 'It's as straightforward as the most exigent detective could wish, surely. Who had a mother who died when she was a small child, whose brother died shortly afterwards? And who was aged, say, between six and nine in 1967?'

Vezey nodded. 'Yes, simple enough, you would think, wouldn't you? I'll buzz them just now and get ages from the statements. And even if she won't come straight out and tell us herself, all we have to do is go to the public records to find out about her family – no nasty fiddly conversations with relatives and friends. Always supposing there isn't a curved ball, like her having assumed another name, or something like that.'

'Surely not!'

Vezey sighed fatalistically. 'It's always when you think you've got it in the bag that things decide to go wrong. Still, assuming that for once the gods are merciful, as soon as we've nailed her, surely we'll be able to get proof?'

'Psychological proof? Probably; I should think her state must be pretty volatile by now.'

'I was thinking in terms of nice ordinary physical proof. The courts like that an awful lot better. We may get prints off the book, or off the wrapper anyway, and given a search warrant it's awesome what forensic can come up with.'

'What are you going to do now?'

Vezey hesitated. 'I have –' he said, and then stopped, as if reluctant to say something which approached the intimacy of a personal confession. He got up, went across to the blank window and stared pointlessly out.

'I can't explain it. I just have an irrational feeling that something's going wrong out there. I don't know why and I don't know where, and I can't justify it. But I feel I should be doing something. Perhaps only something high profile, with lights and sirens, that might make somebody think again . . .

'But on the other hand . . . What time is it now? Well after eleven? How the hell can we go out ringing doorbells, without solid evidence as support? Look,' he picked up the list that had been brought in, 'these are the women who would have been between six and nine in 1967 – eighteen of them! OK, we've homed in on four, but given your sister's intransigence all we can claim is that it's a hunch. And we've interviewed them all recently, each of them more than once and one of them three times. Despite what my gut is telling me, my head says we have to wait either until we have something concrete or it isn't the hour of the night that has people screaming about Stasi tactics. You never know, it's possible Prints might turn up something.'

Moon sighed in his turn. 'I'm sure you're absolutely right, but I confess to sharing your sense of unease. When do you think you might get information through from your HQ?'

Vezey looked at his watch again impatiently, though he knew perfectly well what it would say.

'By the time he's got there – and the fog would make it slow – got it set up, fingerprints taken and compared with known prints – another half hour at least. And even then, we're unlikely to be any further forward.'

It was three-quarters of an hour, in fact, but when the phone-call did come, the result took him completely by surprise.

'Minnie Groak?' Vezey repeated blankly, taking a note of the address then replacing the receiver.

'Is there anything you can tell me about Minnie Groak, whose prints we seem to hold for some reason?' he demanded.

'Minnie?' Moon echoed. 'Minnie's my sister's cleaner, if you could dignify her with that title. You'd have her prints for elimination after the fire.'

'Good God. And what age is the woman?'

'Hard to say. She's one of those grey women who look middle-aged from puberty on, but she's probably around forty-five, I would guess. And her mother is very much, but very much alive, according to Margaret. How does she come into this?'

'That's what I'm going to find out. Her prints are all over everything – the book, the wrapping, everything. Where does that leave our profile now?'

It did not take Robert long to make the connection.

'I think that what has happened is that Minnie has just demonstrated yet again her contempt for Marcus Aurelius's dictum that one should not waste what remains of one's life in speculating about one's neighbours. I think that speculation, in this case, has become investigation. She has taken matters, quite literally, into her own hands.'

'Opened your sister's mail, do you mean?'

'Without a doubt, I should say.'

'Right.' It was the excuse for action Vezey had been looking for, and he leaped to his feet. 'If you're right, she's going to get the sort of fright that will make sure she wouldn't read a love letter from the Prime Minister to Princess Di if she found it lying face-up on the pavement.'

In minutes they were in the police car, with blue light flashing and siren wailing, making surprising speed through the fog to Minnie's door. The turn that it gave her this time made all her previous palpitations insignificant by comparison.

When, after half an hour, they drove off to the district headquarters, leaving behind a hysterically-sobbing Minnie snivelling her statement to a policewoman, they took with them in the statutory plastic bag the crumpled wrapping with its pathetic message, stained now with tea leaves and potato peelings from the Groak dustbin.

Moon smoothed out the covering. ' "Pray for us sinners, now and at the hour of our death," ' he read out. 'Poor creature.'

'Yes, poor creature,' Vezey said grimly. 'But thanks to that repellent apology for a human being back there, we've lost twenty-four hours. And as we know, nothing happened last night; if she hadn't indulged her nasty little habit, we could have had Missy safely under lock and key by now, and I wouldn't be worrying about the pricking of my thumbs.'

'Do you still feel you can't take any action tonight?'

Vezey bit savagely at a rough edge on his thumbnail, then tapped it against his teeth in frustration.

'I suppose you have to accept that the arguments still

apply. They'll fingerprint this at once, of course, but as far as I can make out we haven't taken other prints, apart from yours and your sister's. And now the arachnoid Mrs Groak.'

Robert said, with an optimism he did not feel, 'It was probably the police presence that stopped her last night, you know, and tonight you can't move in Stretton Noble without falling over one of your lads. It will probably be another quiet night and we'll feel foolish in the morning.'

Rod Vezey grunted what might have passed for agreement, but Robert did not think he had convinced him and the knot of tension in his own stomach was becoming a definite pain.

Above the bar in the Golf Club house, the clock was showing five minutes past one. The barman, with his clearing up finished and all the glasses washed, polished and put away, was yawning as he leaned against the bar counter.

The room was deserted, apart from the four men at the table in the far corner, still at their bridge game.

There was money on the table, most of it in front of James Ferrars and his partner. This was not by design; James had been trying hard to lose for more than an hour now, but with the usual perversity of fortune had been dealt nothing but winning cards.

He had tried to bring the evening to a close earlier, but Piers – whose idea it had been to have some money on the rubber 'to give it a bit of interest' – had snarled, 'You're going nowhere till we've had a chance to win it back. Typical lawyer – grab the money and run.'

Colouring, James had sat down again, with a bad grace, for another interminable hour while the other pair's losses only mounted. The sums involved were trivial enough, but Piers hated to be the loser in any game. He had been drinking steadily, though there were no obvious signs that he was drunk, apart from the mottled red of his complexion and his dull and bloodshot eyes.

At last Newton, the Club secretary, appeared, and after a word with the weary barman came over to them. He was a stout, fussy little man who had been a captain in the Pay Corps and insisted on retaining the title. He thought in clichés and was much given to the sort of heavy-handed jocosity which was intended to be ingratiating.

' 'Ello, 'ello, 'ello, what's all this?' he declaimed as he reached the table. 'Still at it, are you? I'm afraid I'm going to have to call time, gentlemen, please. Have none of you lot got homes to go to?'

It was an ill-judged pleasantry. Piers's lip curled and he swung round belligerently in his seat, but before he could say anything James was on his feet and standing between the two men.

'I was just on the point of throwing in my hand anyway. Getting far too old for late-night card sessions, I'm afraid. What about the rest of you?'

The other two men, trapped like himself by Piers's determination, agreed with alacrity and also rose. Piers alone remained seated, glaring resentfully at them all.

The money still lay on the table, at the places where James and his partner had been sitting. Piers looked at it, then at them, and sneered.

'Come on, James, you two had better trouser your ill-gotten gains. Next time remind me to choose my partner a bit more carefully.'

The fourth man, with a vindictive look at Piers, muttered a surly good-night and departed. James picked up his share – some fifteen pounds – and turned to the secretary.

'Put that in the staff box, will you please? We've kept you all far too late tonight,' he said, and his partner, as

248

he had done all evening with such inconvenient success, followed his lead.

With little alternative, Piers at last got up, lurching slightly as he pushed his chair back from the table.

'I can't think why I bother with you lot,' he said contemptuously, and made his way through the glass doors to the foyer, allowing them to swing to with a crash behind him.

Captain Newton looked after him. 'Oh dear,' he said worriedly. 'He's more than a touch the worse for wear, isn't he? I really don't think he should be let loose behind the wheel.'

'I'm sure he shouldn't,' James said sombrely. 'I'll go after him, and try to persuade him to let me give him a lift.'

But by the time he and his bridge partner reached the carpark, Piers's car was gone. There was not even a glimpse of his tail-lights in the fog; he must have moved with considerable speed for someone in his condition.

Newton had followed them out. 'Should I phone the boys in blue, do you think? Not that I'm ever one to want to shop a member, but citizen's duty, and all that —'

'Yes, I certainly take your point. But he hasn't far to go, you know, and he'll be home before the police could track him down, in this fog. He'll be crawling along anyway. Drunk or sober, Piers won't want to damage his precious car.'

'You're not wrong there,' Newton agreed with a laugh, glad to feel that the responsibility had been shifted to other shoulders than his. He had to be careful about his licence, but it wouldn't do to get a reputation for being a copper's nark. 'Good-night, both.'

James followed the tail-lights of the other man at a cautious distance, and they inched off down the golf-course road. Captain Newton, yawning himself, went back inside with some relief to lock up for the night and get home at last.

Swearing at the fog, at bridge partners and club secretaries, at life in general and one woman in particular, Piers edged his car safely home. He had drunk a great deal and his blood-alcohol level would have been off the scale, but habituated to it as he was, it did not incapacitate him and he drove the car into the garage and locked up without noticeable difficulty.

When he came in, the light on the stairs was on as usual – Milla was afraid of the dark and slept with her door open – but that was the only one burning in the quiet house. He did not notice the soft rustles and sighings of his family in bed upstairs, though crossing the hall he heard one of the children coughing in its sleep. Milla, probably; she had kept Lizzie up half the night last night. Or so she said; he had slept through it, himself.

He wasn't ready for bed yet. He'd have played on at the club for another hour, from choice, if those stupid sods hadn't wimped out. He decided to have a nightcap before turning in, and went into the games room.

This was his favourite room. He was proud of the furniture and paintings in the drawing room – he had paid enough for them, God knew – but this was where he felt most comfortable. It was a real man's room, with card table, billiard table, drinks cupboard and a couple of leather wing chairs. He had a small TV there too; he settled himself in the chair opposite with another large Scotch, and searched for the sports channel. He found it; baseball, they were showing, for some unfathomable reason. He zapped it in disgust.

He was being forced back on his own thoughts, thoughts he had been attempting to escape all evening. They gave him no satisfaction. He wasn't so drunk that he didn't realize that he would have been wiser not to tell the woman to her face that she was nothing but a common whore. But how else would you describe someone trying to blackmail you on the basis of favours received? It had wounded his pride, above all; he had been gullible, and now he felt a fool.

He was also very ill at ease. Hayley Cutler was bright enough and hard enough and vicious enough to make sure he paid for that remark, and he found himself speculating uneasily on what form her vengeance might take. He should never have started this; he had known he was playing with fire, but the intoxicating notion that this glamorous woman fancied him – him! – had turned his head. And that was what had flicked him on the raw; whenever he had spelled out that a permanent relationship wasn't on offer, it had become clear that, after all, it had only been about money.

And when you got right down to it, how many relationships did he have that didn't come down to money in the end? How many drinking cronies would he have, if he didn't pick up the tab? How many friends, if he didn't pay for the parties?

Even his wife. She'd never been much interested in the money as such, but did she stay with him only because she was afraid of what his money could do?

He leaned back in his leather wing-chair, swirling the Scotch morosely in the heavy crystal glass, brooding. Perhaps he fell into a light doze. Certainly, he did not hear the door, which he had left ajar, edge cautiously and silently open.

13

It had been oddly easy to break out tonight. Missy wasn't in the habit of considering Dumbo's frame of mind, but she couldn't escape the feeling that her heart hadn't been in the struggle. It seemed almost as if Dumbo actually wanted her to win, to take over. As if Dumbo didn't want her life any more.

Well, no wonder, considering the mess she had just made of it. Missy giggled as she thought about how badly Dumbo had handled the whole business, then smothered the sound with her hand clamped across her mouth like a child. She surely couldn't afford to be discovered now.

Because it had come at last, the moment for the grand finale. There had been a mistake last time – she frowned at the thought that the witch had escaped – but that didn't matter any more. There would be no mistake tonight.

When it all started, whenever that was – she somehow couldn't quite remember – she had felt like a little girl, frightened and helpless in a world where no one cared.

But it wasn't like that any more. She had got her revenge on that hostile world; she, Missy, had everyone terrified and bewildered, and had summoned up all these policemen who were chasing their tails like clumsy puppies as they tried to find her, making themselves look ridiculous because she wasn't there, was she? She had proved to herself, and to everyone else, that she wasn't helpless or vulnerable any more. They were. It was a wonderful sensation.

Missy was strong now. She had felt herself grow stronger and stronger as the days passed, and Dumbo weakened. Once or twice she had nearly managed to break out when people were around, but so far Dumbo had won, fighting determinedly until her energy levels were low at night, and she was just too exhausted to fight any more. Though last night she hadn't let Missy out at all, to her fury.

But tonight – tonight it had been different. It gave Missy a funny feeling when she thought about tonight, about Dumbo just, somehow, switching herself off. It had felt like pushing hard against a door that wasn't closed.

And now there seemed to be nothing any more in the part of her where Dumbo had always been, and she wasn't used to that; she wasn't used to being inside herself, alone. It was as if – as if Dumbo had – died.

She shuddered. That was silly talk. If Dumbo was gone, she should be pleased. After all, she'd been trying to break free of Dumbo for – how long? She didn't do months and years – they weren't a Missy thing – so she contented herself with the reflection that it had been a long, long time. Far too long. And now she had got what she wanted. Hadn't she?

In any case, she had far too much to do tonight to waste time with silly thoughts like these. She had big, serious, important things to do tonight. The other nights had only been a sort of rehearsal, learning her craft, as it were. Tonight was the night of liberation, when everything would be changed. Even if Dumbo did return and wanted her life back, she'd find that it was all different. Better – or better, anyway, for Missy. And if dumb Dumbo was too dumb to see it that way, well – tough. Bad luck. Hard cheese.

She giggled again. She was standing in the kitchen with

the blinds up and the lights off. The fog was swirling outside, and the only illumination was coming dimly from the carriage lamps on either side of the back door. In the eerie half-light she paused to consider her options.

There was, alas, no more barbecue gel, and she had used all the firelighters. You might have thought that Dumbo would have noticed that they were finished and bought in some more, but she hadn't even gone to the shops today. Missy was never quite sure how much Dumbo knew, or guessed; could she have worked out where the last lot went?

But it didn't matter what Dumbo did, because Missy was clever enough to have made another plan. She liked this plan. It was a funny plan, and a sort of – what was the phrase? – poetic justice, that was it.

'Poetic justice.' She declaimed it aloud a couple of times, giving it due weight and pomp, because they were nice words, and it was a neat idea.

She crossed the kitchen to the cupboard by the back door, opened it, and switched on the light inside. It was what he called his cellar, well-stocked, tidy and meticulously maintained with a record book that lay open with a pen beside it on the middle shelf. There were a lot of recent entries after Christmas, and she looked with mild curiosity at the list of vintages and dates.

Then she surveyed the ranks of bottles marshalled with military precision on the shelves: the vintage wines, red and white; the depleted stock of champagne; the gin, the vermouth, the liqueurs; the shelf of single malt whiskies. And on the top shelf the three bottles of the very special, the very old brandy. He had paid more than a hundred pounds for each of these bottles.

She started to laugh again, softly and secretly, as she took up the pen and neatly marked them off, with the date, just as he would have done himself. She gathered them up, then went through to the cupboard where they stored the waste paper. There was a sack of discarded Christmas wrappings; that would be a nice festive touch! She rolled some into balls and filled a carrier bag.

She only needed to lay these along the window ledges, and soak the curtains with the brandy. It would all blaze up as merrily as the Christmas pudding.

She set them on the kitchen table while she put on the hooded coat with the matches in the pocket, and inserted her bare feet into the gumboots that stood waiting beside the kitchen door. Then with the bag over her arm, and clutching the bottles to her, she slipped silently out and was immediately swallowed up in the clammy darkness outside.

'Paula! Paula!'

The child tugged at the edge of the duvet which was snuggled into a tight cocoon round the sleeping form of her sister. She coughed, sneezed, then dismally rubbed her nose. Tears were beginning to well up in her eyes. It was cold in the house now, in the middle of the night with the central heating switched off, and she shivered in her tartan cotton nightgown. There was a funny smell drifting up from downstairs, too, and she was afraid.

'Paula!' she wailed.

Dragged reluctantly from sleep, Paula uncurled from her foetal position and rolled over to peer with disfavour at her small sibling.

'Oh – Milla,' she groaned. 'Do shut up! Go away and leave me alone.'

She tried to turn over once more, but the child grabbed desperately at her arm.

'Don't go to sleep again, Paula, don't!' She was seized

by another bout of coughing, and started to cry in earnest.

'Oh – for heavens' sake!' Paula sat up, knuckling her eyes. 'Why on earth don't you go to Mum? Why pick on me?'

''Cos Mummy isn't *there*!' The wail rose higher. 'I'm coughing, and she didn't come, and I went to find her, and she isn't there, and Daddy isn't, and there's a funny smell and it's making me cough and I'm *frightened*!'

'Don't be silly,' Paula started to say, when at the same moment she caught a whiff of the offending smell and the smoke alarm in the hall began to emit its ear-piercing warning.

Paula's stomach lurched. 'It's a fire! We're on fire!' she exclaimed.

Milla, catching the note of panic in her voice, opened her mouth to scream, and Paula realized, abruptly, that she must take charge.

'Look, don't scream, OK? Honestly, it's going to be all right, Milla. Don't scream. You're a big girl, and you're going to help me. Just wake Peter, make him get up even if you have to shake him, right? Then grab your dressing gown and slippers and meet me at the top of the stairs.'

Milla hesitated. 'Where are you going?' she demanded suspiciously. 'I don't want you to go away.'

Her lip started to quiver again.

'I'm just going to see if I can find Mummy,' her sister told her with a calmness she did not feel. 'I really need you to get Peter, then we'll all go downstairs together. That will be really clever. Off you go.'

Diverted by this notion of her own importance, Milla trotted off to carry out her orders. Paula, sticking her feet in shoes and grabbing a jacket from the back of her door, shrugged it on as she hurried along the landing to her parents' bedroom, hoping against hope that there was some mistake, that her mother would be there, sound asleep, perhaps, but ready to spring reassuringly to their protection.

In her heart of hearts she knew that no one could sleep through the din which was making her ears ring, and the bedroom was, just as Milla had said, empty. Her mother's side of the bed had been slept in; the other pillow was undented, and she remembered that her father had gone off to the Golf Club.

'Mummy!' she yelled at the top of her voice, above the shrieking alarm, but there was no response. She checked her parents' bathroom but then gave up the search. She had other duties that she must perform.

Peter, bemused by his rough awakening into noise and confusion, was shuffling along from the bedroom he and Milla shared, his teddy in one hand and his dressing gown on awry, the belt trailing on the ground behind him. Milla, with her own dressing gown neatly belted, picked it up and tied it officiously round him. With Paula in control, she was almost beginning to enjoy the excitement.

Paula peered over the banisters into the well of the hall below. The light from the staircase allowed her to see that though there were no flames visible, smoke was beginning to seep furiously through the cracks around the games room and drawing-room doors. Her eyes were smarting, and in a moment the hall would be filled with the choking stuff. Milla had started coughing again; there was not a second to lose.

'Downstairs, both of you, quick as you can,' she said, trying to keep her voice steady. 'Straight to the front door. I'm right behind you.'

In fact, she reached the door as they scampered across the hall and was ready to turn the security locks which would have been too stiff for baby fingers. Then they were safe outside, in the wet, smoke-thickened air.

The fog was a lurid, livid orange with the glow of the fire, and now Paula could hear its terrifying roar. The drawing-room windows, to the left of the front door, were broken and blackened, and beyond there was a sea of flame, raging to escape the confines of the surrounding walls. As she watched, a window fell in, the glass jangling on to the floor below, and a flame shot out, like the tongue of a savage monster seeking out fresh prey. She pulled the children back with a jolt of terror.

From round the side of the house, clouds of smoke, held low by the fog, were pouring from the window of the games room. Paula knew she should fetch help, do something, but the sheer magnitude of the disaster held her mesmerized. There was a huge lump gathering in her throat.

Then she heard Milla's shout.

'Mummy! Mummy! Where were you? We were in the house, and it's on fire!'

Paula spun round. There on the lawn, some fifteen feet from the blaze and apparently oblivious to the sparks and floating sooty particles stood her mother, with a hooded coat over her night-gown and gumboots on her feet. She was standing rigid as a statue, staring into the leaping, swirling flames in their beautiful, unholy ballet. There was a strange half-smile on her face, and she did not turn at the sound of Milla's voice.

The sight of her mother should have been a relief, but despite the heat from the blaze Paula felt an icy shiver crawl up her back as she looked at her, and an ill-defined sick fear churn her stomach.

But Milla rushed to her mother, casting herself upon her with arms wide, grabbing her frantically round the waist.

'Mummy, Mummy,' she whimpered. 'I wanted you!'

Elizabeth turned her head slowly and surveyed them: Milla clinging to her, Peter hanging back with fear and bewilderment, Paula behind them, pale-faced and wary. The three livid scratches on her left cheek showed up as dark shadows in the fitful light.

Very deliberately she reached around her waist and coldly detached the small, scrabbling fingers. With unnecessary force, she pushed away the discomfited child.

'Oh, stop grabbing at me and snivelling, will you, you dismal little brat!'

Too shocked for tears, Milla stared, her hands dropping to her side. Peter, under the fierce glittering gaze that was turned upon them, shrank back in fright against Paula.

Steeled by the needs of the little ones, Paula managed to find her voice, staggering slightly as Milla, sobbing now, threw herself at her sister for comfort.

'Mum, are you – are you all right? Your face . . .' she said, then trailed into silence. With the ghastly light from the fire flickering on her shadowed features her mother looked – looked possessed, like the pantomime demon they had hissed last week.

She saw that Elizabeth was eying her with distaste – no, worse, indifference.

'Oh, I'm just dandy,' she said, in a strange, high, childish voice. 'I'm having a great time.'

This was beyond Paula's scope. She was only twelve; her own voice broke as she said, 'Mummy, we were *inside*.' She gestured to the flames as she tried to hold back her tears. 'We could have been killed, and you didn't even try to get us out.'

Slowly, terribly, her mother smiled.

'So?' she said.

For a second the shock overwhelmed Paula. But the urgent little bodies squirming against her in panic were a stronger imperative; she swallowed hard, then bent to clutch them to her so tightly that it was painful, though neither complained.

'Mummy's ill,' she whispered to them. 'Mummy's really sick. We have to deal with this ourselves. I've got to get the fire brigade —'

But as she spoke she heard running footsteps and a young policeman appeared. It was Tom Compton; he was seriously out of breath, and he had lost his cap.

'Oh my God,' he gasped. 'I thought I smelled smoke.'

He snatched his radio from his belt and bellowed into it, 'Fire! Everything you've got to the Lodge – the McEvoy house in the main street.'

Still with the receiver in his hands, chattering out staccato radio commands, he demanded urgently, 'Anyone still inside?'

Elizabeth did not speak or move, but Paula shook her head. 'No,' she said. 'Dad's bed hadn't been slept in. He'll still be at the Club.'

Within seconds there were half a dozen police officers at the scene, and the children were being escorted away, out of the garden. Elizabeth suffered herself to be pulled back but she said nothing at all in response to the barrage of anxious questions, only turning her head so that she could still watch the fire.

Paula tugged at Compton's sleeve. 'She's – she's ill. My mother's ill. I don't know what's wrong with her. I had to get the kids out of the house myself, and she was just standing there, watching the flames, and we were inside.'

The two little ones had been safely removed; she found now that tears were pouring in a torrent down her face.

The young man put his arm round her shoulders awkwardly. 'Don't cry. You've been a real star – done a terrific job. And don't worry about your mum. It'll be shock. Everyone's funny with shock; we see a lot of it. Now look, here's Annie coming to take you next door. You go with her and leave the rest to us. The fire engines will be here any minute.'

Paula had turned obediently to go with the policewoman when Compton called after her, 'You said your Dad was at the Club. Would that be the Golf Club?'

She nodded, shivering and unable to speak now as the tears mastered her, and Annie took off her jacket to hug it round the youngster's shoulders as she led her away.

Compton exchanged a meaningful look with the sergeant who had now appeared.

'At three in the morning?' the older man said. 'Hardly likely the Golf Club's still open at this hour.'

'Won't be the first time Mr McEvoy's gone AWOL in the middle of the night, sarge, not by what they say in the village,' said Compton, parading his local knowledge. 'It'll be a nasty surprise for him when he comes home this time.'

Then the fire engines began arriving, five of them, and police from every quarter of the village. The spectators were starting to gather too, and Compton went off to help bring order to the crowd while the garden filled with lights, hoses and the purposeful professionals who controlled them.

'Looking for me?' the sergeant said to the constable who had taken Elizabeth away, and was now peering anxiously about him in the smoky, foggy confusion. He greeted a senior officer with relief.

'Sir. Bit of a funny thing about the lady there. She's not saying a word, and I can't budge her from the fence there where she's watching the fire. Maybe it's just shock, but it still doesn't seem natural, if you know what I mean. And she's reeking of brandy, though she's not really acting drunk. She looks as if she's been in a fight, or something too; I've seen enough scratched faces in my time to recognize nail marks when I see them. And that's hardly what you'd expect with a lady like her.'

The sergeant looked across the chaos of machines and men to where Elizabeth stood, a little apart, her face impassive apart from that faint, lingering half-smile. He raised his brows.

'Well, well, well. I wonder. Be a bit of a feather in our caps if we cracked this before the clever dicks even got here, wouldn't it?'

'Go and ask her if she'd be prepared to go and sit in a police car – nicely, mind you – charm school stuff – and see there are two of you with her at all times. Grab one of the girls. Then just ask her some gentle questions, and if she starts to say anything, give her her rights quick, in case some smart lawyer comes along later. She's not under arrest, of course. We're just asking her to be a public-spirited citizen and help us along with our enquiries.

'OK? You've heard of finesse, have you, lad? Well, go ahead and use it.'

So when Rod Vezey, with Moon and Smethurst, arrived, it was to be told that Piers McEvoy was out on the town, the children were being looked after by neighbours, and Elizabeth was sitting in a police car, singing like a canary to two frantic officers, one male and one female, both wishing they had done more about learning speedwriting.

He was not pleased. There were so many rules hedging you about nowadays; put a foot wrong, and that was your conviction out of the window. He strode to the car door, flung it open, and said to the startled pair inside, 'Out. Now.'

They hastened to comply. Elizabeth did not move, still sitting unperturbed in the back seat with a trace of that satisfied smile still turning up the corners of her mouth and her hands folded demurely in her lap.

'Mrs McEvoy,' he said.

She looked at him coolly out of the corner of her eye, without bothering to turn her head.

He tried again. 'Mrs McEvoy, we would like to take you over to police headquarters. Would you like us to try to trace your husband, so that he knows where you are?'

She turned her head at that. 'Oh, I really wouldn't bother to do that, if I were you.'

'Very well. Would you be good enough to come with us then, Mrs McEvoy? I know you've been talking to the officers here, but there are a few things I would like to ask you, and it would be easier for you to make a statement at headquarters.'

She looked full at him now, and the smile grew broader. Her eyes danced like those of a little girl.

'Oh, inspector, of course I will. Have I got something to tell you that will make your eyes pop! But call me Missy, won't you?'

It was six o'clock in the morning when, with the fire almost out, one of the firemen – also a local man – was having a break and a cigarette with his friend Tom Compton. It had been a heavy night; both men were weary. The fog was starting to lift a bit now, though it was still dark, and the full scale of the damage would not emerge until the ashes were cooler and daylight came.

'Dreadful, isn't it?' the fireman said. 'It was a beautiful house; McEvoy'll do his nut, won't he?'

The story of the man's imminent embarrassment was too good for Compton to keep to himself, and he told it with relish.

His friend was curious. 'Out, is he?' he said. 'Well, it has to be somewhere local. That car of his – BMW, nice machine – is sitting in the garage; we were dousing it

264

with foam a while back, to make sure it didn't go up as well.'

Compton tapped the side of his nose with his finger. 'That Mrs Cutler, by what I've heard. She's a bit of all right, as they say, and only just down the road there.'

The other man looked startled. 'The American lady? Blonde hair, bit of an armful? I saw her hours ago, standing there in the crowd. If he was round there, it's funny he hasn't come sneaking back before now.'

'Probably waiting until the fuss dies down,' said Compton, but it was an automatic response; they were both uneasy. 'You don't think —'

'Surely not,' the fireman said, then, 'But I think I might have a word with my chief, just in case. It's probably OK, but still . . .'

His anxiety prompted him to break into a run, his heavy boots squelching in the puddles of water and foam as he hurried across to where the fire chief stood beside his little red car supervizing the scaling-down of the operation.

Tom Compton looked after him, easing the cap on his head which suddenly seemed to have become too tight. He stared into the smoking cavities which had once been windows and now showed a chaos of fallen beams and debris.

If anyone was inside there, a minute saved now was hardly going to matter, one way or the other.

14

Margaret Moon had been able to sleep only fitfully that night. She had sat downstairs with the Brancombes till almost midnight, speculating, with Jean mainly, about poor Missy, her sad past and her possible present state. Ted had fallen asleep in his chair by then, and eventually Margaret insisted they all went to bed. A working farmer had to be on the go early, and there was no saying how late Robert might be.

Jean had protested that she wouldn't be able to sleep a wink, but during her own wakeful spells Margaret could hear through the wall her delicate and ladylike snores providing a soprano counterpoint to Ted's basso profundo.

Perhaps it was the painkiller she was still taking, but when she did drop into sleep it was to suffer vivid, confused and anxious dreams from which she woke with relief. She was deeply troubled by her failure to reach this woman who had so needed her help; it was difficult not to blame herself for persisting so long in the dismissive attitude that creature comforts made for an untroubled soul.

She heard the farm noises: the sheep restless in the fields, a cow lowing in the byre. She heard owls, and the reassuring tread of the young policeman as he passed on his round underneath their windows. But the farm lay at the farther end of the village; she did not hear the sirens of police cars or fire engines, and was still ignorant of the night's disturbances when the crunch on the gravel of the police car drawing up, and her brother's carefully-lowered voice thanking the driver jerked her once again into wakefulness. She looked at her watch; it was six o'clock.

Pyewacket eyed her askance from his comfortable nest in the duvet but did not stir as she got up and, opening her bedroom door as quietly as she could, slipped downstairs. There was no way she was going to let Robert sneak off to bed and sleep for hours without telling her what had kept him at police headquarters for such an unconscionable length of time.

When he came in through the back door to the kitchen, she thought suddenly, with a pang, that he looked not only worn out, but old. He was four years older than she, but she was accustomed to thinking of them both as being, like Miss Jean Brodie, in their prime. Tonight his appearance (and no doubt hers too, if she were unwise enough to search out a mirror) endorsed that lady's later discovery, that this prime too swiftly passes.

When he saw her he raised his eyebrows and surveyed her with his characteristic quizzical gaze over the top of his spectacles.

'I couldn't sleep,' she said. 'Look, you're obviously desperate to get to bed, but just tell me if you've found out who Missy is, and what's been happening. I couldn't stand the thought of having to wait until you woke up again.'

'What's been happening?' he said, rubbing his hand tiredly across his face so that it rasped on the greying stubble on his chin. 'What hasn't been happening!'

He collapsed on to a chair by the big pine table in the centre of the kitchen.

'Actually, I'm not ready to sleep yet. It's all still going round and round in my head. Make me a cup of tea and I'll talk to you until I feel I'll be able to fall into bed and crash out.'

She had already lifted one of the covers on the Raeburn and shunted the heavy kettle which always stood on the surface on to the plate to heat, where it began singing almost at once. She set out the big brown teapot, mugs, milk and sugar.

'OK. Start.'

'Start? I don't know where to start.'

'Missy,' Margaret said without hesitation. 'Have you found poor Missy?'

'Oh, we've found her. We've found her because she tried to burn down her own house, with her kids inside it. She very nearly succeeded, and now she's flipped completely. Elizabeth McEvoy.'

'What!' In her shock, Margaret tipped the boiling water she was attempting to pour into the teapot all over the surface, and was forced to leap back before it spilled over the edge and scalded her slippered feet. 'Lizzie McEvoy tried to kill her children? I can't believe it!'

'Oh, not as deliberately as that. As far as I can make out, she just wanted to set the house on fire, and the children being asleep inside was purely incidental. Most likely she'd forgotten all about them.

'She's not Lizzie, you see, she's Missy, and she has no feelings of affection or responsibility or even relationship to Lizzie's children. If it comes to that, I doubt if she has feelings of any kind.

'But if you could see your way to concentrating on the job in hand and coordinating the kettle and the pot, I would certainly appreciate my tea.'

'Sorry,' Margaret said mechanically, resuming the task

which shock had interrupted. 'I feel – gobsmacked, I think is the *mot juste* But I take it there's no doubt?'

'No possible doubt whatever. She's been at headquarters now for a couple of hours, refusing flatly to see doctors or lawyers, and answering any questions we care to put to her. She seems to be revelling in the attention.'

'Does she know what she's saying?'

Robert blew vulgarly on his tea to cool it. 'Who knows? At one level, yes certainly. It's both internally and externally consistent. But she clearly has no sense at all of the enormity of her confession. She is a stranger to remorse, and even the attack on you is justified by the calm explanation that she felt threatened, as if once we grasped that point we would understand.

'She produced the matches from her pocket to show us; she told us that tonight she had to use McEvoy's best brandy because there were no firelighters. She seemed faintly aggrieved that they hadn't been provided.'

'But if she was so afraid that I would realize who she was that she tried to kill me, why is she telling you all this now?'

'As far as you can adduce a rationale, it would be that tonight was her grand finale, the thing she had been rehearsing for all along. That's what she's saying now, though I don't myself think it's as straightforward as that. Whether she admits it or not, she was actually responding to other factors too. She professes to despise Dumbo, but burning down the Boltons' garage suggested itself because Suzanne had upset Lizzie. And as far as I can make out, Hayley Cutler might have been in trouble as well, only Milla had a cold the night before last and Lizzie stayed up and kept Missy in her cage.

'But there's no doubt that Piers was the most important target. It would have ruined everything if we'd caught her before she had a chance to destroy his house. It's not how she put it, of course, but clearly what she feels is that it has been an instrument of oppression for Lizzie as well as a sort of temple he has set up to his personality.'

'Does she realize she's going to end up in prison – or confined, anyway?'

'Ah, I'm not sure that she has really worked that out. Looking ahead is not in general her strong point, and she's just been taking enormous pleasure in explaining to us how clever she has been to outwit us all. I daresay she might think vaguely that if things get difficult she'll be able to retreat again and leave Lizzie to carry the can.'

'And will she?'

Robert shrugged. 'You tell me. Psychology —'

'Is not an exact science,' Margaret finished for him. 'I know. But what a dreadful, tragic business.

'Did you find out anything about the rest of her childhood – what happened after the deaths?'

Robert shrugged. 'Not a lot, I think is the answer. She was well-fed, clothed, expensively educated – had everything she could possibly want, except the one thing she needed so desperately: parental love and attention. Then that was followed by a loveless marriage, and her father's death not long after.

'Missy's our only source, of course, so it's not totally reliable, but it seems the only affection she had was from McEvoy's mother. She was formidable but kind, I think, and there's no doubt that it was after her death that everything started spinning out of control.'

'So there are no grandparents. Those poor children; whatever is to become of them? McEvoy isn't much of a father, by all accounts.'

'He's an absentee father at the moment. He's off some-where out on the tiles, apparently: no one knows quite where. I gather it isn't the first time he's been "at the Club" or "at a business meeting" until the small hours.'

They sat on sipping their tea while Robert told Margaret the rest of the story, including Minnie Groak's share in the responsibility for tonight's disaster.

'It's the problem of disproportion, isn't it?' Margaret said thoughtfully. 'Strange how often some quite minor thing brings the most hideous consequences in its wake.'

' "The little things are infinitely the most important," if you remember your Holmes,' Robert quoted, yawned suddenly, and rose.

'I'm off to bed. Wake me when Vezey phones. I'm no good to him when it comes to pronouncing on Missy's state of mind; I've been too closely involved in the investigation, so he'll be getting in a couple of others to regularize the position, now he's got the information he wants. It should take them most of the morning to get it all tied up and declare that she's unfit to plead. There's certainly no doubt in my mind; spectacular, text-book stuff.

'So I shall expect to be able to sleep through to the afternoon. It's your job to convince Jean that I won't expire from starvation if I miss breakfast and lunch.'

'I'll protect you,' Margaret promised. 'Have a good sleep.'

She washed up his mug then refilled her own and sat down in the old Windsor chair next to the stove, tucking in one of Jean's patchwork cushions at her back.

She realized, with a start, that she had forgotten that today was Sunday, and New Year's Eve. She had reluctantly agreed to cancel the early Eucharist and allowed the diocese to find someone who could take the morning service. But the Watchnight Service was different. She was determined to celebrate that, in the religious sense of the word, if she had to be silent for a week afterwards.

But for the moment, all she could usefully do was pray. She must pray for the children, pray for their father who would now, surely, find a new way of life. And she must try to pray for that strange hybrid, Missy-Lizzie. It seemed foolishly fanciful, but whenever she tried to hold her – them – in prayer, all she could sense was a spiritual black hole, sucking into itself all hope, all light, all love.

Margaret was still wrestling with the problem when the telephone rang. It was twenty-five past seven.

Missy had been quite happy to go to the police station. She had never been inside one before, and her eyes were bright with interest as they escorted her into the purpose-built multi-storey divisional headquarters.

Inside, it was well lit with concealed neon lighting and pale grey walls, a lot of smartly-varnished wood and heavy glass. She had stood with the others as they waited by the counter in the foyer, reading with close attention the warning posters about drugs and security and road safety, but viewing with considerable disapproval the unkempt-looking man sitting on one of the benches opposite. He did not seem to be entirely sober, and he had a black eye.

'He *smells*!' Missy said indignantly in her high, clear, carrying voice to the shirt-sleeved policewoman behind the desk, who winced at this childish candour and spoke hastily to Vezey who, with Moon and Smethurst faithfully at his heels, had escorted her here.

'Interview room five, sir; that's vacant now. It might be best if you were to take her through right away.'

The interview room was small, bare and grey, an environment which should have been neutral but which by the absence of moveable objects suggested at the very least the expectation of violence. The disinfectant they used was pungent, but did not altogether mask another, grosser smell.

The intrusive eye of a camera poked into the room from one corner of the ceiling, and in the middle was a table joined to the wall and two chairs on each side which were bolted to the floor.

Missy sat down on the farther side, gesturing graciously to the men that they might be seated. Vezey and Moon took their places opposite her; the other man leaned against the wall by the door.

They explained to her about the recorder and she eyed it curiously but did not object, sitting tranquilly enough while they set it up with the appropriate identification, and asked her the first question.

She had decided privately that it would be more fun if they played it like a game. She remembered, dimly, a game she had played a long time ago which was about asking questions, though the details were fuzzy now in her head.

So she had to make up her own rules. If they asked her something, she would tell the truth, but they had to think of the questions to ask. That would be fair, wouldn't it? They couldn't expect her to do it all for them. And her challenge would be to see if she could manage, without cheating, to save up her big surprise for the end.

They were all very nice and polite, though one of them was impatient. She was a little bit wary of him; she thought he might get angry, and she didn't like people who got angry and shouted. She really hated people who got angry and shouted. Like horrible Piers.

But for the moment, it was fine. They listened to her, and even seemed to understand when she explained how difficult it had been, and how clever and careful she had needed to be.

They didn't laugh much, though, even when she did – she had laughed a lot when they asked her about the scratches on her face – and she decided they were just a bit stuffy.

They liked the matches when she brought them out of her pocket, though, and made her put them in a plastic bag. They hadn't asked about the matches, but that was a little extra she gave them, because they had played so nicely.

At last, one of the men got up to go. He was the older man with spectacles; she liked him. He had asked her lots of interesting questions about herself and about Dumbo and seemed to listen properly to the answers. She had never had the chance to talk to anyone about the things she thought and the feelings she had, and she was sorry to see him go.

Then a little later, someone came in and whispered something to the other man, the impatient one, who said a very rude word and rushed out. And someone else brought her and the young man who was left a cup of tea.

But they still hadn't asked about her surprise. She giggled out loud. Perhaps she would have to tell them about it herself, after all.

Piers McEvoy's body was lying on the rug in front of what had been the hearth. The ceiling of the bedroom above had collapsed as the fire burned through the ends of the joists and the bedstead of antique brass – Paula's bed – had fallen through, landing oddly in protection of the body like a parody of an ancient flat tombstone.

It was still dark. The interior, once they got the beam of the arc lights trained through the gaping window cavity, was a hell of fallen beams, plaster and rubble. But they were lucky in that Piers's leather chair had burned through to its framework, and a probing torch almost immediately picked out beneath it the sole of a foot clad in a heavy brogue. They were lucky, too, that the body beneath its curious canopy was not going to prove charred beyond immediate recognition.

The sergeant was less sure how lucky he was going to feel once Vezey got there. He had, after all, informed the man authoritatively that McEvoy was out on an amorous adventure when all his daughter had said was that he was at a club which everyone knew closed hours before. If anyone could prove the man was alive – drunk, perhaps, and then overcome by smoke – while they stood outside and made no attempt to get him out, he could kiss his police pension goodbye.

Vezey was certainly in a towering rage when he arrived, a rage which was the more alarming for being tautly controlled. His face was white, his jaw rigid, and a muscle was twitching in his cheek, but he said absolutely nothing in response to the sergeant's anxious explanations, shouldering him aside to swing over the window sill on to the sodden embers that formed a thick spongy layer on the floor of the ravaged room.

'Be careful, sir,' the hovering fire chief cautioned. 'These beams are smouldering still, and the fog's lifting; if we get a gust of wind they could go up again in a moment.'

Vezey gave no sign of having heard him. Ducking under one beam and stepping over the end of another he reached the back of the skeletal chair. The bed, its water-saturated mattress and covers scorched but not burned away, concealed most of the body from him, but by crouching and craning his neck and flicking on his powerful torch he gained a foreshortened view from the feet in their brogues, up the scorched cavalry twill trousers as far as the edge of the cashmere sports jacket.

The fingers of the right hand, the arm and the part of the shoulder protruding from below the hanging covers on one side, had not escaped the fire, and he averted his eyes. Years of criminal investigation had cured him of excessive squeamishness, but the detail was the job of the scene-of-crime unit and he never chose to dwell needlessly upon horrors. He had registered the stench of charred flesh when he came in, but the olfactory characteristic which means that any smell is blunted after a few minutes was a mercy for which he had frequently been grateful.

From what he could tell in this position, it looked as if McEvoy was lying on his front, his right arm at least in a position which suggested that he had fallen forward on to his face.

Squatting back on his haunches, Vezey frowned. He lowered his torch for a moment; the waiting shadows dipped and gathered once more in the gruesome cavern beneath the bedstead.

The instinctive feel for something not quite right, which is the shrewd detective's greatest talent, gripped him now as he scanned again such details as he could see without disturbing anything.

In policework it was not uncommon to have to deal with the victims of fire. Often they were drunk; sometimes they were drunk and incapable, and these you found still sitting in the chair where the fatal stupor had transfixed them. If they were sober enough to move at all, there would be obvious signs of some attempt at escape, like poor Tom so pathetically trapped by the unyielding garage doors. Even under the effects of extremely toxic fumes, Margaret Moon had made it to the threshold of her bedroom.

But not McEvoy. McEvoy, it seemed, had stood up and immediately pitched forward on to the hearthrug. That was strange.

He forgot his anger now in concentration. The itch to understand all mysteries might, without charity, be as nothing, but it was most surely the core of his professional being. That, rather than a grand and abstract passion for justice – whatever that might be – was why the abuse, the violence and the squalor did not send him hunting for a desk job. This was what it was all about.

Oblivious to the watchful fire chief and the sergeant, still murmuring nervously behind him, he leaned forward as far as he could. Beneath the man's body was a Persian rug – a Qashgai, beautiful and valuable – burned around the edges, blackened and stained with water. It was hard to tell in this unreliable light, but surely that deeper stain, which seemed to have seeped out round the fallen body, was neither water nor soot?

Ignoring the fire chief's protests, he climbed round to the other side, penetrating deeper into the ruins of the study. He was conscious of the heat still lingering there; automatically he loosened the collar of his shirt. But he gained the vantage point he wanted at the farther end of the bed.

It was darker here, of course, away from the lights directed in at the window. But when he pointed his torch under the head of the bed, he saw what he was looking for.

Piers McEvoy's head was turned to one side, his left hand and arm flung up in reflection of the position of his right. His face was drained of colour, greyish-pale, and the upper part of his jacket, his shirt and his tie were so saturated with blood that there was no longer any pattern to be seen. From the side of his neck protruded a skewer; a long, thick barbecue skewer with a handle like a Spanish sword's at the end.

Robert Moon was waiting at headquarters when Rod Vezey arrived back. He had believed he felt terrible when he retired to bed two hours ago; now he realized that, compared to his state at the moment, he had been feeling terrific.

They had shown him to Vezey's office and given him a cup of coffee; in his own interests, he was trying very hard not to drop off to sleep again when the door was flung open and Vezey strode in.

'This had better be good,' Robert said with quiet menace, but Vezey hardly heard him.

'She's killed him,' he said savagely. 'She's run a barbecue skewer through his neck and she's killed him, and she's talked to us for hours without even mentioning it.'

'Ah. That's – unfortunate.'

'Unfortunate!' Vezey exploded. 'Is that all you can say – *unfortunate?*' Then he stopped.

'Sorry,' he said tiredly. 'I know that was deliberate understatement. I didn't mean to take it out on you. I'm just raging with frustration at the incompetence of the moron at the other end who didn't take any steps to investigate where McEvoy really was, and the moron at this end who is supposed to be leading the enquiry and failed even to elicit the fact that a murder had taken place.'

'But she was pouring her heart out, I thought. How come she didn't even mention it? And a skewer; something long enough so that there wouldn't be blood on her hands to give her away. Is it all a front, and she's actually not half as loopy as she seems?'

'The Hamlet syndrome, only mad north north-west, you mean? No, I don't think so. In my opinion she couldn't tell a hawk from a handsaw if one of them pecked her on the leg.

'What does strike me, though, is that what she was doing was answering questions, not volunteering information. She responded very fully to what we asked her, but not once did she instigate a topic. And we simply didn't ask the question.'

'Well, we're going to ask it right now. Come on, I'm sorry to have dug you out of bed, but I'm keen to continue with the same social dynamics as before – that's the jargon, isn't it?'

When they reached the interview room once more, Smethurst slipped out to talk to them. The tiles on her roof, he explained graphically if inelegantly, had started slipping. She had become restless during their absence, talking about games and surprises, and looking for someone who wasn't there, which had distressed her. He had sent for a policewoman who was with her at the moment; she slipped discreetly away when they went in.

Missy was looking different now; the bright eyes had become opaque, the jaunty air replaced by a brittle nervosity. She was tired, naturally, and on the waxy pallor of her skin the crusted scars stood out.

Forestalling Vezey, Moon asked her gently about Piers, and for a moment the eyes danced again, she clapped her hands and, shockingly, laughed.

'Oh, well done! That was my surprise, and I won, because you didn't guess, did you? He was in the games room, wasn't he?'

Vezey nodded, unable to speak for the revulsion that choked him as he remembered the body, the charring, the pool of blood.

She was delighted to tell them that she had known Piers was at home; she had set fire to the house, and killed him. But she denied, with increasing vehemence and indignation, all knowledge of the skewer.

He had died in the fire, she told them again. She had waited till he came home, then she had locked him in and killed him. 'Just like that stupid old man,' she said more than once.

'And he just sat there while you broke the window and lit the curtains,' Vezey sneered. 'Why would he do that?'

She stared as if the idea had not occurred to her, then faltered. 'I – I don't know why. Because he was drunk, I expect. I didn't look, but I listened and there wasn't a sound.'

'Because he was dead.' He pressed home his advantage. 'You knew he was dead, because you had killed him before. With a skewer.'

'No! No! What skewer? Why do you keep saying that? You're trying to upset me. I killed him, I killed him in the fire, because if he was dead Dumbo couldn't just go on the same way. But there wasn't any skewer. I don't know what you mean.'

'So are you saying that it wasn't you? That somebody else killed him?'

'No! No! I did it, and you shan't say I didn't!'

The voice was becoming higher, louder, hysterical, and she began beating her small fists on the table.

Moon's hand, vice-like, gripped Vezey's in warning before he could speak again.

'Now don't worry, Missy. We'll get all this sorted out. You say you don't know anything about a skewer. Could Lizzie have done it, do you think, to help you?'

The soothing voice had an effect and she became calmer, though her expression was still hostile. 'Dumbo?' she said, a world of contempt in her voice.

'Would you have seen her if she did?'

'Well, of course I would. She can't see what I do, but I can see her any time I like. Dumbo couldn't skewer a fish finger if it squeaked. I'm the one who does exciting things. You shan't say she did it, you shan't!'

'Missy,' Moon said, 'could we – would you let us speak to Dumbo?'

At his side he felt Vezey draw in his breath. Missy stared at him for a moment, then, 'Oh, why not?' she said dully. 'I don't like this, anyway. She's welcome.'

The tension in her body suddenly seemed to disappear, as if a puppet-master had let go of the strings. She sagged in the chair and closed her eyes.

Moon found that he too was holding his breath. A long, long silence followed.

Suddenly her eyes flew open, wide and blank. 'She's not there,' she said in a strange flat voice. 'She's not there. Dumbo's not there. She's dead, she's dead.'

And then she began to scream, scream upon endless scream.

Once the paramedics had gone, they walked back, shaken, towards Vezey's office.

'And what do we make of that?' Vezey demanded despairingly. 'I'm out of my depth here. Why would she be desperate to take the credit, as she sees it, for murdering him, but deny the skewer?

'Perhaps it's a social thing. Perhaps People Like Us don't skewer their husbands, they just kipper them. That class has all sorts of taboos that normal people couldn't begin to understand.'

Moon looked at him shrewdly. 'I would have thought you would be as likely as anyone to know what they were, Rod?'

Vezey coloured, then said defensively, 'I've spent my life forgetting everything of that sort that my mother tried to instil into me. But never mind that – it was only a throw-away remark. Where do we go from here?'

'Back to the drawing board?'

Vezey looked at him aghast. 'You're not seriously suggesting she – they – didn't do it?'

Moon shrugged. 'You heard her. She wanted us to think she'd killed him – though it seems to me, from her account, that if he'd been alive he could easily have escaped – and was outraged at the suggestion that she hadn't. She was totally certain that Dumbo hadn't done it either. Why should she lie?'

'How the hell would I know? I'm just a humble copper. You're the shrink – you tell me! But it seems a touch unlikely that we've found the person behind all this – one death, one attempted murder, three fires – and now there's suddenly some other homicidal maniac who just happens to be passing by pure coincidence and nips in and does this, presumably just to put Missy's nose out of joint. Do me a favour!'

They had reached Vezey's office by this time. Moon said, 'Would I be very wide of the mark if I suggested that you are what is fashionably termed "in denial"; that you are simply refusing to entertain the thought that you are at the beginning of a new investigation, and not at the successful conclusion of the old one?'

Vezey had sat down at his desk.

'Dear God!' he said, almost reverently. 'Please not. Please, please not!' and bending forward he banged his head on the blotter in front of him.

15

As a small gesture towards his bodily needs, Rod Vezey went down to the canteen in the basement of the police building and had breakfast.

He had sent both Moon and Smethurst away. Robert had gone thankfully, without even a token protest, but he had needed to be much more forceful with his junior officer.

'You're no use to me when you're clapped out, Dave,' he said brutally. 'You're infinitely replaceable, you know, and you'll see things a lot straighter when you've had a few hours' sleep.'

He did not encourage friendships with his sergeants, but he worked more often with Dave than the others, and they worked together well: both taciturn men, who were blunt if they must speak.

Now Dave said, 'And doesn't the same apply to you, guv?'

'Cheeky sod,' Vezey said without heat. 'The difference is, you're replaceable and I'm not. Go to bed.'

But he was aware of the light-headedness of extreme tiredness as he shovelled down the greasy, undercooked bacon, the frizzled egg and the baked beans without actually tasting them. He stared ahead unseeing as he ate, his mind racing over this latest problem.

He must at least make his own mind up about what he

thought before he reported to his super later today. If it was still unresolved, Our 'Enery would get twitchy about perceived importance as denoted by rank and insist that one of the divisional chief inspectors took over the running of the investigation. Reasonably enough, to be fair, but if it was the one he was afraid it would be, it would make life distinctly uncomfortable. Much easier just to say that their murderer was even now in a secure ward under serious sedation.

Perhaps she was. He accepted Robert's logic, though whether you could usefully apply logic to Elizabeth McEvoy's thought processes was another question altogether. He was less convinced than Robert appeared to be that Missy knew everything done by Dumbo. He was no expert, but it seemed conceivable that Missy might believe she did, while Dumbo hid somewhere in the thickets of their psyche and refused to come out to answer awkward questions.

By now the SOCOs should be coming up with some hard evidence. If he drove across there it would be a two-birds-with-one-stone job. He would find out sooner what they had to tell him, and he would be out of reach of any superior officer until he was in possession of a few more of the facts.

Vezey opened the window as he drove, despite the chilly drizzle that blew in. He had cleared up after too many accidents caused by people who believed they could function without sleep, including one of his own colleagues, now wheelchair-bound, who would infinitely have preferred that the crash had killed him.

There were still a lot of police vehicles at the scene, as well as the usual crowd of gawpers and a couple of newspaper stringers hanging about. They hadn't put out a statement yet; they couldn't hold off much longer, but since that would inevitably bring the whole of Fleet Street down on them, the more stalling they could do the better. He strode past them with a nod to the constables on guard, ignoring shouted pleas for information.

Men were still working in the study, where debris had been carted away and McEvoy's body was now lying exposed. They directed him round to the back of the house when he asked for the man in charge.

The back of the house – kitchen, dining room and bedrooms above – was not seriously damaged by the fire. One or two windows had cracked with the heat and there was the inevitable smoke damage, but in contrast to the devastation elsewhere, the normality was somehow macabre: the dishwasher, waiting to be emptied, the table providently set for a meal which would never now take place. The only incongruity was a rickety, old-fashioned typewriter which was sitting in an open, dusty black plastic bag beside the espresso coffee machine.

Nolan, the officer in charge, was a big man run to seed, with fleshy jowls and a soft paunch sagging over his waistband. He had thinning black hair draped hopefully across a bald patch, and plump hands. Vezey found him personally repellent, but held him in enormous professional respect. He was famous for what he called his 'two-minute job'; a precise analysis of the features of a case most likely to repay immediate attention.

With him was the police pathologist, a Scot with fair hair and baby-blue eyes veiled by gold-rimmed spectacles. He had a reassuring bedside manner – wasted on his clientele – and the shrewdness of his judgement and astringency of his tongue belied his mild and youthful appearance.

He found the pair sitting drinking coffee at the kitchen table in a parody of domesticity. Vezey, with a mixture of distaste and impatience, would not join them.

'The two-minute job? Right.' Nolan clasped his pudgy hands, flexed his fingers till they cracked, and considered.

'First thing – position of the deceased. No attempt at escape. You noticed that?' as Vezey nodded. 'OK. Next thing, the weapon. No problem about provenance – seven others identical on that rack over there.'

Vezey followed his pointing finger. Attached to the kitchen wall was a decorative rack made of wrought iron with brass trim, and across it, in fitted spaces, were laid the barbecue skewers with their Spanish-style hilts. One space was eloquently empty and the rack showed the metallic traces of fingerprint powder.

'You can have a look at one if you like. They're all the same – sturdy, well-made, lethal. No problem about getting purchase for the thrust.

'No fingerprints on the skewer that was used, though. Smudges which we haven't analysed yet, but Chummy definitely wore gloves.'

'What?' Vezey, who had taken down one of the skewers and was fingering it thoughtfully, spun round.

Nolan cocked an eye. 'Touched a nerve, have we?'

Missy had no gloves with her. And there had been no glove smudges on the matchbox.

'What about the brandy bottles she used to start the fire?'

'Oho, we *are* well-informed, aren't we? Spoiled one of my little surprises, that has. They're covered with prints, though we haven't had time to check whose.'

Vezey knew whose they would prove to be. And could he really believe that she was organized enough to use gloves for murdering her husband, then conceal them somewhere before carrying on bare-handed with the bottles and the box of matches? It seemed unlikely. More than unlikely.

'There are dozens of unidentified prints everywhere,'

Nolan went on. 'You'd expect that. But the handle of the door to the den, or whatever they like to call it, has smudges uppermost. Although, interestingly, that door was locked and the key shows fingerprints.'

'OK. What else?'

'The body itself. I'll let Hoots Mon! here tell you himself. Take it away, Jock!'

With the infinitely patient smile of the Scot who has heard that joke a hundred times before and found it minimally amusing the first time, the pathologist outlined his findings.

He was used to a lay audience, and his explanation was commendably clear and simple. The skewer, passing in front of the vertebrae which might have deflected it and behind the windpipe, had penetrated the carotid artery. Bleeding would be instantaneous and profuse. The immediate loss of blood to the brain would produce confusion and loss of control of the limbs, and death would follow in around three minutes.

'He must, I would say, have been asleep – or drunk, maybe, though I've not had time to check – because there's no sign of struggle or alarm. He'd hardly know a thing about it. A sudden jab, a moment's panic as he clutched at his throat – there are signs of blood on the charred right hand – and then struggled to his feet. Hands instinctively forward as he felt himself falling. After that – oblivion. I will say I can think of nastier ways to go. Quite a lot of them, truth to tell.' The blue eyes gleamed ghoulishly. 'But I don't expect you'll be wanting me to tell you about those.'

'No,' Vezey agreed absently, thinking it through. 'I suppose if you planned to kill someone it's a pretty effective way to do it.'

'Ah!' A finger was wagged in caution. 'Not necessarily.

It could be, but on the other hand you could put a spike through someone's throat and miss all the vital organs quite easily. You could hit the backbone, without doing fatal damage. I'm not saying your victim would enjoy it, right enough, but he'd still be in a state to come out fighting.'

'Right.' Vezey digested that. 'So you reckon this was just a lucky thrust?'

'Lucky for some, you could say. Yes, unless you think the perpetrator was likely to know precisely the right spot to hit.'

'So let me recap. You're saying it was either someone who was so inexpert they didn't know it was difficult, or someone who was so expert they knew precisely? Thanks, doc, you're a great help.'

'My pleasure. And hoots, mon!, as we don't say in Scotland.'

Vezey had made his mind up by the time he got back to his car. The fingerprints clinched it; he didn't believe that the woman he had been dealing with last night would – in whatever manifestation – be capable of planning this pointless deception. So he must, after all, cast the net wider. There were the other women he must question; Suzanne Bolton, with her nurse's knowledge of anatomy, came to mind. And they must question the people who had been at the Golf Club; someone there must, apart from his murderer, have been the last to see Piers McEvoy alive.

He drove away quickly to evade the group of reporters. It had grown; word was obviously getting about, and a camera flashed in his face before he could turn aside. He gave his orders over the radio as he drove. There were plenty of officers he could deploy, mercifully, and he could have everything well in hand by mid-morning.

*   *   *

290

Ted and Jean Brancombe had gone off to church, but Margaret had declined to go with them. She felt, she told them, obliged to stay in case there should be another summons for her now-slumbering brother, who could sleep through an earthquake let alone a ringing phone, but in fact she was still feeling far from robust and dealing with well-meant enquiries and sympathy would deplete the strength she felt she might need to cope with other demands as the day's events unfolded.

She was in the sitting room trying hard to focus her mind on the morning epistle with Pyewacket dozing on her knee when the doorbell rang. He gave her a death stare as she unceremoniously tipped him on to the hearth rug and went to answer it.

Andy Cutler, of course, she recognized immediately. The girl beside him, a thin wiry child in her early teens, wore the surly expression the young adopt when they are deeply uncertain, and she was pulling the dark grey jersey, which all but covered her micro-skirt, down over her hands, thrusting her thumbs through the holes they had worn in the seams. The heavy mascara on her eyes was smudged, as if she had been crying.

Andy, too, was very pale. He said without preamble, 'Can we come in and talk to you? There isn't anyone else, and I told Martha you were OK. We went to the church but it was someone else doing the service, so we came away.'

'I'm glad you knew where to find me. Come through to the kitchen. Would you like coffee, tea–?'

She chose the kitchen rather than the sitting room deliberately; its sturdy, practical furnishings were reassuring, and they took seats at the table without waiting to be asked. They both shook their heads at the offer of coffee, but Martha, in a show of defiance, asked if she could smoke.

It was clearly a test; Margaret passed it by saying

indifferently, 'Sure,' and found a saucer to use as an ashtray, hoping that Jean wouldn't have a fit when she returned and found her kitchen polluted.

Andy burst out, as if this were a burden too heavy for him to bear a moment longer, 'It's the police. I think they're going to arrest Hayley for killing that sod McEvoy, and she didn't do it. I can't stop them; they won't listen to me.'

'The pigs never do,' Martha put in, but he ignored her.

'Would you speak to them?' he begged. 'They'd listen to you.'

Martha, stubbing out the cigarette she had just lit, added, 'She's a rotten mother, actually. Everyone thinks that, and it's quite true, she is. But she hasn't done this, I swear she hasn't.'

Margaret looked at their tortured faces, in which the pain showed as clearly as the colour of their eyes. Was there no limit to the agony some parents chose to inflict on their children, the sins of the fathers – and mothers – visited so directly and horribly on these hapless innocents? Robert had outlined briefly the later developments, and it seemed all too hideously plausible, given Hayley's involvement with Piers, that she might have been moved to kill him. A man who treated one woman as badly as he treated his wife would have had few scruples about the way he used his mistress. But Margaret could hardly say that now.

'Tell me everything that's been happening, and I'll try to think what we should do.'

They poured it all out; it was the fourth time the police had questioned Hayley, and this time they had taken her away. She had an alibi for the night of the fire at the Boltons', she had reminded them, but apparently they weren't interested in that any more. They had evidence that Hayley had quarrelled with McEvoy last night, and Hayley's airy explanation that it was just a little misunderstanding between friends hadn't cut any ice.

292

'And was it?' Margaret asked gently.

They exchanged glances. 'No,' said Andy. 'She was fit to be tied when she came home last night. It's her business, you see: it's like – well, a bit iffy just now. With Piers being loaded and –' he hesitated on the word, 'a friend, she thought she could get him to sub her so she could keep it going. She wouldn't tell us what he said, apart from no. But she was spitting tacks.'

'Did she go out afterwards?'

'No, of course not,' Martha said fiercely, then without warning burst into tears. 'She couldn't have, I'm sure she couldn't have.'

Andy absently patted her shoulder, but his own olive skin had taken on a greenish tinge.

'That's the problem,' he said. 'We wouldn't actually know, once we were all asleep. I wanted to ask you, when we know she didn't do it, should we, like, invent an alibi for her that we can tell the police?'

'No,' said Margaret, sick at heart. 'You must never lie to the police. Leaving aside the fact that it's simply wrong, you couldn't do it well enough. They'd trip you up in five minutes, and that would make everything much, much worse.

'But –' she paused, trying to frame the question in such as way as not to alienate them, 'I know she's your mother, and of course you believe what she's told you, but is there anything – anything at all – that the police might take account of, that might show them that she didn't do it?'

Then Martha, her husky voice further thickened by tears, said, 'She didn't want to kill him. She just wanted the money, and she'd decided exactly how she was going to get it. And she surely couldn't get it from him if he was dead.'

Andy's head had gone down. 'We might as well tell it like it is. She was going to blackmail him. Our mother was going to blackmail her former lover. That's a great thing to have to live with. Not.' He raised his head, and his eyes were blazing at the injustice of it all. 'But I'd rather that than be the son of a murderess.'

Vezey took Jackie Boyd with him to take notes while he questioned Suzanne Bolton. She was looking surprisingly calm if somewhat drained this morning, and Patrick sat close at her side on the sofa throughout the police interview, exuding husbandly support.

Yes, she was prepared to tell them all about last night, about the strain she had been under and the upset at the hospital, and – with shame – about her attack on Elizabeth. It was difficult, looking at the neat, composed woman, to imagine her as an avenging Fury.

'I think, I really think I must have had some sort of brainstorm,' she said. 'I just can't believe I did that to poor Lizzie. As if she hasn't got troubles enough! Are you – are you going to charge me with assault?'

No, Vezey didn't think it was likely that charges would be brought, and her relief was obvious.

'We'd had a very bumpy time in our marriage,' she said, looking affectionately at Patrick, who squeezed her hand.

'But Patrick came after me last night, in all that fog: he searched and searched until he found me. I'd just parked the car up by the reservoir at the top of the common, and cried and cried. I don't know what I'd have done if he hadn't coaxed me to come back. We talked half the night, and I've promised to see the doctor and talk to him about depression. And it wouldn't be the end of the world if I had to give up my job, either.'

She smiled at Patrick again.

Vezey did not feel that it was part of his police duties

to preside over a love fest. 'And exactly what time was it when you found your wife, Mr Bolton?'

'Time?' Patrick looked to Suzanne for help, and she shook her head. 'I'm sorry, I haven't the faintest idea. I seemed to be driving round for ages, but that could have been because of the fog. It probably wasn't as long as all that. I really couldn't say.'

'Thank you very much, sir.' Vezey tried not to sound heavily ironic, and failed. She didn't have an alibi, but then she really didn't have a motive either.

They left, and went on to Laura Ferrars. James had been interviewed at his office, and had given a precise, lawyer's account of Hayley Cutler's contretemps with McEvoy. But he had been hesitant about what had happened after he went home, and his wife's statement was a loose end Vezey wanted tidied up and out of the way. He had directed that Cutler should be taken to headquarters, and he was hopeful that he could have the whole thing tied up in pretty pink ribbon by the end of the afternoon.

Laura Ferrars seemed somehow different. He was not a man who paid much attention to feminine appearance, but he had her filed as cool, well-groomed, understated. When last he had seen her she had been both nervous and defensive.

This woman was none of these things. Her feet were bare; she was wearing jeans and a Garfield sweater which might have belonged to one of her children. Her hair, normally smooth and sleeked-down, looked as wild and fluffy as a dandelion clock. He had the impression that the appropriate expressions of concern for Elizabeth McEvoy cloaked an emotion that was almost elation, and he wanted to know why.

'We have reason to believe,' he said brutally, 'that some

third person was involved in Piers McEvoy's death. According to our information you bore him a considerable grudge because you believe he cost you a professional promotion which you coveted. Is that correct?'

Colour stained her cheekbones, but she did not lose her composure. 'Yes, I'm quite prepared to accept that's a fair enough way to put it. I made one or two resolutions last night, and since one of them was not to fudge things any more, I have to say that the man was a wart on the face of humanity. I can't think of anyone who won't be better off without him.'

'That's straight enough, anyway. And may I be equally direct, and ask you whether your sense of duty to humanity might have compelled you to run a barbecue skewer through his neck?'

This was plain speaking with a vengeance. She had invited it, but even so recoiled instinctively.

Recovering herself, she said, 'Not my duty to humanity, no. At one stage, I'd probably have done it on my own account, if I'd had the guts. But as it happens, I didn't.'

'And can your husband confirm your movements during the hours in question?'

For the first time, she seemed flustered. 'Well no, not really, I suppose. We had a bit of a row – no, that's not true, and I said I would be honest, didn't I? We had the mother and father of all rows, and he slept on the sofa in the sitting room, because he was scared I might throw something else at him if he came upstairs. So I daresay I could have got up and murdered half the population of Stretton Noble in their beds and he would have been none the wiser.'

So she had no alibi either, and she had been more than frank about her motive. But somehow he couldn't see it.

He was very tired. He was looking forward to interviewing

Hayley Cutler and getting it all wrapped up, but in deference to his exhaustion he let Jackie Boyd take the wheel on the journey back to district headquarters.

When he reached his office Robert Moon was waiting for him, looking disgustingly spruce. He was bathed, freshly shaved, and had the well-fed air of someone who has just consumed a farmhouse breakfast and lunch rolled into one. He looked up with concern as Rod Vezey came in, hollow-eyed and gaunt, with a day's growth of stubble, and stumbled over a pile of files which had been left on the floor beside his desk.

'Good grief, you look terrible!' Moon exclaimed. 'Haven't you had any sleep?'

Vezey shook his head. 'Soon,' he said. 'I've just got to sort out Hayley Cutler – they've picked her up for me, and she's waiting for questioning downstairs. And after that I can sleep for twenty-four hours while some other poor sod gets it all down on paper, secure in the knowledge of a job well done. Are you coming with me to talk to her?'

'Hayley Cutler?' Moon sounded startled. 'Look, I think you'd better listen to this first, before you find yourself doing something you might regret.'

He told Vezey what the Cutler children had said, and watched with considerable sympathy the doubt growing in his heavy eyes.

'But for God's sake, man! It has to be her!' He rubbed his hands over his face, as if he could wipe the tiredness away. 'She's the only one left – there just isn't a case against either of the other two. Oh, you could argue back and forwards intellectually, but in fact it's perfectly obvious that they're non-starters. And you may well say that there are umpteen other women who fit your profile, but these are surely the only ones in the frame —'

'Rod,' Moon interrupted, 'you really should get some sleep you know.'

'Oh, don't waste my time! How can I, before I get a line on this? I'm the only person in possession of all the facts of the case.'

'You're not in possession of all the facts of the case – or at least, I suppose you may be, but you're certainly proceeding on entirely the wrong premise.

'I'm gratified to find you paying such slavish attention to my profile, but that was to help find Missy. And we've found her, remember? This – McEvoy's murder – is an entirely new and separate crime.'

As Vezey stared at him blankly, he continued, 'You're simply too tired to think clearly. Have a rest. The killer is most unlikely to strike again while you're asleep.'

Blankness had given way to despair. 'If you think there's the remotest chance that I could sleep, after that bombshell, you're off your trolley. I'll have to report to the super, and how can I say, "I'm sorry, sir, I've just wasted a day of the investigation and however many hundreds of pounds of the taxpayer's money it is in barking up the wrong tree, and I haven't the faintest idea where to go from here"?'

Robert Moon sat back in his chair, folding his hands across his well-rounded stomach, and said gently, 'Oh, I don't think it's as bad as that. That's exhaustion talking. If you were in anything like your normal form, I'm sure you'd have realized that it's all remarkably obvious, really.'

16

Patrick Bolton opened the door. Robert Moon, who was observing him minutely, thought he saw a dilation of the pupils of his eyes, but there was no other visible reaction beyond a natural surprise.

'Well, good afternoon, gentlemen. I must confess I didn't expect to see you back so soon.'

'Just a few more questions, Sir, if you don't mind.'

Rodney Vezey had got his second wind; he had washed, shaved, had a cup of black coffee and a couple of sausage rolls and now looked, to his companion's admiration, as if he were fit for another twenty-four hour stint.

A frown crossed Bolton's brow. 'I did hope my wife could be left alone for the rest of the day, after cooperating with you so fully this morning,' he said stiffly. 'She's very tired, you know, and I've persuaded her to go upstairs and lie down.'

Moon saw Vezey smile. 'Oh the shark has pretty teeth, dear . . .' The line came irresistibly to mind.

'Not her, sir,' he said genially. 'You.'

There was no mistaking the dilation of the pupils this time, but still the man did not flinch.

'Me? Well, in that case you'd better come in, and I'll do whatever I can to help you.'

He led the way through to the sitting room. 'How is poor

Elizabeth, do you know? The rumour mill has it that she's having some kind of breakdown.'

Vezey ignored him, striding ahead and taking control of the room by the force of his presence.

'May I sit down?' he said, and did so without waiting for permission, choosing a hardback chair which would give him, seated, the highest position in the room.

The tightening of Patrick's lips betrayed his annoyance. 'Please do,' he said sarcastically, and sat down on the edge of one of the armchairs, as Robert stolidly seated himself in the other one opposite.

'We're busy men, Mr Bolton, so I won't waste time, yours or ours. Perhaps we could start by talking about your relationship with Mrs McEvoy. How long had it been going on?'

'Relationship? It was hardly that. I was sorry for her – very sorry, because though Piers was a good friend of mine I could never say he was a considerate husband. She is a gentle soul, very easily upset; she was crying last night when I went round to see if she was all right.'

'Wasn't it a little strange to go round to see her when you knew her husband was out?'

Bolton was gaining confidence. He obviously believed in his own ability to talk himself out of trouble, and Robert noted the body language as he sat back in the chair and crossed his legs. But he noted, too, the nervous plucking of his fingers at the pile of the chair fabric.

'No, absolutely not. Well, with hindsight I suppose it was a mistake, but at the time the whole point was that I was concerned about her being alone when she was so nervous. And then, of course, she started to cry, I had taken her hand to comfort her and in burst Suzanne.'

He essayed a laugh. 'Oh, I know it sounds like the classic joke, "And that, me lud, is the case for the defendant." But ask Suzanne! She accepts that she misinterpreted the whole thing and with the stress she's under she just went right over the top.'

He smiled at Vezey. It was meant to be an easy, man-to-man smile, but his upper lip was fractionally curled back in the ape's placation gesture.

Vezey was implacable.

'Were you at all worried about Mr McEvoy's reaction to the scratches on his wife's face?'

Patrick shifted uneasily. 'Well, yes, I suppose I was. After all, I felt to a large extent responsible for my wife's actions. I offered to stay and explain, but Lizzie felt this would only make matters worse.'

'Oh? For some reason she felt that her husband would find it hard to believe in this very innocent relationship? A difficult and unreasonable man, you would say?'

'Perhaps.'

Vezey produced a notebook and made a show of consulting it, though to Robert's certain knowledge he had made no notes on the information which he had so rapidly gathered about Patrick Bolton.

With an abrupt, unsettling change of direction, he said, 'You were in a nearby supermarket last Wednesday, the 27th. Is that right?'

'I – I may have been. It's perfectly possible.'

'And you were observed in the coffee shop engrossed in an extremely intimate conversation with Mrs McEvoy. Was this another manifestation of your social conscience?'

The shaft went home, and Bolton lost control of his temper.

'And what pernicious bastard sicked up that disgusting little piece of snooping?'

Robert tried not to look conscious as Bolton raged on. 'This is entirely ridiculous. I've tried to be patient, but I really don't see why I should have to defend myself against what is simply the sort of gossip that people invent when they haven't enough to do with their time.'

Vezey let him bluster himself into silence, allowed the pause to lengthen, then said mildly, 'Oh, I think you would be well-advised to cooperate. I'm trying to decide whether we should take you in for questioning straight away, or whether we can clear everything up in this little chat. It's up to you.'

Bolton's outburst had shattered his facade of coolness, and it was not easy to establish it again. His eye movements became rapid in one of the classic signs of nervousness, and he moistened his lips.

'Look,' he said at last, spreading his hands palm up in the gesture which denotes openness, 'I'm sorry about that. I didn't mean to lose my temper.

'Let me be completely frank about the whole thing. My "relationship" with Lizzie, as you choose to call it, amounted to precisely one cup of coffee and the visit which Suzanne interrupted. No affair, no secret assignations.

'I admit, I was very drawn to her. Suzanne and I, as she told you this morning, were going through a bad patch. She's always been very competent, very self-sufficient, and I had felt, wrongly as I now know, that what she was telling me was that she could look after herself, that she didn't need me.

'Lizzie was very sweet, very vulnerable.' His voice softened instinctively. 'She had a pretty tough time with Piers, and you couldn't help but feel protective, which I did. But that was it; there you have it. Ask Lizzie; she told me herself that Suzanne needed me, and I must go to her. She can confirm that I left her right there in the sitting room and did just that.'

He had managed to sound sincere, but Vezey was unimpressed. His eyes were cold and hard.

'Mrs McEvoy, unfortunately, is not in any condition to tell anyone anything. She is suffering, as far as we can tell, from the psychological condition known as dual personality, and at the moment the second personality – the one who wrote the poison pen letters and started the fires – is in the ascendant. We have no means of knowing whether or not her original personality will ever return.'

They had kept this information restricted, and Vezey used it now to deliberate effect.

There was no mistaking the shock, and then the agony, which Bolton experienced. The colour drained from his face and he whispered, 'Are you saying Lizzie – *Lizzie* – is mad?'

It was Moon who replied. 'It's not a very useful term, Mr Bolton. She was severely traumatized as a child, and she has clearly had to struggle with this fractured personality for a long time. She is certainly not – normal.'

Mercilessly Vezey pressed on. 'You mentioned the word "protective", Mr Bolton. Mrs McEvoy, as a result of your – attentions, shall we call them, was left with these scratches on her face which, as you acknowledged, she would have to explain to her husband. He was difficult and as you have also hinted, probably violent.

'So did you, perhaps, feel that the only way you could safeguard her was by making sure he didn't survive till the morning, when he would see those marks, and she would have to take the consequences? Could you not bear to think that she, towards whom you felt so gallantly "protective", was going to suffer physical violence because of you?'

Patrick Bolton was ashen now. Robert watched, with clinical interest, as a bead of sweat formed on his upper lip. In a nervous movement his tongue shot out and licked it away.

'That's – that's nonsense. You're simply inventing a situation that didn't exit.'

'And have I also invented a body? Piers McEvoy was lying dead in a pool of blood in his games room – but then, I don't need to tell you that, do I?'

The human instinct for self-preservation is very strong. Before their eyes, Bolton began to pull himself together again.

'Yes, I'm afraid you do have to tell me, actually.' He spoke savagely, and his expression had hardened. 'I know nothing about that, nothing. And I would have to say that if you have established, clearly to your own satisfaction, that Lizzie McEvoy is – is disturbed, and has been responsible for fires and attempted murder, it's more than a little perverse to go looking for someone else to blame for the death of a husband who's bullied her for years.'

He had been unable to say her name without a telling hesitation, but self-interest had triumphed. If he had been in a troika pursued by wolves and his companion was already dead, he would have been similarly undeterred by sentiment.

Vezey surveyed him with contempt. 'Nice try, Mr Bolton. But for reasons which I won't go into, we are satisfied that it was not, in fact, Mrs McEvoy who killed him.

'Let's not beat about the bush. I think it was you.'

The muscles in Bolton's jaw were standing out and he countered Vezey's accusatory stare with flinty, narrowed eyes.

'You *think* that, do you? I assume that means you haven't a shred of evidence. If you did, we wouldn't be sitting here, would we? You'd have dragged me off to one of your dungeons and clapped me in irons.

'In any case, my answer to you is that no, I didn't kill

Piers McEvoy. So you'll have a hell of a job to find evidence that proves I did.'

It was a shrewd response. Vezey got to his feet, and Robert Moon followed suit. He smiled, and once again Robert was reminded of the shark.

'Oh, but we will, Mr Bolton. That I can promise you.'

Bolton did not get up, but he turned his head to watch them go to the door.

With his hand on the handle, Vezey turned. 'Oh, just one more thing. You were in the army, weren't you? In the SAS, to be precise? Trained to kill swiftly and effectively, isn't that right?'

The wolves were closing on the troika once more, and fear flared in the man's eyes.

'You needn't say anything, Mr Bolton,' Vezey said over his shoulder as he went out. 'We know you were. And by the way, don't go off and try to do something clever. There's a chap out there who seems to have developed a real attachment to you.'

Stretton Noble had never been so busy on a Sunday afternoon. The pub had done a roaring trade, but had kept to its usual two o'clock closing time, and up and down the main street were groups of disconsolate reporters and photographers, their shoulders hunched against what had now become a sleety drizzle.

They had the murder house staked out, of course, and had taken turns to phone in their copy ('The champagne-swilling class in toffs' village Stretton Noble was in shock this morning . . .') from the call box near the church.

Opinion was divided as to the other areas that would repay press attention. A couple of the more enterprising hacks went to the Golf Club and bribed a waitress – who had no recollection of ever having seen Piers McEvoy but who knew a sucker when she saw one – to tell them he was ever such a nice man and everyone was ever so sorry.

Bertie Bignall was a sharper operator altogether, which was why his scandal sheet paid him the sort of money that brain surgeons can only dream of. He had chatted up one of the barmaids at lunch time, and elicited the name of Minnie Groak as the biggest gossip in the place.

Taking care that none of his fellow-members of the Fourth Estate was watching, he made his way to Minnie's door, noting with satisfaction when she opened it her greedy eyes and slack mouth.

'Miss Groak?' he said ingratiatingly. 'I've been told that you're the person I have to ask if I want to get the low-down on this place. I hear there's nothing you don't know about what they get up to around here.'

He winked conspiratorially. 'Now, how about you and me having a cosy little chat? I can make it well worth your time.'

He took out a wad of notes. Experience had taught him that nothing loosened the tongue faster than the sight of the notes on offer being riffled seductively.

He was astonished, therefore, when Minnie, with a gasp of shock and a terror-stricken look around, said, 'I don't know what you're talking about, I'm sure. I can't think who can have been telling you such wicked lies, and I certainly wouldn't demean myself by gossiping to trash like you.'

She slammed the door in his face, leaving him with much the same emotions as the drunk in the gutter when the pig beside him got up and walked away.

'The trouble is,' Vezey said grimly to Robert Moon as they went back to the car, 'that he's right. It's just a theory. We haven't a scrap of solid evidence to tie him in.

'And he's obviously been careful. Presumably we were

meant to assume that the maniac lighting the fires was responsible, and he wouldn't be able to believe his luck when he heard about the fire last night.'

'He certainly had no idea about her. That was a bombshell.'

'Didn't take him long to make use of it, though, did it? Cold-blooded bastard!'

'Pragmatist, certainly. But look, surely you could make out a strong case against him?'

Vezey grimaced as he started the car and drove off, escaping a posse of reporters who, spotting him, came running up.

'Yes, of course. And perhaps they would issue a search warrant on that basis. Perhaps. But when it's a case of taking apart the house of an upright citizen in the speculative hope that forensic will come up with something, they tend to be a bit stroppy.

'I need something, just some link, however tiny. I haven't the least doubt that once the forensic boys get into his wardrobe they'll find something – they always can – but it's a question of getting them the chance.'

He braked suddenly, then swung the car back into a road end to turn round.

'Let's go to the McEvoys' house,' he said. 'You don't mind, Robert? Just one last look to see if anything suggests itself. Then I really will knock off, I promise you.'

They had to shoulder their way through the press, slavering like hyenas at the gate.

'Why don't you just arrest them for obstruction?' Robert, disgruntled, reached the haven of the garden adjusting the coat that had almost been pulled from his back and smoothing his ruffled hair.

'I wish!' Vezey led the way round the blackened shell of the front and side to the back of the house. Robert looked at it curiously as he passed, though there was little to see. The body had been removed, and now with darkness coming on they were sealing up the rooms with improvised shutters and leaving the site for the day.

There were still people working inside the undamaged part of the house, though the kitchen was empty.

Robert felt, just as Rod Vezey had, the eeriness of this pretty domestic room, with its bright pottery plates and gleaming copper pots and everything in its usual place. The recessed lights in the ceiling were on, and with the soft terracotta wash on the walls gave the room a warm intimacy. There was a large, business-like electric cooker and below an arched recess, backed by white and terracotta Italian tiles, a dark green gas-fired Aga.

Robert eyed it with interest. 'It's fascinating, you know, the fashion for these things. It performs precisely the function of the piano in a Victorian parlour; it doesn't matter whether you use it or not, but it makes a statement about the sort of person you want people to think you are.'

Vezey grunted. He was pacing around the room, fixing with a fierce stare the tidy surfaces and the primly-closed cupboards, as if they held secrets he could force them to disclose. He was looking very tired again; he had put his last reserves of nervous energy into the interview with Patrick Bolton.

'Can we touch things?' Robert was looking about him with bright-eyed curiosity.

'Sure.' Vezey yawned, and gestured to the greasy evidence of the silvery powder. 'They've checked this for latents. We'll get Bolton's prints for comparison, of course, but finding them in a friend's house wouldn't prove a thing.

'But surely there has to be something . . .' He opened a drawer, then slammed it shut dispiritedly. Robert was engaged in systematically opening and closing cupboards.

'Come on,' Vezey said wearily. 'You're the psychologist. What did he do? Talk me through it.'

Robert considered. 'All right. Lizzie tells him to go after Suzanne, and he agrees. We know that, because he thought she could confirm it before we told him she couldn't confirm anything. I would guess she must have been upset, anxious to get him out of the house; from the tone of his voice when he talked about it, he was reluctant to leave her to face the music alone.

'He feels protective and responsible; guilty as well, no doubt. So what does he do? He's a soldier – a highly-trained man of action – and it wouldn't take him long to come up with the idea of neutralizing the threat.'

Vezey was listening intently. 'And all he would need to do was see to it that he unlocked a door before he left – the back door, probably – so that he could get back in to wait for McEvoy. He could have gone back home, hung about for a bit —'

Robert shook his head. 'No. He couldn't have known Suzanne wouldn't be there. So perhaps he just hid out here – but then the car would give him away. No, he must have had to move it, then come back and hide out somewhere to wait for McEvoy coming home.'

'An easy target, because he knew he was fairly drunk. Right! He would wait around till the lights went off in the sitting room and Lizzie went upstairs – she, of course, mustn't be involved – then he lets himself in, puts on the gloves and – well, all that's speculation. It's only at this point we get to the evidence. We still have the problem of bridging the gap between the two.'

Robert, who had been examining one of the skewers, dropped it with a crash.

'But where did he get the gloves from? He didn't go home —'

He turned to the sink. There was the washing-up liquid, the scourer tucked into the wide mouth of a green pottery frog. There was the dishcloth, wrung out and laid to dry. And lying folded behind the drying-rack, an innocent pair of pink rubber gloves.

' "The little things," ' Robert murmured as Vezey fetched the men who were still working next door.

They produced long tweezers, a plastic sheet, a large fluffy fibreglass brush and a jar of the ubiquitous powder. The sheet was spread out, the gloves laid on top, and delicately, one of the men began stroking the powder across them while they all crowded round to watch. Painstakingly, he dusted one side of each glove, then with the tweezers turned it over and repeated the performance. Then he straightened up.

'Nothing, Sir,' he said. 'I'm sorry, not a thing. Not a print of any kind.'

Vezey swore, thumping his fist down on the countertop.

'The bastard's washed them, that's what he's done. He's scrubbed every inch of them.'

With Robert's round face and spectacles it was hard for him to look shark-like, but when he smiled Vezey found himself, bizarrely, thinking of spreading scarlet billows.

'Inside as well?' he said.

And after it was all over, there was the candle-lit service in St Mary's. It seemed hardly credible that only one short week had intervened since the last one.

Margaret Moon found it almost unbearably poignant, and her damaged throat ached still more with the tears she must not shed. The church was fuller than last week, but her thoughts were not with the ninety-and-nine within the fold.

There was still the familiar smell of dampness from the stone, and the jam-jar candles flickered and danced, casting wavering shadowy grotesques on the walls as the congregation rose in their pews for the hymn which Penny Jackson was cajolling from the organ, wheezier than ever tonight.

> O God our help in ages past,
> our hope for years to come . . .

But what hope was that? So many futures blighted. Two hours ago, armed with a warrant, the forensic team had discovered – 'just for starters' they said – a pair of blood-spattered shoes ineptly concealed behind a wardrobe, and Patrick Bolton had been arrested.

His killing had been for love, of a sort; a love which was illicit, illusory, and whose object had vanished like the mermaid dissipated into sea foam. There was nothing for him now but the legacy of his evil: ruin and despair.

And an hour ago, Margaret had looked into hell itself, as bundling a devastated woman into an escape car, she saw the blood-lust of the jackal press, the men and women whose eyes showed that they had lost their souls by selling human agony for pieces of silver.

With a sense of outrage, she recognized some of them now, mingling discreetly with the worshippers at the back of the church. It was her impulse to drive them out, to pronounce anathema, but she must not. She must, after all, believe them to be more gravely in need of grace than any. The blood on Patrick Bolton's hands was clean by comparison.

But the McEvoy children were in care tonight through his agency, being given 'counselling' which was what in the modern world was offered to those who grieved instead of love. The Ferrars were missing too, but she could see Andy, Martha and Mike Cutler in a group of youngsters. Martha's face in the candle-light was wet with tears, and she was not alone in that. Anthea and Richard Jones were there, his face shadowed and her head buried in his shoulder.

How wrong she had been about them all, and how she had failed her flock! She had stood here last week projecting on to them her own smug prejudices, when a more skilful shepherd might have gone out and brought back the one who was lost. *Mea culpa, mea maxima culpa*!

Before the hills in order stood . . .

Yet perhaps she wasn't as important as that. It had all happened long, long ago, with another disaster, when a child lost her mother and a father was too selfishly engrossed in his pain to comfort her. But then, what had happened to him, to make him as he was? There was no clear beginning, and tragically no foreseeable end.

A thousand ages in Thy sight
are like an evening gone . . .

The singing was noticeably faltering. Isaac Watts' great vision of eternity was all too apposite, and Margaret was glad of the excuse of her sore throat. She could not have sung those words without tears, nor those of the next verse.

Time, like an ever-rolling stream
bears all its sons away;
They fly forgotten, as a dream
dies at the opening day.

A dream – and that, however they might all feel at the moment, was true. Tomorrow for most of them life would return to normal, and the memory and the horror would fade.

But for the others . . . 'Pray for us sinners, now and at the hour of our death,' poor, poor Elizabeth McEvoy had written in her despair.

Was it sin, where there was no moral judgement? And could there be forgiveness, where there could be no remorse?

She was too tired, and it was too difficult. In her hoarse, painful voice, she joined in singing the last verse of the hymn.